PRAISE FOR *NIG*

"All those who love thrillers will find in Nichael Alexiades's first novel a source of great pleasure and satisfaction. It combines suspense and knowledge, experience and imagination. His grateful readers will now wait for the next."

—Elie Wiesel, Nobel Laureate and Award-winning Author of *Night*

"This book is a fun, scary ride. Written by a prominent New York surgeon, *Night Harvest* serves up a strong cocktail mixing the author's unique knowledge of those terrifying black holes, big-city hospitals, the godlike Caesars who run them, a satanic villain or three (one of them a critic, of course), and a platoon of smart, young, and gorgeous residents for us to root for, and worry about. It is great fun, smartly written, and hard to put down. Pick it up."

—Brian Dennehy, Award-winning Actor

"First-time author Dr. Michael Alexiades has written a medical thriller that will set your pulse racing, your blood pressure rising, and your temperature shooting through the roof. What a debut!"

—Michael Takiff, Author of *A Complicated Man: The Life of Bill Clinton as Told by Those Who Know Him*

"Michael Alexiades may be a first-time author, but his writing is a match for the very best. *Night Harvest* is a powerful story of success and failure, of dreams realized and broken. The book is about choices . . . and the mystical way our choices become our life story. Read it carefully; it's worth your time."

—Rev. Dr. Joan Brown Campbell, Director of the Department of Religion at Chautauqua Institution

"Raymond Chandler once observed that crime novels could be fine literature. Michael Alexiades proves Chandler to be correct. His debut novel is written with humor, insight, and a truly sardonic view of humanity. It is a superb thriller that delivers more than any reader could ask."

—George Minkoff, author of *In the Land of Whispers Trilogy*

NIGHT
HARVEST

A NOVEL

NIGHT HARVEST

MICHAEL ALEXIADES

TURNER
PUBLISHING COMPANY

Turner Publishing Company
4507 Charlotte Avenue • Suite 100 • Nashville, Tennessee 37209

www.turnerpublishing.com

Night Harvest

Cover design and book illustrations: Maxwell Roth
Book design: Kym Whitley

Library of Congress Catalog-in-Publishing Data

Alexiades, Michael.
  Night harvest / Michael Alexiades.
     pages cm
  ISBN 978-1-62045-485-5 (pbk.)
  1. Medical students—Fiction. 2. Police—Fiction. 3. Tunnels—Fiction. 4. Manhattan (New York, N.Y.)—Fiction. I. Title.
  PS3601.L3593N54 2013
  813'.6—dc23
                          2013024462

Printed in the United States of America
13 14 15 16 17 18 0 9 8 7 6 5 4 3

To Aliduke,
best friend and savior

PROLOGUE

PERVIS

F. J. PERVIS III KNEW HE WAS ON top of his game. He was the best damn drama critic New York had seen in decades. No Broadway show was safe from his lacerating prose. Just last month he'd slaughtered a multi-million-dollar musical in his column in the newspaper, the *Metropolitan Post,* and on TV. It closed after one performance, delivering all those mediocre actors and musicians to the unemployment they so richly deserved and leaving those sanctimonious producers in the red, big time. All due to yours truly, he thought. He was so respected . . . no, feared was more like it. After the mayor and the police commissioner, he figured, he was the most powerful man in Gotham.

How he ended up on the short end of a scalpel, in an operating room getting his knee scoped, was beyond him. At 5 feet 5 inches and 250 pounds, he was in the best physical condition of his life—a member of the world's most elite athletic club, where he regularly kept in shape before enjoying a well-lubricated lunch in the club bar. Yesterday, however, was different. One minute he was at the club playing squash with his editor; the next he was on the floor, in pain, unable to straighten his knee. A trainer ushered him into the locker room, but, after twenty minutes of ice, the knee still couldn't bear weight. Fortunately, he had his orthopedist's private cell number on his speed dial. He didn't hesitate for a moment, despite the club's strict no-cellphone policy. Screw them, he thought, it's not their knee.

"Warren, it's Pervis. My knee is locked. I need to see you *now.*"

"Can't do it. I'm in the OR all day. Head over to the emergency room. I'll have one of my boys look at it."

"No fucking way am I heading to the ER. And your 'boys' won't be satisfactory. I'll see you in your office in a half hour."

With that, Pervis ended the call then yelled at the trainer to help him to the elevator and to the lobby to hail a taxi. A beat-up Crown Vic yellow cab pulled up. After cursing the trainer for not being more gentle as he helped him into the backseat, he shouted at the driver through the Plexiglas divider, "Eastside Medical Center! Pronto!" The cab lurched forward while its drive train ground and groaned like a food processor on its last ball bearing. Another taxi with no AC and an immigrant driver who smells like curry, Pervis thought. The cab ride was bumpy and painful, courtesy of New York City streets perfect for off-road rally cars but not old Fords with 250,000 miles on them and worn-out suspension. After the driver helped him out of the cab and into a wheelchair at the hospital, Pervis handed him a ten-dollar bill, which covered the ride plus a tip of 50 cents. The driver is probably an illegal, thought Pervis, and should be thankful that he didn't call the feds to have him deported.

Although it normally took two to three weeks to see Warren Nathan, M.D., Pervis saw him right away, between surgeries. One of the top sports-medicine orthopedists in the city, according to *New York* magazine, widely considered the authoritative source for such judgments, Nathan owed Pervis some big favors because the critic occasionally mentioned him in a column, thus helping to build up his Q rating. Warren was a pathetic publicity hound—in addition to Pervis, he also kept close to the paper's chief crime reporter, a hack named Bigelow. Pervis hoped that Nathan spent half as much time studying medicine as he did burnishing his public image. But Pervis thought he must—after all, he was a "full clinical instructor" at one of the city's premier academic medical centers. Little did Pervis realize that the title designated Nathan as occupying the lowest position on the academic food chain—comparable in status, among those in the know, to an adjunct instructor of comp lit at NYU.

"Your knee is locked."

"No shit, Sherlock."

"You probably have a torn meniscus cartilage and need arthroscopic surgery, but I can't tell for sure based on the exam. We need an MRI."

"Is the MRI going to change the fact I need surgery?"

"Not really. We call it internal derangement when we know something is mechanically wrong inside the knee but don't have a definitive anatomic diagnosis."

"So why are we wasting time? Let's get this derangement done ASAP."

AT FOUR THE NEXT AFTERNOON, they were in OR number 11, the ultraclean laminar-flow room often used for joint-replacement surgery. Warren and the anesthesiologist both recommended regional anesthesia, but Pervis wanted general.

"I want to hear nothing, see nothing, and say nothing. But no online stock trading on my time. Capisce, anesthesia man? And Warren, you do the entire surgery, no one else, including the students or residents over there."

"Don't worry, they're only here to assist."

Nathan told Pervis to enjoy the nap then prepped the leg for surgery. "You should lose some weight," Nathan said, groaning as he lifted the morbidly fat leg for the nurse. Pervis felt burning in his IV and had the oddest taste of garlic in his mouth. As he drifted off to sleep, he let out the words "I'm king of New York" then thought he heard the anesthesiologist whisper, "What an asshole."

THE NEXT THING PERVIS KNEW, he was on a gurney heading down a hallway. Strange dreams during the surgery had him perturbed: he dreamt of being pounded on his chest until his ribs cracked and being electrocuted multiple times. He tried now to lift his head but could not muster the strength. Strange, he thought, the knee didn't hurt at all—his surgeon must be damn good after all. Strange also that his peripheral vision was blocked by what seemed to be black sheets. As he looked between them, he expected to see the anesthesiologist, a preppy white guy with horn-rimmed glasses, wheeling him, but this man was Asian. Nor did he recognize the man leading the way at the foot of the gurney. As they entered the elevator, Pervis realized they must be residents or nurses taking him to the recovery room. But he could swear that the last time he had surgery here, gastric bypass, the recovery room was on the same floor as the OR, and the anesthesiologist took him there. Well, he thought, this is a teaching institution, where the doctors-in-training do all the work while the attendings trade stocks all day on their BlackBerries. Just wait until I receive the anesthesia bill—that doctor will have some explaining to do.

As the elevator door opened, the transporters continued to chat and laugh. Pervis noted that the hallway they entered was much darker than the other parts of the hospital. The medical center was probably trying to cut power costs. The hallway was also much hotter and stuffier than usual, and his body felt very damp and clammy, no doubt a lingering effect of the anesthesia. They passed what looked and sounded like kitchens and rounded a corner to enter an even darker corridor, with overhead steam pipes.

He tried to speak to the transporters, but they continued to ignore him as they rolled along. Why can't they hear me? Pervis thought. He tried to yell and even grab the transporter's arm but to no avail—he felt physically and psychologically paralyzed. He started to feel severe pain in his chest and ribs, as if the pounding was no dream, and his neck was sore. Pervis realized something had gone very wrong.

The two men hit a button on the wall to open a large door. They went through it into a room that was practically freezing. The two men transferred him roughly to another stretcher, one that was cold and hard. He labored to shout out or sit up, but the efforts ended at his brainstem. The transporters turned and were exiting the room when the Asian one said something to the other, then turned, walked up to the gurney, and zipped closed what was apparently a black plastic bag surrounding Pervis, leaving him in utter darkness. As Pervis heard the two men leave, the door slam shut behind them, and the lock clicking, he recalled that there had been a sign over the room's entrance:

SUBBASEMENT
MORGUE

AUTHORIZED
PERSONNEL
ONLY

NIGHT
HARVEST

1

DEMETRI

DEMETRI MAKROPOLIS WAS DEAD TIRED. A fourth-year medical student taking an orthopedic elective, he was working what amounted to slave labor, eighteen- to twenty-hour days, just to impress the intern, resident, and especially the attending orthopedists, in hope of receiving a glowing recommendation for a residency. Invitations for interviews at all the major orthopedic programs were being sent out any week now, and the best in the country was the one right here at his medical school's teaching hospital, the Eastside Medical Center. It all led up to "Match Day," in March, four months hence, when all U.S. medical students are assigned their internship and residency. Soon he'd be able to let up, coasting to graduation with electives in psychiatry, dermatology, and ophthalmology—undemanding fields, with civilized hours and no contact with blood and gore. But for now, he had to keep busting his hump. Competition for residencies in orthopedics was always fierce; he didn't want to be one of those poor bastards who get stuck at a community hospital in a tumbleweed border town, reading X-rays of Mexican illegals struck by truckers on the Interstate.

He'd just finished a thirty-six-hour tour of duty. The last few hours, he was barely conscious as he scrubbed on one surgical case after another. He was like a car on cruise control—everything would be fine until you fell asleep at the wheel . . . then *wham!* Crash and burn. It had been particularly hard to stay awake during Dr. Warren Nathan's twelve knee arthroscopies. Demetri had been assigned to "cover," or assist, on those cases, and he had no idea why. Nathan could breeze through them without assistance from anyone, let alone a lowly medical student. Nathan was, by Demetri's estimate, a below-average arthroscopist with an above-average ego; in other words, your basic, everyday New York orthopedic surgeon. Demetri was more interested in joint-replacement surgery than arthroscopy anyway, because of the complex engineering, metallurgy, biomechanics, and biology involved. He also saw it as a life-altering procedure, where a virtual cripple became able to lead a normal, productive life. The days of relegating arthritic people to wheelchairs on the back porch were long over. Dr. Mortimer, an old-movie aficionado, told him during a total hip replacement that Lionel Barrymore probably suffered from rheumatoid arthritis.

"How do you know?' Demetri asked.

"In his later movies, he was always in a wheelchair—remember Mr. Potter in *It's a Wonderful Life*? And just look at his hands. The deformity is classic for rheumatoid arthritis. What it's called, Demetri?"

"Ulnar drift?"

"Well, what do you know? A med student who has done his reading."

But that was yesterday's case. Today, Demetri was playing sports orthopod.

Although a Nathan knee arthroscopy rarely yielded any pathology amenable to correction by a Nathan knee arthroscopy, at least this doctor was fast. The team was on its final case by 4 P.M., a last-minute add-on, which meant Demetri should get back to his student-housing apartment and bed by 6 with any luck. That would mean ten hours of sleep—if only he didn't have to prepare a patient presentation for tomorrow morning. Web searches for the supporting literature alone could eat up two hours, plus at least an hour to put it all together. Well, he thought, seven hours of sleep is better than none.

That was the plan. But the last case did not go according to plan.

THE INDUCTION OF ANESTHESIA WENT smoothly. The leg tourniquet and holder were applied by Demetri and the resident, Tom Carter, as Nathan scrubbed. Then it was Demetri's and Carter's turn to scrub.

Standing over the sink in the scrub room, which was separated from the OR by a glass wall, Demetri's mind wandered—he thought he heard Carter say that the rotund patient lying on the operating table was some kind of celebrity. Carter was a tall, lanky young man. At 6 feet 3 inches tall and 190 pounds, he wasn't slight of build but rather lean. He had smooth blond hair and light blue eyes to go along with his elongated face and perfect nose. A definite contrast with Demetri, who was 6 feet tall, big-boned, and muscular, with a light olive complexion and thick, curly, jet-black hair. His face mirrored his body, broad with prominent cheekbones and dark brown eyes, but his nose was uncommonly narrow for a Greek's.

Demetri knew the Eastside Medical Center was one of the last bastions of the WASP elite—every department chairman's roots were in Essex or Sussex or some other -sex. No one ever said a word to Demetri disparaging his roots on the Aegean Sea, but he did wonder. No one on the premises embodied the WASP ideal more than Carter, but Demetri enjoyed his company nonetheless and admired his work ethic. Carter had played point guard on his college's basketball team—some small northeastern college across a lake from Cornell University whose name Demetri could never remember.

Finished at the sink, Demetri tossed the scrub brush into the wastebasket and started to rinse his arms when someone in the OR started to yell. He looked up and saw that it was the circulating nurse, barking orders as she hit the panic button on the side wall. Mayhem followed. Actually, organized chaos was more like it. As Demetri and Carter entered the room, it was clear the patient was in big trouble. The anesthesiologist, Greg Toll, was working frantically.

"Carter, get the crash cart in here now!" he yelled, and Carter was out the door.

"Greg, what the hell is going on?" said Nathan, running around like a madman and gesticulating wildly with his hands. It was a nervous disorder of Nathan's that Demetri noted and disliked.

Toll screamed at Nathan, "Your patient just arrested on me, and I haven't yet established an airway, godammit. Get over here and put some pressure on the trachea so I can intubate. I hate these fucking short, fat, fucking necks. I should make you do this, Warren. You're the one who brought this whale in here."

After at least thirty seconds, which seemed like sixty minutes, spent fighting Pervis's spasming vocal cords, Toll finally was able to snake the tube down the trachea into the lungs.

"Okay. We're in business. Hey, you, the student, you trained in CPR?"

"Yes."

"Start compressions. Five to one."

With that, Demetri began what was to be an hour of adrenaline-fueled hard manual labor, with short breaks for the Lifepak paddles that delivered electric shocks intended to jumpstart the heart. The crash team, with five anesthesiologists in tow, tried every trick in the book, from atropine to amiodarone, from intracardiac epinephrine to ever-higher energy on the paddles.

All to no avail. The EKG strips continued to show flatline, albeit with a rare odd beat—not a pattern either sustainable or compatible with life. One thoracic and trauma surgeon, the white-haired, charismatic G. Thomas Waits, sauntered in. Rumored to have been on the surgical team in Dallas's Parkland Hospital when JFK was brought in, he never spoke about it. Waits argued in his best Texas drawl for cracking the chest open and starting open cardiac massage. After much discussion, the idea was dropped, as Demetri continued his chest compressions and the respirator ran on auto. Unfazed, Waits remained in the room, not giving up hope for a shot at the dying patient. Settling into his chair, he began talking about his favorite subjects, Texas—pickup trucks, big-haired nurses, chicken-fried steak—and himself.

"Did I ever tell you about that time on I-30 when a semi was tailgating me?"

The lack of an answer didn't stop him from going on.

"Well, he was on me for at least ten minutes at 90 miles per hour. So I opened the window of my pickup and gave him a squirt from a 60-cc syringe I'd filled with axle grease."

Nathan took half a second to picture the event then asked, "So what good would that do? Sixty ccs is not enough to make a truck skid."

"No, sir, it ended up on his windshield. The driver turned on his wipers to clear it, but that only smeared it all over. He hit the brakes and had to pull over—no more tailgaiter! I always keep a syringe of the stuff in my car."

Multiple blood-gas specimens were sent; results looked progressively worse. Carter offered to relieve Demetri, but Demetri refused—the majority of orthopedists had been athletes at one time or another and most stayed in great shape compared with other physicians. Demetri, who went to the gym at least every other day, wanted to look and act the part of the jock orthopedist. He thought he might be taking that role too far when periodically the compressions were interrupted by the loud snap of a rib cracking.

"Easy does it, pal," said Carter, who added that rib fractures were common with CPR in older patients.

All the while, Nathan sat on a stool in the corner, seemingly in a trance. He hadn't been certified in advanced cardiac life support in years. As a matter of fact, he hadn't used a stethoscope in the last five.

After an hour of persistent asystole, Toll, over Nathan's objection, called the code at an end. Nathan was already complaining of the bad press he'd receive, and the inevitable lawsuit to follow. He was positive that the patient's family, even though they no doubt hated Pervis as much as he hated them, would descend like vultures to pick Nathan clean.

"Anesthesia's in trouble, so's the hospital," Nathan said to Demetri and Carter as they all exited the operating room while the nurse and room attendants cleaned the mess up. "My exposure should be minimal—we didn't even start the case yet—but forget it. The last newscaster to die after orthopedic surgery in this town meant weeks of bad press for everyone involved. Demetri, if you're going to be a doctor, you should know that the media have been anti-physician for years. Investigations? Unbiased reporting? It's all yellow journalism. It contaminates the jury pool, so when you finally get your day in court, you've already lost."

Nathan stopped in front of the doctors' locker room and fidgeted with the combination of the lock.

"This case is going to the medical examiner, then to the state. OPMC will call me in to explain it all." After a couple of seconds, Demetri realized that OPMC stands for the Office of Professional Medical Conduct. "My malpractice insurance costs me ninety-five grand a year. Do you think it covers my legal representation for that? And now I have to call the family."

Still ranting, Nathan disappeared into the doctors' locker room. Sleep deprivation was catching up to Demetri; the adrenaline high during the code was gone.

"I'm leaving, Carter. Bedtime."

"Poor you. Try not to think of the fun I'll be having on my date with that nurse from ICU."

"Not the hot brunette?"

"You've noticed her then."

"Hard not to. Her nurse's clothes are one step removed from a Penthouse centerfold."

"Yeah, but she has the body to pull it off. Besides, I like the way she says, 'Oohh, doctor . . . ' If I'm late for rounds tomorrow morning, you'll know why. I'm outta here like a bad dream."

ONCE CARTER AND HIS SHIT-EATING grin had gotten into the elevator, Demetri headed for the Third Avenue exit and his apartment, half a block away. This was not his first death of a patient, and besides, he was too tired to think about it now. An older man, stooped over a walker, was crossing the avenue; Demetri knew he wouldn't make it to the other side before the light changed. The cabs and trucks were already rumbling up the avenue, timing the traffic lights to minimize stops. Demetri saw the head-lights approaching.

"Let me help you." As Demetri hustled him across the street, he noted that the man, whom he'd seen before in the neighborhood, was not as old or infirm as he'd thought. The man had a white bandage on his cheek and mumbled nonsensical words. Through the man's clothing, Demetri felt the distinct feel of aluminum foil. Probably a schizophrenic trying to ward off evil cosmic rays, Demetri thought. Once across, the man simply turned away.

By the time Demetri got to his building, the cold air had revived him, so he decided to hit the gym before turning in. The place was crowded: first- and second-year students in the weight room, third-year students vs. residents on the basketball court.

One of the basketball players invited him to join the game, but Demetri declined. Basketball as played in this gym was more martial art than sport—people played it to blow off steam, and that showed in the type and frequency of injuries. Demetri had stopped playing a year ago when one of his room-mates, Allan, got elbowed in the head and sustained an orbital-floor fracture of his left eye. The fracture had been fixed, but the guy still suffered from double vision, eye fatigue, and headaches. Those symptoms had ended his chances of going into cardiac surgery like his dad. He was now applying for residencies in radiology. Demetri had worked too hard too long to blow it all with a sports injury.

His parents, both immigrants from Halkidiki, Greece, had worked for years to send him and his younger siblings through school. They now put in twelve-hour days in a dry-cleaning store they had recently opened when his dad retired after twenty-five years with the NYPD. Few Greeks were in the department at all, let alone as detectives in Manhattan North's narcotics squad. Demetri had heard all about his exploits. As a younger detective, his dad often spent his days undercover, wearing filthy clothes and sporting long hair and a greasy beard. Demetri's mom would not let him into the house until he looked and smelled presentable, so they had a sink and shower in-stalled in the garage. Demetri would meet his dad in the garage and debrief him while he cleaned up.

Despite his parents' hard work, Demetri had had to take out major loans to get through medical school—$200,000 worth, and that wasn't as bad as the debt some of his classmates were carrying. His smart undergraduate class-mates went into the financial racket, already pulling down six- and seven-figure salaries and bonuses, driving Porsches, summering in the Hamptons.

One grammar-school buddy had done even better: he lived in London, drove a Ferrari, and had married a Victoria's Secret supermodel.

Many of his med school classmates came from rich families that could afford the tuition. But those kids were going into radiology, pathology, and dermatology—they wanted limited work hours that would not interfere with their social life. The country needed doctors willing to work nights and weekends, thought Demetri, and not punch clocks at the end of the day. He was optimistic about his future practicing the noble art and science of medicine. He could do good for his patients and make a buck at the same time, even if his investment-banker friends could buy and sell him a hundred times over.

Besides, it was better than driving a dry-cleaning truck.

2

CARTER

LIKE HIS FATHER AND GRANDFATHER before him, Thomas Carter III loved being a preppy. He bought his clothes at P. Elliot, an East Side institution even more faithful to the prep ideal than Brooks Brothers. The manager and staff had the perfect sense of what was required: the proper length of sleeve on a blue blazer and of inseam on a pair of khakis were crucial to showing off the proper pastel shirt or argyle sock. When wearing a double layer of polo shirts, the color combination was critical.

Tonight, though, the occasion called for something simpler: a single white polo shirt and sockless Docksiders. A socialite's daughter, Beth Johansen loved all preppy men but specialized in doctors, who rewarded her with a much-discussed reputation for nymphomania. (Naturally, they referred to her by her initials.) Any male resident at the Eastside Medical Center who wanted to cut his teeth with a nurse could count on Beth to show him a thing or two. Normally the soul of discretion, six months ago, she was caught in the ER giving head to an intern during a lull in the action on the midnight shift.

She wasn't fired—perhaps the fact that her mother's family had built half the medical center had something to do with it. Also, she was the Emergency Department's best nurse. The hospital had to take some action, however, so she was transferred to the Surgical Intensive Care Unit—the day shift, where, presumably, she would be under better supervision. The intern's punishment was two weeks' lost vacation. Not a bad tradeoff, Carter thought.

Dinner, Carter knew, was hardly necessary to get into Beth's pants, but he did not want a one-night stand. He knew that, by treating her well, he could have her "on call," as needed. So tonight he planned on a meal at Luzzo's, a trendy Lower East Side eatery that had great, if unadventurous, Italian food. The fried oysters and homemade buffalo mozzarella pizza were to die for. With luck, they would be back at his place by 9, in bed by 9:05, and asleep no earlier than 3.

He picked her up at the main hospital entrance at 6:30 as she came off shift. She was dressed in a low-cut pink cashmere sweater with pearl drop earrings and a tasteful strand of pearls that emphasized her cleavage to full effect. Tight black capri pants and black stilettos finished the outfit. He could tell she was wearing thong panties. The night was looking promising.

"Nice Mini Cooper," she said as she got into his car. "I had a Benz AMG until I totaled it."

It was a cool November evening, and Carter noticed her nipples poking through the inviting cashmere. A honk from a nearby cab broke the spell, bringing him back to the business at hand.

The drive downtown via the FDR didn't take long as Carter weaved the Mini through traffic like a rattlesnake through grass. Since the 14th Street exit had been closed probably since 9/11, he got off at 23rd and headed down Second Avenue. They just beat the crowd in the door and took a booth up front, since the wood-burning oven in back made it too hot to sit there. He ordered the minestrone and oysters; she had a salad followed by the pizza. They drank a bottle of Nero d'Avola.

"The hard crust and the dripping cheese are making me hungry," she said as she slowly wiped the mozzarella off her chin with her index finger, shoved it in her mouth, and swallowed.

Carter took the hint. He ordered two cannolis to go, which they devoured in the car as he slalomed his way back uptown. Beth slipped off her clogs and put her feet up on the dashboard, wiggling her painted toes. Carter hadn't been this exhilarated since he'd first found out that the Medical Center had an active nursing school with a hundred kittens per class.

Entering his apartment building through the garage, Carter was happy he met no one on the elevator who might make this whole thing public. He had a one-bedroom apartment on the nineteenth floor of resident housing, with a decent city view. He turned on his music system, a Bang & Olufsen that had cost him a pretty penny. But the women loved the styling and the sound was good.

He returned with two vodkas and found her standing by the couch.

He'd been right about the panties.

3

NATHAN

HE HATED TEACHERS AS PATIENTS—they know a little about everything and think they know everything about medicine. Even worse was a teacher as parent of a patient. Nathan had already spent forty minutes this morning explaining to an adjunct professor of comparative literature at NYU why her fourteen-year-old daughter needed ligament reconstruction surgery on her knee.

"Her ACL was torn because of the twisting injury and because she's a girl."

"What does being a girl have to do with it?" asked the mom. "Are you saying that only boys should play soccer? Maybe girls are only fit to be cheerleaders."

"Not at all. But girls do have a much higher rate of injury than boys of the same age playing the same sport. It may be hormones, it may be anatomy. Either way, it's a matter of medical statistics, not sexism."

The woman looked down at her many annotated sheets of paper, which were obviously printouts from the Internet. Nathan sighed. This was not over yet.

"Do you routinely do double bundle?" she asked.

There was a knock on the exam room door. A reprieve from this purgatory, Nathan hoped.

"Doctor," his nurse said, "an urgent call."

Nathan excused himself before the professor could object.

"It's Dr. Mortimer," the nurse told him in the hall.

Nathan slipped into his office and closed the door. He knew his department head was calling about the death the previous day.

He picked up the phone. "Joe?"

"What the fuck happened yesterday in the OR? And why the fuck didn't you tell me about it?"

"I never got to operate on the patient. He arrested before we started."

"Get your ass up to my office. Now!" Nathan had never heard the chief so angry. He sped past the receptionist and into the elevator.

"What about your roomful of patients?" said his nurse.

"Reschedule them all," said Nathan as the elevator door closed. This is going to be a fucking long day, he thought.

The elevator opened on the top floor, the twentieth. The offices of the top hospital administrators and the department chiefs were huge, ornate turn-of-the-century rooms with 12-foot ceilings. Dozens of portraits of prior hospital and departmental chiefs lined the long carpeted hallway. The carved wood paneling oozed decades of oil used to burnish every surface to a fine patina. If the purpose was to intimidate lesser personages who visited the floor, it worked on Nathan. His palms were sweating and his heart was racing as he turned the antique brass knob to Mortimer's suite.

"Good morning, Dr. Nathan. Dr. Mortimer is expecting you."

Abigail Peabody, Mortimer's imposing secretary—she shunned the more modern term, "executive administrative assistant"—had been here thirty years, through half a dozen heads of orthopedics. Nathan had known her almost a decade, since he was a student rotating on an elective. She hasn't changed a bit, he thought. Slim, with salt-and-pepper hair, impeccably dressed and mannered. She could be 55 or 70. All-powerful, she could make or break any orthopedist in the department with a single comment or one stroke of her pen.

As Nathan walked into Mortimer's inner office, he noticed that he and the chief were not alone.

"Warren, I believe you've met Dr. Pear."

So the president of the hospital was here, too, thought Nathan. They've decided to castrate me and feed my balls to the pigeons outside the main entrance.

Nathan sat down in the seat Mortimer indicated for him—opposite the two occupied by his bosses.

Mortimer began. "Warren, I want to make it perfectly clear, this case is not about your having done anything wrong, especially since you never even started the surgery. But in medicine as in any other business, perception is everything. Now, I understand that you didn't order an MRI before the surgery."

Nathan started to explain. "No, but . . ."

"I'm sure there's a perfectly good reason, Warren, and I want you to know that we'll back you up 100 percent. However, the press can ruin a hospital if it wants to, digging through and second-guessing the medical decisions made at every step. The media can bring down the best institutions and the best doctors with nothing more than innuendo and flimsy circumstantial evidence."

Then it was Pear's turn. "Dr. Nathan, you're one of the department's rising stars. It would be a shame to throw that away because of a small misstep in the aftermath of Mr. Pervis's demise. Please do not say anything to anyone, especially anyone in the media, until you have cleared it with Dr. Mortimer or myself —and the same will be true for the entire team that was in the OR. It is vital that we stand united on this. Our counsel is preparing a statement for this afternoon's press conference."

"A press conference?"

"Yes. Thank you, Warren. I know we can rely on your discretion."

As Nathan walked down the paneled corridor past the portrait of Cornelius Duff, the hospital's founder, his hands balled up into tight fists, and his blood pressure started to rise. He was angry and he knew why. He had little pull in the hospital and no multimillion-dollar NIH grant. He didn't advise any professional sports team and didn't do 300-plus inpatient surgeries a year. His ambulatory cases were worthless to the hospital's bottom line. He didn't even have a board member as a patient.

In other words, he was the perfect fall guy.

He got back to his office and closed the door. He took out his BlackBerry and dialed.

"Bigelow? Nathan. I have something you might be interested in."

4

MORTIMER

DR. JOSEPH MORTIMER WAS NERVOUS. His six years as the Leopold Johann Stanislaus Chair of Orthopedic Surgery at the Eastside Medical Center hadn't seen a single incident to tarnish his reputation. In fact, no chair of any specialty in the hospital had done better: on his watch, the department had more than doubled in size, to eighty attendings and ten residents per year, making it one of the hospital's most consistent producers of cash. NIH grants had exploded to $24 million per annum. He'd just been elected vice president of the American Academy of Orthopedic Surgeons, putting him on track for the presidency in five years.

Standing next to Pear on the podium, he looked out on the reporters assembled for the press conference on the Pervis case and knew that any one of them could destroy all he'd worked for.

Pear stepped to the microphone and began.

"Yesterday, during a surgical procedure, Mr. F. J. Pervis III sustained a cardiac arrest and could not be resuscitated despite the best efforts of modern medicine. Next to me are Dr. Nicholas Rizzuto, chairman of our anesthesia department, and Dr. Joseph Mortimer, chair of orthopedics. Please hold your questions until after they have read their statements. Dr. Rizzuto."

Mortimer had glanced at enough of the statement the lawyers had prepared for him to know that it was sanitized poop. No doubt Rizzuto's was the same.

Rizzuto began. "Yesterday, at approximately 4 P.M., the patient . . ."

"Doctor, is it true that a resident and a medical student scrubbed on the case?"

Mortimer recognized the face of the questioner. Even more, he recognized the braying voice. It was Jack Bigelow of the *Post*. Two years ago, the obnoxious bastard had forced the resignation of the CEO and two department heads at St. Anthony's Hospital, Eastside's crosstown rival, with his exposé on the death of Julie Davidoff, teenage daughter of the violinist Artur Davidoff. Admitted to the emergency room late one night, the girl was shot up with tranquilizers to treat seizures and hallucinations. Nurses and attendings didn't bother to take her temperature for three hours. When they did, it was 106.5. The meningitis killed her by morning.

"Also, Doctor, hasn't the Medical Examiner been called in to do the autopsy instead of your obviously biased pathologists?"

As Bigelow's colleagues started to follow his lead, the commotion of questions reached ear-shattering proportions. Pear pushed Mortimer and Rizzuto out of the way and stepped to the microphone.

"Written statements will now be handed out. We will provide additional information on the case once the medical examiner has determined the cause of death. Thank you for coming."

Pear grabbed Mortimer and Rizzuto by their arms and pushed them through the room's back exit as security guards blocked the reporters from following.

"What a bunch of fucking jackals," said Pear once they had reached safety.

The three men entered the elevator together. Rizzuto got off on the nineteenth floor for a squash game in the hospital's executive gym with the assistant chief of interventional cardiology. Pear and Mortimer headed back to their offices on twenty.

Mortimer reached his office and sat down in his chair to contemplate his future. He'd been staring out the window for ten minutes when Peabody buzzed.

"No calls, Ms. Peabody."

"I think you should take this, chief, it's the loading dock. He says it's urgent"

The loading dock? Urgent? What the . . . ? He hit the speakerphone button.

"This is Dr. Mortimer."

"Sorry to bother you, Doc, but I don't know who else to call. This is Frank Lombardi, supervisor of the loading area."

"Yes?"

"Well, sir, it's like this. We're missing something down here that was to be picked up this afternoon."

"And?"

"And I believe the missing item is something very important to your department."

"I'm a busy man, Mr. Lombardi."

"Yes, sir. The medical examiner came to pick up a deceased person, and it's—well, it's missing from the morgue. Mr. Pervis has been . . . misplaced."

5

DEMETRI

DEMETRI AWOKE STARTLED AND STILL exhausted when his clock radio turned on at 4:30 A.M. He was still in yesterday's scrubs. At his side was half the dinner he'd microwaved the night before—his mother's pastitsio—and in his hand was a fork. This was not the first time he'd fallen asleep in the middle of a meal.

He got up and quietly placed the dish in the already full kitchen sink so as not to wake his two roommates, Allan and Cheryl, also both fourth-year students at the medical school. Although the school allowed coed apartments, Demetri got an earful from his mother on the subject. Her lecture on the wiles of the fairer sex was long and arduous and totally in Greek, indicating she was deadly serious: no Greek mother worth her spanakopita would lecture her son on the birds and the bees in English. His dad merely smiled and said, "Listen to your mother," although Demetri thought his father secretly approved. "Just be careful," he said, before giving his son a playful slap on the back of the neck.

Demetri washed his face, grabbed a granola bar, and sat down at his desk to finish his PowerPoint presentation on acromioclavicular joint injuries, aka shoulder separations. Twenty minutes later, he headed over to the hospital to scan some digital photos and radiographs into the file. He was done at five minutes to 6, just in time to start rounds with the service fellow, residents, and physician assistants. Once all the dressings had been changed and the notes and orders entered into the hospital's computer system, they all headed to the lecture hall for the morning conference.

Tom Carter joined them at this point. He looked like crap.

"Sorry, I must have overslept."

"Yeah, six hours of porking your girlfriend can make one sluggish in the morning," responded the fellow, as everyone started laughing.

Demetri scarfed up a cinnamon raisin bagel and a black coffee before the start of the lecture. The best way to ensure a good audience in medicine, he thought, is to offer free food—although not too much; otherwise, people feel they can come late and still eat. After a forty-five-minute lecture on idiopathic scoliosis delivered by the chief of pediatric orthopedics, it was Demetri's turn. He completed his presentation in the allotted ten minutes. Three minutes into it, Mortimer showed up. He stood at the back of the hall then left when the question-and-answer period started. Demetri answered two simple questions posed by two residents but was surprised that the attendings in the room asked nothing. This meant they either found Demetri's presentation thorough and authoritative or were unimpressed by his work or uninterested in the topic.

Leaving the hall at 7:05, Demetri was paged—he was being called to cover a scoliosis case. It was a combined front-and-back approach that would last six hours. He'd already been pressed into service to cover a surgery that would take begin in the late afternoon, a long-revision hip replacement that would add another four to six hours to his day. He'd barely have time in between to use the bathroom and eat a Power bar that would serve as both a late lunch and an early dinner.

In both cases, Demetri held retractors and used the suction tip. It was the most boring day he'd had in orthopedics to date; staying awake was his biggest challenge. As he dozed off on his feet toward the end of the second procedure, he was interrupted by the voice of the circulating nurse, who was yelling through the laminar airflow panels.

"Makropolis! Chief Mortimer wants to see you in his office at 5 P.M. sharp, whether the case is done or not."

Demetri turned to the attending surgeon, Beezmer, who was busy removing cement from the patient's femur with a Midas drill.

"I heard," said the surgeon, looking up. His headlight shone in Demetri's eyes. "I heard even through this blasted helmet and the noise of this blasted drill. You can help for another fifteen minutes before you have to go."

Demetri was wide awake now, overjoyed that he would avoid another four hours of holding retractors while Beezmer used his high-speed drill to remove bone cement millimeter by mind-numbing millimeter. The fellow and the surgical technician who were assisting watched with envy as Demetri left to scrub out.

Demetri grabbed his white coat out of the locker and headed straight to Mortimer's office. As he walked through the paneled hallway, his happiness over his release from Beezmer's tool-and-die shop gave way to apprehension over this unusual summons. He'd never before been called to the chief's lair. Was it some royal fuck-up in the presentation this morning?

He walked into Mortimer's outer office to find Carter, Nathan, and Toll, all also, apparently, ordered to see the boss. Something was going on.

The intercom on Peabody's desk buzzed at exactly 5. "You may all now go in," she told the four of them.

As they entered the inner office, Mortimer was pacing. "Sit," he said. He did not lift his gaze from the floor as he continued tramping from one end of the room to the other. Noticing the worn carpet in the chief's path, Demetri recalled twice covering Mortimer's cases in the OR—whenever a problem came up, he paced the room two or three times before making a decision. Nervous son of a bitch, thought Demetri.

Two other men, one from security and the other from services, stood against the wall behind Mortimer's desk. The chief finally looked up, although he did not break stride. "I need not tell you that whatever is said in this room stays in this room."

Okay, thought Demetri, this was something bigger than his misidentification of a pathology slide in his PowerPoint. Pervis? Yes, Pervis.

Mortimer went on. "We have a problem. Let me introduce to you Frank Lombardi, supervisor of the hospital's loading dock, and James Murtaugh, our chief of security. They will be integral to the search."

Nathan stopped biting his nails. "The search? For what?"

"Quite simple, Warren. Pervis's body is missing."

"What?! How does a 250-pound body get lost?"

"Let's not say 'lost,'" said Murtaugh, "let's say 'misplaced.'"

"Well, that clears it up," said Nathan. "I feel much better." The gesticulations began in earnest.

Murtaugh ignored the interruption. "It was last seen yesterday at 6 P.M. when the attendants deposited it in the morgue. At that time, the door to the morgue was locked. Except to allow one pickup of another body by a funeral home yesterday evening, the morgue was not, to our knowledge, unlocked until 3 P.M. today when personnel from the medical examiner's office came to pick up Pervis's remains. Mr. Lombardi handles all the transfers personally.

When he arrived to deliver the body over to the ME's people, he noticed it to be missing."

"Okay," said Nathan, "the body was stolen between 6 yesterday and 3 today. You do have security cameras, don't you?"

"We do, of both the morgue entrance and the loading dock. My security team is reviewing the tapes."

"The tapes? The tapes? You think that maybe someone should have been watching the monitors *while this was happening*?" Nathan emphasized the point by jumping up and down. His head looked like an overripe tomato about to burst.

"Dr. Nathan, we have over a hundred cameras throughout the medical center. We have twenty-five monitors. We therefore alternate views approximately every fifteen seconds, with everything recorded on hard drives. We're checking for any and all traffic in and out of the morgue. It's entirely possible that the funeral home came for another body and took Pervis's by mistake."

"Not possible," said Lombardi. "I double- and triple-check every time."

"Or maybe he was abducted by aliens," said Nathan.

Mortimer finally stood still. "Enough, Warren. The four of you know what Pervis looks like. You will help identify him when he is found, and you will answer any questions Mr. Murtaugh has for you. And, let me repeat, you will tell no one of this."

Nathan stood up. "Wait a minute. The hospital kills my patient—before I even start the surgery. And now the brass will make me the patsy. Don't deny it—Pear has done it in the past to I don't know how many others." Mortimer tried to interrupt but was waved down by an insistent Nathan, "And now the hospital *loses the fucking body.* The media will have a field day with that: 'Dr. Warren Nathan denies all knowledge of loss of body prior to autopsy.' I'll be finished in this town. And you're asking for my help?"

"I'm not asking, Warren. I'm ordering it."

"Before I do anything, I demand a letter from the chairman of the hospital's Quality Assurance Committee, co-signed by both you and Pear, finding that I was in no way responsible for Pervis's death. Otherwise, I think it's time the police knew about all this."

"Are you asking or ordering me, Warren? You know your promotion is coming up for review, as is your OR block-time utilization."

Mortimer had finally silenced Nathan. Loss of block time would relegate him to operating nights and weekends, if at all. It would kill his practice,

Warren's only response was a shrug that Demetri thought could be translated one of two ways: "Screw you" or, more likely, "I'm screwed."

Demetri's mind started to wander. He recalled a case his father had worked in the early '90s, dubbed the Poppy Murders by the tabloids. Eight male heroin addicts had been found in northern Manhattan with their throats slit and a single poppy flower stuffed into their tracheas. His dad was a first-grade detective at the time in narcotics.

After the eighth body was found, the city and the tabloids braced for number nine. As all the victims were Latino or African-American, Ed Scarfton, the city's premier preacher/activist/rabble rouser, denounced the police department as racist for its failure to apprehend the killer. By the fifth day of waiting, a crowd of several hundred was picketing City Hall nonstop. With the mayor and the commissioner breathing down their necks, practically every detective in the NYPD was working overtime to find the perpetrator.

On day nine, the case was broken, thanks to the work of one Michael Makropolis. Something about the seventh victim seemed familiar to Demetri's dad. He spent twelve hours in his files to find the guy: he'd busted the junkie eighteen years earlier after his girlfriend had died of an overdose. It turned out the girlfriend was the daughter of a kosher butcher from Crown Heights, in Brooklyn. After her death, the man had become mentally unstable and was institutionalized. He'd been released to his family just months prior to the start of the poppy murders. Detective Makropolis, who as a young immigrant in Queens had earned a few dollars as a *shabbos goy* at B'nai Israel of Bayside, had seen the bloodletting of kosher chickens and recognized the technique. Two days later, he stood behind the mayor, the commissioner, and the chief of detectives as the case was pronounced solved. Then came a commendation and a promotion. The stature of Micky Makropolis, as his buddies on the force called him—Mic Mak for short—landed his son a scholarship from the department's Honor Legion Society to help finance his education.

Demetri's daydream ended with the ring of the security chief's cellphone. Murtaugh grunted a few *yeahs* and *okays* into the phone, then replaced it in his pocket. "Security recordings show the one documented body pulled by the funeral home, but otherwise no bodies taken from the morgue since Mr. Pervis was deposited there and nobody leaving the premises from any known exit with a stretcher, crate, or anything that would resemble a body. Also, one of our people just visited the funeral home in question—not Pervis."

"Then the body is still on the premises," said Nathan. "Joe, I want that letter."

"There's something else," said Murtaugh. "Except for the one pick-up, the security camera shows no one entering or leaving the corridor to the morgue since the body was deposited there last evening, and that includes the ME's people who we know were there two hours ago."

"No corridors to the morgue?" said Toll. "No back exit?"

"None."

"I don't get it," said Carter. "What does this mean?"

The son of Mic Mak had an answer. "Obviously, the security cameras have been tampered with."

6

McMANUS

THE CALL CAME IN AT 8:30 P.M. to the precinct, an anonymous tip delivered directly to the executive officer on duty. The XO called the precinct commanding officer; the precinct commanding officer called the chief of detectives. The whole process took six minutes from start to finish—record time. All the squad's detectives were ordered to report forty-five minutes later for a briefing. Detective Patrick McManus got the call via his cellphone while eating a not-so-leisurely dinner at Sparks, his favorite hangout, with his soon-to-be ex-wife, Marcia, an officer in the Transit Bureau.

They were engaged in a heated debate regarding the custody of their only child, Angus, a five-year-old, 220-pound English Mastiff—the Arnold Schwarzenegger of dogdom, as McManus called him. Although he hadn't had a dog as a kid, he'd learned to love Angus despite the damage done to his trousers by the slobber he dispensed by the gallon and the hair he shed by the bushel. A clothes hound, McManus preferred Italian suits and Hermès ties. Unfortunately, on his salary he had to wait for warehouse sales to get them. Fortunately, as an NYPD detective, he'd accumulated multiple sources over the years he'd spent working the Garment District, so any time a designer was selling off merchandise, he got in before the doors opened to the public.

This evening he was wearing a dark navy Armani suit with an Ike Behar shirt and an Hermès yellow tie, topped with a Loro Piana overcoat. He headed out the door of the restaurant, peeved that he'd finished neither his steak nor the argument.

His unmarked Monte Carlo was parked in front. He checked his watch: 9:20 P.M., ten minutes until the meeting. He should make it with time to spare, he thought. Then he hit Second Avenue and the Midtown Tunnel traffic.

"Damn it!" He hit the lights and sirens. "Move!"

He made the meeting, twenty minutes late.

"Detective GQ. Glad you could join us. Your partner will catch you up." That was Inspector Mary McCarthy, NYPD's only female CO of a detective squad. She was finishing up the briefing. "He's been missing for over twenty-four hours, so get over there now. The press is onto this story, gentlemen. It is your top priority. Dismissed."

McManus looked around; Thompson, his partner, was nowhere to be seen. Just then his cellphone vibrated. It was a text: "Sick with flu. Tomorrow. Big Joe." McManus knew he was screwed. The only information he had was that someone had gone missing—obviously a VIP if ten detectives were sent after him when he'd only been gone a day. He walked over to the inspector. "Mary, Joe is on his deathbed again. Sorry I'm late."

"I suppose you were at his bedside nursing him personally?"

As she spoke, McManus's gaze lingered on her chest.

"I'm up here, Pat."

"So you are."

Two other male detectives, lingering to load up on doughnuts, guffawed.

"Here's a printout of what we know so far, Detective McManus," the inspector said. "Now, if it's not asking too much, perhaps you could get to work."

With that, she turned and catwalked away to talk to the precinct CO, who had just arrived. When she reached the commander, she turned her head to look back at McManus for a moment. McManus thought he saw her wink.

McManus sat on a chair to review the printout. He was careful to make sure his cashmere coat did not touch the floor as he sat. The seventy-five-year-old stationhouse might be "cleaned" daily, but a thick layer of crud held on tenaciously to the floor. He scanned the brief and the photo. Five foot 5 inches and 250 pounds. The photo looked familiar, but the name brought him into focus. F. J. Pervis. McManus had seen him on the news reviewing plays and movies. A snob, full of himself. *Last seen in the morgue . . .*"

"The morgue?"

The Inspector turned from the CO. "Is there a problem?"

"Problem? You mean, like a dead body lost by a hospital morgue?"

McManus left the stationhouse and got into his car. Before moving he listened for a radio traffic report. The accident in the Midtown Tunnel had been cleared. He headed over to First Avenue, drove north a few blocks past the UN, then turned left toward Midtown. The emergency room entrance was on the right. A brightly lit sign indicated no parking except ambulances. He pulled into the only open spot and got out.

The case was urgent. So instead of entering the hospital, he went to the diner across the street. The Crime Scene Unit would be hard at work, and they found his presence annoying. Besides, he really needed a cup of coffee.

7

DEMETRI

AFTER THE MEETING IN MORTIMER'S office, Murtaugh took Demetri, Toll, Carter, and Nathan to the operating room where Pervis had met his demise. The OR was not in use at the moment. Murtaugh had the four reenact every step of the procedure, from Pervis's live entry into the room to his dead exit. Waiting outside the OR door were the orderlies who had delivered the body to the morgue—Murtaugh had the two men reenact that step, too, with the entire group in tow. Once inside the morgue, Murtaugh ordered Lombardi to open each refrigerated drawer. If it contained a body, Murtaugh had Demetri and the doctors confirm that it wasn't that of the late Mr. Pervis.

When they came across a cachectic female, Toll said, "This isn't the King of New York. More like the Dowager Queen." The operating team got the joke. Murtaugh didn't.

"Is this the respect you people have for the dead?"

Nathan responded on behalf of his colleagues. "Look, Mr. Super Serious Security Chief, we spend our entire day working to aid the sick and the dying. We're selfless in our dedication—saintly, really." By this time, Nathan's colleagues were doing their best not to burst out laughing. "So I hope you won't begrudge us a morsel of comic relief to make our trials and tribulations just a bit more tolerable."

Rolling his eyes, Murtaugh turned away. "And doctors wonder why people hate them," he muttered.

Murtaugh, the three doctors and Demetri, and a handful of security personnel then combed the basement, the operating areas, and the loading dock for any sign of a misplaced body. Finally, after three hours and no dinner, the four men refused to go any further.

"Keep looking, Murtaugh," said Nathan. "When you find something, page us."

The security chief stared at Nathan. He said nothing.

Toll exited the main entrance of the hospital and headed toward the faculty housing where he lived with his wife and two sons. Nathan flagged down a cab headed uptown.

Carter flagged down Demetri. "Dinner, my treat. Lots to tell you about my night of delight with Beth."

"As long as you spare me the gruesome details. I want to be able to sleep tonight."

The two crossed the street to the Eastside Center Diner. It was a typical all-nighter seen all across America in the vicinity of hospitals. Medical personnel need to eat at all hours of the day and night; the food has to be good and filling; and it has to get to the table, or delivered to the hospital, fast. The Eastside met all those criteria. Of course, it was owned by Greeks.

They sat up front near the window. Carter ordered a burger and fries while Demetri ordered the lamb and potatoes special. Carter spared few details, gruesome or otherwise, as he told Demetri about his date with Beth. Mercifully, just as the story was reaching its climax, the waiter arrived with their orders.

"I should have ordered that," said Carter when he saw Demetri's plate.

Demetri thought that, if Carter had ordered the same dish, it wouldn't look as good or be piled as high as his.

Carter noticed a man in a long cashmere coat enter and take a table against the far wall and order a coffee.

"Check out that coat," he said. "Two thousand bucks, at least. Buy me one for Christmas, Demetri boy."

Demetri turned and took a long look at the customer. He immediately saw the man for what he was but made no mention of it to his buddy across the table. The remainder of the conversation centered on the mysterious disappearance of Mr. Pervis. When they were settling up the check, Carter said, "So your dad was a detective. What would he make of this mess?"

"He would gather the facts as we know them, build a chart, draw several hypotheses, then try to rule things in or out."

"Well?"

"Well, what?"

"You've got the genes. What do you think?"

Demetri sat still and thought long and hard. He lifted an eyebrow and said, "The only possible answer is that an alligator came through the drain from the sewer and took the body in one gulp."

"Weak, Makropolis, weak. Come on. What does your gut say?"

"My gut says that it's probably something mundane, like the body was never put in the morgue by the orderlies in the first place. They left it in a hallway somewhere while they took a break. They screwed up and are lying about it. Or else . . ."

"Or else?"

"Or else someone went to great lengths to steal a body."

8

McManus

OVER HIS COFFEE—LEADED, WITH milk and two sugars—he reread the sheet detailing the case. The patient died the day before during minor surgery, was last seen in the morgue, then disappeared. The security tapes showed no one entering or leaving the locked morgue except for the pickup team from one funeral home accompanied by hospital personnel—and the body they took checked out as the body they were supposed to take.

Maybe this Pervis isn't dead. Maybe he's home watching TV. Maybe he's walking the halls of the hospital with no memory of who he is. Or maybe he *is* dead and his doctor got rid of the body to destroy evidence of malpractice. It was probably dumped into the garbage chute and is now feeding rats in a New Jersey landfill. McManus remembered a case where the remains of a patient were placed in a garbage bag and that bag, instead of the bag containing his personal effects, was sent to the family. That cost a hospital in Brooklyn $2.5 million.

In other words, this was one huge clusterfuck. In a medical complex this size, it could be days before the stiff showed up. One thing was certain: the papers would have a field day.

No doubt the squad's other detectives were already onsite with the Crime Scene Unit. In an hour, their work would be finished, after which McManus planned on reviewing the scene himself.

In the meantime, he decided to take a stroll through the medical center. He left $2 on the table, walked out, and crossed the street. He flashed his badge to the guard at the main entrance. Inset into a sandstone wall in the lobby he saw a large bronze plaque, dated 1855, dedicating the Eastside Medical Center to "the care of the indigent." Once upon a time, he thought, the surrounding neighborhood was a slum; now it was the wealthiest ZIP code this side of Dubai. Another wall held a larger plaque, from 1998, dedicating the new wing to Samuel Stiel, the banker who, McManus remembered, had forked over $100 million for the privilege just prior to his indictment for insider trading. He walked past the gift shop, now closed, to a hallway that led to the building housing the medical school.

The door was locked. McManus waited until three students came through, then slipped in before the door closed. The school had an altogether different feel to it compared with the hospital. The hallways were more narrow, everything appeared more functional. No fancy stone floors or special lighting to impress patients and their families. The doors were metal, the drop-ceiling lighting industrial. About half the doors were unmarked aside from their room number. Some had nameplates—mostly M.D.s, a Ph.D. or two.

After turning a few corners, he walked into a large atrium, practically empty at this hour. The atrium did have the requisite stone floor and walls— the Stiel family had to have something glitzy to show off to their friends on the social circuit. On the walls were portraits and busts of old white men— great doctors, he supposed, in the history of the Eastside Medical School. He walked over to the portrait of Winston Stevens II, M.D. The painting was at least a hundred years old, he surmised from the old boy's starched clothing and sour face. He leaned over to read the small writing under his name: "Dean 1905-1918." Further down the atrium were pictures of the school from its inception in 1880 to the present day. He walked to the security station that stood beside two sets of revolving doors. He flashed his badge again.

"Is this the main entrance to the medical school?"

"You got it." The guard was sixtyish. He had a beer belly and alcohol breath, with severely stained and misaligned teeth. He had a long pink scar down the right side of his face. A knife fight not so long ago, thought McManus.

"How many other entrances and exits?"

"Half a dozen fire exits, one for the faculty club. There's a loading dock; there are connecting hallways to the hospital on floors one through five."

"Is that all?"

"It ain't enough?"

"Are they all locked or guarded?"

"Yeah, but the exits to the hospital open without a passkey from the medical school side. They're locked only from the hospital side. No one wants patients or pain-in-the-ass families walking into the labs by mistake."

"You're a sentimental man."

"I do my job."

"Security cameras?"

"All over."

"Monitored where?"

"Central station, Parker Pavilion basement across the street."

"How many blocks and buildings does the center encompass?"

"Eight square blocks, eighteen buildings, not including the Pediatric Hospital and the Ruff Rehabilitation and Nursing Center."

"Why wouldn't you include them?"

The guard decided he'd had enough of the third degree. "Why don't you go fuck yourself, you dumb Irish prick?"

McManus reached for the guard's face. He pressed his thumb into the man's scar, "Wrong answer." The guard tried to throw a punch with his left hand, but McManus caught that one. McManus increased the pressure.

"Anything else I should know?" he said.

"Yeah," said the guard, his face looking as comfortable as a jellyfish on a bed of nails. "All the buildings are connected."

"And how would they be connected?" McManus tightened his grip.

"Bridges and tunnels. What else could there be, asshole, ropes and ladders?"

"Thanks. Pleasure making your acquaintance."

McManus let go, wondering how so many ex-cons managed to get hired as security guards.

He left the building, beginning to realize that, if someone wanted to steal and hide a body, there were a thousand ways of doing it.

THERE WAS LITTLE TRAFFIC ON the street, automotive or pedestrian. He felt for his Glock 9mm on his right, strongside hip. It was there as always, tucked against his body in his custom-made Galco Deep Cover holster. He'd never liked Kydex and the other plastics used for holsters—they had none of the tactile feel of leather. Although, as a former Marine captain, the 1911 .45 caliber was his first choice in handguns, the Glock he carried was reliable and approved by the department. For backup, in case the cavalry didn't arrive in time, he wore a compact Smith & Wesson .38 special with +P+ Speer hollow points in an ankle rig. He'd never had to pull the .38 out, but there was a first time for everything.

He entered the Parker Pavilion and asked directions to the security station. Stairway to the left. Right turn downstairs. Room B12. He was met at the door by a gorilla, former NYPD; McManus didn't recognize him, but he recognized the type.

"The chief will be arriving shortly," grunted the ape, who then led the visitor through a large communications room filled with people watching what seemed to be about two dozen monitors. They came to a glass-enclosed office marked "Chief of Security." The gorilla opened the door, had McManus take a seat, then stood beside him.

Obviously, thought McManus, the ex-con with the beautiful bicuspids had phoned to announce that a visitor was on his way.

McManus looked at the pictures on the wall and the nameplate on the cluttered desk. As do many officers who retire after twenty years in the NYPD, former Deputy Inspector James Murtaugh had gone into the private security business. Chiefs and deputy commissioners made the big bucks working for Wall Street, but Murtaugh was doing just fine here—pulling down low six figures, McManus imagined. McManus remembered Murtaugh as a back-office type of cop. The type who abhors the streets, preferring paper, pencils, and protocol. He also recalled Murtaugh trying to get out of the PD on a disability retirement after his twenty years for a back injury he'd sustained fifteen years prior. He was denied that substantial perk due to "a lack of objective physical findings." Though not much liked by his peers, Murtaugh was a good-enough suck-up to his superiors to become a deputy inspector. He was also a backstabbing son of bitch who routinely peddled innuendo and hearsay to the Internal Affairs Bureau in order to keep innocent men in his command, including one Patrick McManus, from advancing up the ranks.

After ten minutes, Murtaugh arrived. "Patrick McManus, the hot shot cop who goes it alone. What the fuck are you doing here?"

McManus stood. "And good evening to you, too, Murtaugh."

9

MORTIMER

THE CALL CAME IN JUST as he was nodding off with a book on the making of *Gone With the Wind.* He usually read about old Hollywood for fifteen to twenty minutes prior to bedtime to calm his nerves, although tonight he also needed a double Glenlivet on the rocks. His wife was already asleep next to him and did not stir when the phone rang. Thirty-eight years of marriage had gotten her used to calls at all hours.

Mortimer picked up the cordless phone and slipped out of bed. He headed into the library of the eight-room prewar Gramercy Park apartment and closed the door.

He sat there as the phone continued to ring, staring at the caller ID. The corner lamp, the only light on in the room, cast multiple shadows throughout. This was Mortimer's favorite room in the apartment, with its solid walnut paneling and carved cornices. He sat in his comfort chair near the fireplace. He thought back to 1971 when he and his wife bought this apartment for what was then considered a fortune. Now the amount wouldn't even make up a down payment. On the walls, he had hung many of his old awards, but he cherished most the pictures of his family taken over the years at the house in Maine. He and his wife had bought it just after he'd been named to the Eastside faculty. His two sons and eight grandchildren had always loved summers there, sailing or just sitting on the porch that overlooks the rocky coast.

On the eighth ring, he pressed the speak button: "Yes, Fred." Pear had bad news. Someone—most likely that fool Nathan—had alerted the police to the Pervis disappearance. In fact, a detective had already been nosing around the hospital. Pear wanted Mortimer to deal with him. "Tell him to be in my office at 7 A.M.," said Mortimer before ending the call.

He could only hope that by then the body would have been found in some hallway, causing the hospital only minor embarrassment and Nathan to do some explaining when his biennial hospital appointment came up for renewal next month. Come to think of it, his own faculty appointment was coming up for review as well.

He looked to the wall on his right and saw class photos taken of him with his graduating residents. Present and future leaders of orthopedics stood in those pictures. Even if the Pervis mess sent his career to hell, he knew that more than one of those residents would remember him with kindness.

10

McManus

"TYPICAL, MCMANUS. YOU WALTZ AROUND my hospital like you own it. Did you ever hear of a warrant?"

"Calm down, Murtaugh, I haven't even started my official investigation. I just wanted to get a feel for the place."

"A feel. Was there ever a cop more full of shit? First, all that happened is that we're temporarily missing the corpse of a guy who died of natural causes. There's no evidence of foul play. So let me ask you again: what the fuck are you doing here?"

"The department was called, I was assigned. I came to investigate while forensics was finishing its work on an already contaminated crime scene."

"Crime scene? How many times do I have to tell you: there was no crime."

He looked as though the blood vessels in his brain were about to explode. McManus supposed that this hospital had experience dealing with stroke victims, although it wouldn't have bothered him if it didn't.

"Okay, Murtaugh, I'll speak slowly. Just because a crime has not yet been documented does not mean that a) one didn't happen and b) the evidence can't be destroyed, intentionally or not. You'd know that if you'd spent your time on the force being a cop instead of a professional pencil-pushing pussy."

"Get. The fuck. Out of here."

McManus turned and headed out the door of the office. He paused and looked back. "If I do find that a crime was committed and that you or your staff have contaminated the site to the point that it's useless to us, I will make sure every television station and every newspaper and every ten-cent website knows the name of the fuck-up security chief in charge. Goodnight, Murtaugh."

He headed back the way he came, up the stairs, across the street, then through the medical school into the main hospital. He reached the elevator banks and pressed the down button. Above him the glass-and-steel atrium rose all the way to the building's top floor, with a large skylight showing the night sky above.

The elevator to his left opened. He entered the empty car and pushed B for basement. As the door started to close, he saw McCarthy rounding the corner with the precinct CO. He hit the close-door button while looking the other way.

Getting off in the basement, he ran into one of the Crime Scene guys getting on with his equipment.

"Anything?"

"Hairs, fibers, dust, you name it, none of it worth shit. Multiple prints but all of them smudged."

"What a surprise. Where is it?"

"Down the hall, past the kitchen, make a left."

McManus hurried, knowing he had only moments to come up with something to tell the inspector and the CO, who were on their way. He slid under the crime-scene tape that had been strung from wall to wall about 10 feet in front of the morgue's entrance. Two detectives, Ruggiero and Fernandez, were sitting on folding chairs.

"Here's a riddle for you, McManus," said Ruggiero. "When is a case not a case? Answer: When a guy is dead; tagged and bagged; signed, sealed, and delivered—and then he's gone. Christ. The security tape shows the orderlies wheeling him in."

"Five minutes later, they leave," said Fernandez, "wheeling nothing, carrying nothing, dragging nothing. Since then, no one takes anything out."

"And the body is still missing," said McManus.

"Like Jimmy Hoffa," said Ruggiero.

The inspector and the CO appeared. McManus backed away.

"Gentlemen," said McCarthy, "what do we have?"

Ruggiero and Fernandez began to regurgitate the story in detail. As they entered the morgue with the two supervisors, McManus remained outside. He looked down the hallway. The morgue was at the end of a long corridor, which had no exit other than back toward the elevator he'd just taken. He looked up at the ceiling—it was covered by a mass of pipes, conduits, and wires that ran on both sides of large fluorescent light fixtures that gave off so little light they should be called fluorescent dark fixtures. At the entrance to the hall, he noted up in the corner a standard interior security camera. Connected by coaxial cable to the server, no doubt.

He looked around for something to stand on. He found a stretcher. He moved it into place then locked the wheels.

He scrambled up, his prematurely arthritic knee, courtesy of the United States Marine Corps, complaining more than usual. He'd asked an orthopedist about a knee replacement after his honorable discharge from the Corps. Too young, the doc had told him. But today his forty-two-year-old body was being schooled by his sixty-five-year-old knee. He reminded himself to pop two Advil and discuss it with himself in the morning.

The housing of the camera was intact, as was the cable attached to it.

"Something, detective?"

He looked down to see McCarthy then looked back up, tracing the cable from the camera as it led to the line of cables on the ceiling. He noted a glint of chrome. He pulled out his Surefire flashlight.

"Maybe."

He shined the light toward the piece of chrome.

"Inspector, if you and the CO don't mind, please unlock the wheels and push me ahead 5 feet. Slowly."

"Really, Pat."

"A hunch, Mary. Indulge me."

As they rolled the stretcher, McManus kept his eyes glued to the jumble of cables.

"Stop." He placed the Surefire in his mouth and pointed it upward as he felt for the piece of chrome that had caused the glint.

"Wanna let us in on the secret, Detective?" said the CO.

That instant, Patrick McManus, NYPD detective with a bum knee, jumped off the stretcher as if he were fifteen years old.

He held out his right hand and opened it to reveal a small metallic object. With his left, he took the flashlight out of his mouth.

The blank looks on the faces of McCarthy and the CO showed they had no idea what they were looking at, so McManus told them. "It's a video A/B switch."

The CO's face still didn't register comprehension. "So?"

"So this is now a criminal case."

11

PERVIS

HE AWOKE IN A LIT chamber that looked like OR 11 but seemed older, damper, warmer. He recalled lying in the dark, covered and cold, for what seemed hours.

Perhaps it was all a bad dream.

With great effort he lifted his head. The move triggered a tidal wave of nausea. After a few moments, the room stopped spinning, and he was able to look around—but only a bit: his head felt like it was locked into a vise. He found himself naked, strapped down tight to a metal table, with an IV in his right arm and a small white tag attached to his big toe. His body reeked of urine and feces. And he was parched. His thirst was beyond description.

This was no dream.

He felt a slight vibration as he heard a distant rumble. The subway? Was he underground? Was he in the same hospital? He couldn't even tell the time of day in this windowless chamber.

"Good evening, Mr. Pervis." The voice came floating from behind him.

"Who are you?" These were the first words he'd been able to utter since surgery.

"Why, Mr. Pervis, I am your doctor, of course."

"Warren? This isn't funny." Pervis twisted his neck as much as he could to see where the voice came from but saw no one.

"No, I am not Dr. Nathan. He is an orthopedic surgeon. Do you know, Mr. Pervis, that orthopedic surgeons used to come from the bottom ten percent of their medical school classes? They were the gorillas of the profession, the ones with their knuckles dragging on the ground, the jocks with too many injuries to continue their sports careers. How times have changed. Now they all come from the top five percent, performing high-tech joint replacements and arthroscopic surgery. Still, they will never be anything more than over-paid carpenters."

Pervis heard the squeal, and felt the vibration, of screws tightening at the head of the stretcher. He felt some pressure and pain, as if screws were directly attached to his skull, which they, in fact were.

"Neurosurgery, on the other hand, is infinitely more rewarding. The secrets of the brain are unending. The brain holds the center of human reason and emotion. Its structure mirrors our species's development, from proto-plasm to masters of the world. Did you know, Mr. Pervis, that the brainstem is the key to life and longevity?"

"What does this have to do with me? Do you know who the fuck I am?" The words barely escaped his parched throat.

"Oh, yes, Mr. Pervis. I'm a big fan of your writing. But, you see, I was in need of a new subject to continue my work and you became available. True, your celebrity makes you not the optimal choice, since people are looking for you as we speak, but I have reached a crucial stage. Time, as I'm sure you can appreciate, is of the essence."

New subject? His work? Pervis began to panic.

"Money? Do you want money? I can arrange . . ."

"Oh, no, Mr. Pervis, this isn't about anything as sordid as money. It's about life."

Though dehydrated, Pervis felt himself urinate involuntarily—painfully, as though he were expelling dry urine crystals. He looked at the instrument tray to his right. On it lay drills and saws, as well as scalpels, clamps, and what looked like a power saw. He tried to swallow, but his throat and mouth were cotton dry. His hands and feet were numb from the leather straps holding him down, and the queasy feeling had returned.

He looked at the walls of the brightly lit room and saw shelves full of huge specimen jars containing what seemed to be tissue samples floating in fluid. In the room's darker recesses were shelves with even larger jars. Were those human remains in them?

"Did you know, Mr. Pervis, that some fish live for hundreds of years? And that amphibians can hibernate for generations before resuming a normal life? The brainstem, Mr. Pervis, the brainstem. It is the most primitive part of our brain, with an array of neurotransmitters unlike those found in any of the brain's other areas." It sounded to Pervis like a lecture an old professor might deliver to his students—except that this old professor was clearly mad. Pervis felt the taste of bile in his throat as the dry heaves overtook him.

"The drugs I utilized to feign your death have now left your system, so let us begin. I have already applied, through a halo device, four large-diameter screws to your cranium to keep your head still. I will apply local anesthetic to the skin and subcutaneous tissue for the surgical approach to minimize initial reactive movements, but no general anesthesia. You will be alive and totally awake for the entire procedure, with no drugs in your system. The harvest will be of higher quality that way."

Pervis noted a bright light being moved over his head and then was temporarily blinded as a shape bent over him wearing a mirror attached to a headband, as though this doctor came straight from one of the original Dr. Kildare movies from the '40s.

"No, this is insane. This must be a joke. Warren, where are you, you sick fuck?" He began to cry like a little baby. "There has to be another way."

"I assure you, Mr. Pervis, this is the only way. Decades of trial and error have gone into perfecting my technique."

Pervis felt his head being held down by a powerful hand then squeezed by the tightening screws.

"It is essential you do not move at all, Mr. Pervis. Brain tissue, as you know, is extremely delicate."

The squeal of the screws again reverberated, even more loudly, through Pervis's head. Pervis then noted the doctor leaning toward him with a large-bore needle and syringe in hand.

"This will hurt, Mr. Pervis. In fact, it will hurt a lot. But it will be over soon. Feel free to scream as much as you need to. No one can hear you."

12

PEAR

HE DREAMT OF BODIES WASHING up on the shore of the Central Park Reservoir, within eyesight of his Fifth Avenue duplex. All the bodies were the same: each one the bloated corpse of that fucking Pervis. The cover of the *Metropolitan Post* featured a photograph of the scene with the headline "INVASION OF THE BODY SNATCHERS." Inset at the upper right was a close-up of the hospital's CEO, Dr. Fred Pear, Photoshopped into zombie make-up.

He awoke at 3 A.M. in a cold sweat, his heart racing irregularly like a nervous mouse skittering across an open floor: speeding, stopping for a sniff, then speeding off again. He was in atrial fibrillation again. He would need to see his cardiologist in the morning. Although a trained cardiologist himself, he hadn't practiced in years and would leave the medicating to others even if the problem was obvious to him: His Toprol dose was too low. Unfortunately, upping it made him impotent; Pear hated impotence of all kinds. He also hated living on Coumadin to prevent clots from forming in his heart; the blood thinner meant he had to avoid his favorite vegetables, like broccoli and kale. In addition, his high cholesterol meant he could eat only minimal amounts of red meat, so practically every dinner consisted of chicken, overbaked potatoes, and soggy peas. Even fish rarely passed his lips because of the mercury. It was a wonder he was able to eat anything at all; yet, even so, he was unable to lose weight. In all likelihood, his chief of cardiology, Richard Landau, would place him on Amiodarone, a drug implicated in the lung complications that killed that sports commentator right after a knee replacement a few years ago.

Fortunately, that train wreck had taken place at another hospital in the city.

As he lay back down, his mind raced along with his irregular heart. The medical center's attorney and PR guy were to meet with him and Mortimer at 6:30 A.M. Twenty minutes later, he would check in with Murtaugh. At 7 was the sit-down with the ineffectual Mortimer and the NYPD.

He didn't fall back to sleep until after 5. His dreams were better now, of ribeye steaks, buttery mashed potatoes, and sautéed broccoli. The alarm interrupted the meal at 5:30 sharp. He rose and checked his pulse; it had returned to normal sinus rhythm. He could put off that visit to Landau.

In forty minutes, he was on the street and into his waiting Mercedes S600 sedan with blacked-out windows.

"Good morning, Dr. Pear." It was Dan Lee, his driver, gopher, and bodyguard. "Have you seen this?"

Lee passed a copy of the *Metropolitan Post* back to him.

On the cover was a photograph of Fred Pervis with the headline, "DEATH AND DONUTS." The article, by Jack Bigelow, took up most of page 3:

Two days ago F. J. Pervis III, drama critic for this newspaper, entered Eastside Medical Center for minor arthroscopic surgery on his knee. He died on the operating table. No one at the hospital has been able to explain why.

A massive string of mistakes might be funny if those making them were the Keystone Kops, but the multiple screw-ups by medical "professionals" at Eastside carried with them tragic consequences. The "irregularities" (as these so-called healers call them) uncovered by this reporter's investigation include: Failure to presurgically clear the patient. Administration not of regional anesthesia, the norm for such cases, but rather of general anesthesia delivered intravenously. That risky step, outside experts have concluded, was most probably the worst goof in the whole sad story, causing complications that led to Pervis's demise.

Department chairs of both anesthesia and orthopedic surgery appeared at a news conference yesterday. Donuts and coffee abounded, but neither a solution to the mystery nor a hint of accountability was to be found. As this reporter pressed for answers, the hospital's top dog,

*CEO Fred Pear, abruptly ended the presser, hustling the two depart-
ment honchos out a rear door.*

*The city medical examiner has stepped in to conduct the autopsy,
rather than risk a cover-up by hospital pathologists.*

*F. J. Pervis was a member of this newspaper's family. This reporter,
and this newspaper, will not rest until the truth is told.*

Pear put down the paper. It was clear that Bigelow and the rest of the hyenas
were not going to sit idly by while the hospital figured out its story. A concise
and definitive course of action was required.

The stakes were enormous. If the body was not recovered by midday,
the hospital's hard-earned reputation was down the tubes. Medical centers all
over the metropolitan area would seize the opportunity to grab market share.
The financial blow would cripple the institution, leaving it ripe for takeover.
That was unacceptable, because it meant he, Dr. Fred Pear, CEO of the largest and most prestigious medical center in the United States—architect of
a decade's worth of expansion—would be unemployed. No doubt he could
get another job: running a 200-bed community hospital in some backwater
swamp, 300 miles from nowhere.

He was ready to sacrifice the surgeon, the anesthesiologist, and their department chairs to clean up this mess. But other heads—those of the chief
of security, the head of the loading dock, or anyone else he could find to
plausibly or implausibly blame—would roll first if the corpse was not found
this morning.

He had too much to lose.

13

McManus

HE HEADED HOME TO QUEENS.

No prints had been found on the video switch. The device was a cheap one, available at any Radio Shack, and thus untraceable. The splicing job had been done with precision, probably during overnight hours, and at least a week prior to the body theft: the security server recorded a week's worth of video before going back and overwriting, and both Murtaugh and the Crime Scene guys had assured him that all available video for the compromised camera had been reviewed with nothing out of the ordinary found. That meant the theft had been planned long before it was performed. However, the theft of this particular body had not been planned—Pervis had gotten injured and died within forty-eight hours of the body's disappearance, well after the camera had been tampered with.

In other words, any corpse would have done just fine.

McManus recalled a documentary on the History Channel he'd seen on body snatching. During the nineteenth and early twentieth centuries, doctors and medical schools, in the U.S. and in Europe, were notorious for stealing freshly buried bodies to use for anatomy dissections—often with the connivance of the grave diggers themselves. Families would stand vigil over graves, not to grieve but to protect the body from theft until it had decayed sufficiently to render it useless to doctors. The novel *Frankenstein* was a fictionalized account of the grave robbing that terrorized helpless populations.

That was then. Why would someone go to such lengths to steal a body now?

THE INSPECTOR HAD REWARDED MCMANUS for his
find of the switch by assigning him and his partner the case. The last time
Big Joe had had "the flu" he'd been out two weeks, so success or failure in the
matter of Dr. Frankenstein was going to be McManus's alone.

He didn't mind. In fact, he liked the action.

What he needed once he got home was sleep. What he got when he
arrived at his Bayside split level was the completion of an argument with his
wife. She'd been waiting up in her nightgown to finish flaying him for his
alleged neglect of Angus, who slobbered all over McManus's fine cashmere
coat as soon as he opened the door. "Thanks, buddy, I appreciate that."

Ten seconds later, Marcia bushwacked him. "You appreciate nothing but
a good case. The dog means nothing to you other than dry-cleaning bills and
responsibility you can't handle."

McManus thought he couldn't handle this discussion right now. It was
almost midnight; he had to be back at the hospital by 7. The thought also ran
through his mind that living in the same house with your soon-to-be ex is a
bad idea. But having nowhere else to stay gave him no alternative.

McManus knew how it was. The highest-stress jobs led to the highest
rates of divorce and heart attacks, and being a homicide detective was number
one on the list. Lately their different work and vacation schedules had made
it seem as though he and Marcia were leading two completely separate lives,
occupying the same space at different times. He still loved his wife, but so
does the mate of a black widow spider. The poor male spider has it easy compared to McManus: its head only gets bitten off once, whereas, lately, Marcia
bit her mate's head off every time he saw her.

"I love Angus as much as you do, and you know it. What are you doing
here, anyway? I thought you were working the overnight shift."

"Nope. After you ran out in the middle of dinner, I realized you hadn't
walked and fed Angus the way you said you would, so I did. Then I called in
sick. This dog needed some quality time—from someone."

"Angus knows I couldn't help it. A body was stolen at the Eastside Medical Center; a real-life grave robber went to great lengths to get it. If there's a
thunderstorm tonight, Boris Karloff will be on the loose in the morning."

Marcia cracked a smile. McManus smiled as well, sensing a chink in her
armor. Through everything, she'd never lost her appreciation for his sense of
humor. He missed the mad lovemaking they used to have at every opportunity. He started developing a hard-on that became quite visible, even through
his hair-covered overcoat.

"It seems the monster has arrived," she said as she grabbed him and kissed him forcefully. McManus, surprised, backed into and fell onto the couch as Marcia yanked his coat off. The trousers went next as she reached under his briefs and squeezed hard. "Which body did this come from?" she said as she straddled him and let him penetrate her.

The excitement rubbed off on Angus, who started running circles on the carpet. McManus ordered him to lie down, which he did, his eyes glued to the spectacle before him. When it was over, he walked over to check out the olfactory sensations.

"It's late, we'll talk tomorrow," Marcia said as she arose and pulled down her hiked-up nightie. She headed to the master bedroom with Angus in tow then closed and locked the door. McManus could not figure how she could be so hot for him one moment then turn ice cold the next. Did she love him, or was it only physical satisfaction that she wanted from him? He wouldn't figure it out tonight.

He gathered his clothing and headed to the guest bedroom on the second floor. His BlackBerry vibrated, and he checked the message. It was Joe, his partner, texting him that he would be home again tomorrow with "the flu." More likely, McManus thought, it was too much fried chicken from Sylvia's or some nymphomaniac from Highway Patrol that was keeping Joe from his duty.

Once in the guest bedroom, he sank into the bed and stared at the ceiling. He felt powerless to change the course he and Marcia were set upon. Marcia had given him till the end of the week to fill out the separation papers.

HE OVERSLEPT AGAIN. HE QUICKLY got dressed in a Ralph Lauren Black Label gray-flannel three-button suit, with a red Hedgehog Hermès tie, a white Behar French-cuff shirt, and Ferragamo burgundy wingtips. He finished the look with gold-and-silver filigreed cufflinks he'd found at a street fair on Sixth Avenue. He got into his unmarked RMP and hopped onto the Parkway, on which where he didn't average more than 10 miles per hour all the way to Manhattan. The good doctors of the Eastside Medical Center would just have to wait for him.

14

THE DOCTOR

KILLING INVIGORATED HIM: THE ADRENALINE rush was almost as thrilling as the rush he got when he self-injected his youth concoction intrathecally at the base of his neck. That was always the hard part, placing the needle through his skin, epidural space, and dura into the cerebrospinal-fluid–filled space surrounding his spinal cord. Back in the early years, he used a set of mirrors to place the needle directly in the midline of his spine. Today he used computer-assisted placement: a monitor showed him exactly where the needle had to be. He looked forward to a host of medical advances throughout the twenty-first century, and beyond.

After pushing the combination of drugs and human brain matter into his body, every nerve ending came alive, as though he'd placed his finger in a wall socket, but without spasm or pain, only ecstasy. In the early days, as he was developing his formula, he'd found it did not work nearly as well when used intravenously.

And so he now felt revitalized.

He had a bit of housekeeping to attend to: he needed to get rid of the body. He could dump it in the river, as he had so many others over the years, but where was the fun in that? He decided to leave it in a conspicuous area and cause his nemesis, Pear, some heartburn.

Nighttime would be best for the disposal. The halls and offices at the medical center were mostly empty those hours; the medical school was deserted.

Wheeling his prize in a laundry hamper, he passed the main lecture hall,

Paige Auditorium. It was dark except for the dimly lit stage. Built like an amphitheater so all could look down at the action, the auditorium was where generations of medical students had seen lectures, demonstrations of physical diagnosis, cadaver dissections, and even, in the early days of the school, surgical procedures. What better place for drama than a stage, thought the Doctor. He stopped, removed his keys from the pocket of his maintenance-staff uniform, and quickly opened the door. He wheeled the hamper in.

He lifted the body bag without hesitation or effort, his life force pulsating at maximum, and laid it on the table adjacent to the lectern. As he was about to unzip it, there was a sound from the corridor: footsteps, male, alone but authoritative. Security, no doubt, making rounds. How fortunate.

The door opened. The security guard entered and turned on his flashlight. He looked in the hamper, found it empty, then pointed his light to scan the seating area. "Hello," he called out. "Anybody here?"

No response. The guard shut off the flashlight and placed it on his belt before stepping behind the laundry hamper. "First that pain-in-the-ass detective and now this," he said through clenched, crooked teeth. He began to roll it toward the door when he heard a faint sound. He stepped back and yelled out into the dark auditorium, "I know you're in here. Come on out. I ain't gonna report you."

He waited, hearing nothing.

"My shift is over. I got no time to waste on rich-kid students wheeling each other around in canvas dumpsters because they can't find a girl to pork. Will you just get out of here so I can go home?"

More silence. He grabbed his flashlight and tried to turn it back on, but it didn't light. "Cheap plastic shit from China," he muttered. " Biggest-ass hospital in the world—this is the shit equipment they give us?" He fiddled with it some more then flipped it up toward himself so he could see the bulb. He tightened the top and it went on, immediately blinding him as the beam torched his retinas. "Fuck me!" he yelled from the neurogenic pain.

Moments later, his vision began to return, in time to see the silver flash of the knife as it arced towards his throat.

Now the Doctor had two bodies to dispose of. He'd double Pear's heartburn: one for the lecture hall, one for the anatomy lab.

15

DEMETRI

A BIG EVENING MEAL ALWAYS helped him sleep—the glucose tide, a wave of rising blood sugar, was way better than Ambien. He'd need the rest tonight; he'd been summoned to appear at Mortimer's office at 7 A.M.— "SHARP," as the text message said.

Both roommates were out, in all likelihood working late. He brushed his teeth in the communal bathroom then went to his room, stepping over Allan's size-14 sneakers, strewn as usual in the hallway. He didn't bother changing; his scrubs were as comfortable as pajamas.

Despite the late hour, he wanted some sage advice, so he called his dad.

"Demetri? Are you alright?"

"Yes, Dad, I am alright." It was his father's first question no matter what time he called. "Just calling to shoot the shit."

From the silence on the other end of the line, Demetri knew his dad already knew he wasn't all right. Whose twenty-five-year-old son calls at 11 P.M. when everything is hunky dory? Michael Makropolis, the former NYPD detective, was surely surveying the possibilities. Either his son has decided to drop medicine and join the NYPD like his dear ol' dad, or, more likely, his roommate is pregnant, and his son wants to do the honorable thing.

"What's the problem?"

"Dad, something strange is going on here at the hospital."

"Oh." Little did Demetri know he'd just spared his father a myocardial infarction.

A moment passed as the older man recovered from his near-death experience. "Okay, son. Shoot."

Demetri took twenty minutes to recount all he knew about the missing body.

After a pause of ten seconds, his dad responded. "In the 1980s, at the same hospital, there was a missing body of a patient who had died. It was never solved; it was eventually classified as a cold case. Thing is, it turned out there were two similar incidents about twenty years earlier. Neither of them led anywhere, either."

"You mean dead bodies have disappeared from this hospital before?"

"Yeah, the last one was a homeless man—no friends, no family. I'd forgotten all about it. We didn't go overboard investigating. New York was spilling blood in the streets back then. We had other thing to do besides look for a body that was going to Potter's Field."

"Look, tomorrow morning I'm to meet with the detectives assigned to the case. The hospital brass will all be there."

"Be cooperative, don't volunteer information other than that I'm your dad."

With just minutes remaining before his blood sugar knocked him out, Demetri quickly said goodbye to his father then opened his laptop and began to search for prior losses of human remains at the Eastside Medical Center.

What he found in newspaper archives were missing bodies documented as far back as 1890. They seemed unrelated—most were years apart—but the poor hospital management and record-keeping of earlier years made it hard to tell.

The hospital's archives and medical records department would have more information.

16

MURTAUGH

AT 7:05, DR. JOSEPH MORTIMER was pacing his usual path as everyone else sat or stood by. "He's late," Mortimer said.

"He'll be here," said Pear.

Warren Nathan sat in the far corner, quiet but fidgety. He was regretting at that moment that he'd gotten the NYPD involved, bringing into the public realm the case and the consequences it might have to his reputation. Toll and Carter stood by the window chatting about the code—how it could have and should have been done differently, even though they agreed that the outcome would have been the same. Carter felt that open-heart massage would have helped. "Typical surgeon," was Toll's response. "Everything can be solved with the knife." Demetri stood quietly behind them.

Seated directly in front of Mortimer's desk was Murtaugh, the security chief. His cellphone rang; he answered. "Find him yet?" It was his second-in-command. Murtaugh listened, then he yelled into the phone, "I don't give a flying fuck. Unless he's got an airtight excuse for leaving his post in the middle of the night, his ass is fired. Call his cell and get him in here."

Murtaugh ended the call then turned to Pear and said, "The missing guard."

The man they'd been waiting for finally arrived; now the party could start.

"Good morning. I am Detective Patrick McManus of the New York City Police Department. I have asked you all here since, to one extent or another, you are all involved in this case."

"We're here to help in any way possible," said Pear.

McManus nodded and continued. "Overnight there were some developments in this criminal investigation."

Murtaugh stood. "This isn't a criminal case."

McManus turned away from Murtaugh as if he didn't exist and told the group of the tampering he'd found in the video surveillance system. "This is a criminal case until proven otherwise."

Murtaugh's phone rang again. "What?" he growled into it.

He listened for a minute then hung up. "Well, Detective Patrick McManus of the New York City Police Department, the case is solved. You can head for the exits. The show is over."

17

JAY SILVERBERG ARRIVED AT THE lab early. He had a lot of ground to cover if he wanted to be the year's top student in anatomy. His group of four students had to finish the head and neck dissection this week on their cadaver before they could proceed to the extremities.

Anatomy was the make-or-break course for first-year medical students, taught as it always had been: four students per cadaver, five cadavers per professor. In any particular year at any particular institution, a handful of students drop out of school within a day of starting anatomy. The skinning of the cadaver convinces them they'd wanted to be lawyers all along. Not Silverberg. Blood and guts didn't faze him. Anatomy was the basis for his future career in surgery, preferably in reconstructive plastics.

He'd brought his breakfast with him: an egg and bacon on a roll and a black decaf. Leaded coffee gave him the shakes, an unwanted affliction for a budding surgeon. He sat down at the counter across from his cadaver to enjoy his meal before starting the dissection. The odor of formaldehyde that permeated the lab and the hallways leading to it no longer bothered him, as it had saturated every shred of clothing he owned except one set he never wore to the lab. Those threads were reserved for special occasions, like visiting his mother at her condo in New Hyde Park, on Long Island. Early in the school year, he'd gone home for Rosh Hashanah. Before he got through the door, she'd pushed him out. She grabbed her car keys and threw them at him, ordering him not to return until he'd bought a new outfit at the Roosevelt

Field Mall and thrown his malodorous shirt, pants, socks, and underwear in the trash.

He took a bite out of his sandwich as he slouched back in the rolling chair and opened up an old copy of Hollinshead's *Anatomy* to review the day's dissection. He finished off half the sandwich, pulled a latex glove onto his right hand, then picked up the other half with his left. Taking another bite, he wheeled himself over to his cadaver and, with his gloved hand, unzipped the body bag. The cadaver reeked more than usual today, he noted. He finished his meal as he started to unroll the bag off the cadaver.

"What the . . . ?"

Something was definitely wrong; this was not his cadaver. George, the janitorial attendant, must have mixed them up when he was cleaning. Silverberg would have to open all the cadaver bags to find the right one.

He turned and yelled down the hallway, "Hey, George! George, get down here!"

George entered the lab to find a partially exposed cadaver he didn't recognize, and he knew them all by sight. Silverberg's cadaver was thin, this one was portly. In fact, it was pinker and fleshier than any of the twenty-five bodies that had inhabited the lab this semester.

"Where did you move my cadaver?" said Silverberg.

"I cleaned last night, just like always," said George. "Didn't move a thing."

He looked up and down the lab, five rows of five cadavers each. He walked over to Silverberg and peered at the uncovered legs and abdomen of the cadaver.

"This isn't one of ours," he said.

Silverberg reached to uncover the head and neck but paused when he noted another body bag on the lower level of the stainless steel stretcher. "George, what's going on?"

"I don't know."

Silverberg pulled the rest of the bag off with his ungloved hand. As George blurted out "Holy Christ!," Silverberg vomited his breakfast.

The puke landed directly on what used to be a human face.

18

MURTAUGH

THEY ALL WAITED BY THE elevator bank impatiently. Murtaugh stood by the call button, his chest expanded. "I knew we'd find him. The anatomy lab, of course. Some orderly found the body in the hallway and thought it belonged in there."

Demetri didn't seem so sure. "If the body has been in the anatomy lab all this time, why didn't someone report it earlier? The class was there yesterday, and George cleans up every night."

"Make you a deal," said Murtaugh. "I won't perform surgery if you don't play security chief. Obviously it wasn't in the anatomy lab 'all this time.' It was left in the hall overnight and then taken to the lab early this morning. The point is, the body's been found."

"I agree," said Pear. "Job well done."

Murtaugh puffed up even more as he leered at McManus. "Guess it's back to the streets, McManus."

"I think I'll join you at the lab anyway," said McManus. He leaned toward the security chief and whispered, "Just to make sure you don't totally fuck it up."

Murtaugh mouthed the words "Eat shit" as the elevator arrived and they all piled in.

Mortimer hit the fourth floor button. "We'll take the quick route through the medical school."

Standing in the back of the car, Nathan was apprehensive, thinking ahead to what the medical examiner might find. He needed protection. He took out his phone and started texting—first Bigelow, then a contact in the mayor's office.

The group exited left from the elevator, passing the Parks Wing housing the inpatient general surgery cases. Mortimer swiped his ID at the door to the medical school, and the lock clicked open. The group passed through, entering the Poldark Wing of the school. McManus didn't know why it was called a wing, let alone why some rich donor needed to have his name all over it.

Demetri took the lead at this point since he walked these halls every day. Multiple rights, lefts, and doors led to elevators 101 and 102. McManus, feeling completely lost, was wondering how the body could end up so far from the hospital without anyone seeing it.

The read-outs indicated that the elevators were on floors eight and twenty; the men were on four so Demetri headed for the stairs. "This will be much faster. It's only two floors down."

Nathan, still texting, walked at the back of the group while Pear, slightly short of breath, mentioned he had not been in this part of the medical center in years. He'd been spending too much time with big-money philanthropists who wanted their name on new wings of the hospital rather than getting the medical school its fair share of the donations. In truth, the hospital and the medical school were two different institutions, with separate boards and administrative structures, even though they were linked by an affiliation agreement dating back over a hundred years.

They got to the entrance of the lab to find two security guards, one of them the brute McManus had met at Central Station the night before. Next to them stood an orderly and a medical student, both as pale as the student's short white coat.

"Chief, these are the two who found the body," said the non-brute. "George is the orderly in charge of the lab and Jay Silverberg is a first-year student."

Murtaugh grabbed the boy by both shoulders to congratulate him, but the student appeared to buckle under the pressure. "What's the matter? You've seen cadavers before, haven't you?"

"Not like this one." It was the brute.

"What are you talking about?" said Murtaugh.

"The brain surgery he died from must have been nasty."

Nathan stopped texting. "Brain surgery?"

"He died with the induction of anesthesia," said Toll. "He was in for arthroscopy of the knee, which we never even started."

Murtaugh pushed the security men aside and entered the room, followed by McManus, then Nathan, Toll, Pear, Mortimer, Carter, and Demetri.

What they saw turned the stomach of each of them. The retching in the back by Pear and Mortimer was uncontrollable. Murtaugh's speech was unintelligible. Only McManus and Demetri were able to inch forward and take a closer look at the body on the stretcher. The stench of partially clotted blood, vomit, and formaldehyde, with just a hint of coffee and bacon, filled the room.

Murtaugh, McManus, and the others could not believe what they were seeing. The front of the skull had been removed, and the frontal lobes of the brain appeared to be missing. The upper half of the face was split in two and spread apart all the way back. The body's back was arched upward, and the bloody mouth was locked open in what appeared to be an agonizing scream. The open cranium was filled with vomitus, courtesy of medical student Silverberg.

"Mother of God," Murtaugh said, while Demetri, with a quivering hand, made the sign of the Greek Orthodox cross.

McManus had seen countless dead bodies in the last twenty years, both on the job and in the first Gulf War with the Marines. He'd seen bodies that were shot, strangled, poisoned, blown to bits, and decapitated, but never one like this. Determined to maintain his poise, he collected himself then turned to the others. "No one is to touch anything. Keep both guards at the door. Everyone is to stay together until further notice. For now, we'll all wait here until the Crime Scene Unit and the medical examiner arrive. Then I'll need witness statements from every one of you."

He turned back to stare at the grotesque carcass on the steel cart. "Well, Murtaugh, the ball is my court now."

EVERYONE SETTLED INTO SEATS AS far away from the body as possible—except for Nathan. Holding his cellphone in front of his chest, he managed to shoot a dozen pictures of the body without anyone noticing.

Murtaugh's phone rang again. "Murtaugh." He listened and became rigid, standing back on his heels, jaw clenched, almost catatonic. He looked as though he could be pushed over with a finger, as though he were a plank of wood balanced on end.

Murtaugh put away his phone. He said nothing until McManus spoke. "What is it?"

"They found my missing security guard," Murtaugh said, moving his lips but otherwise still frozen. He gazed past McManus, focusing on the blank white space of the far wall. He hesitated a moment, then resumed. "He was seated in the back row of Paige Auditorium with his throat slashed."

19

Demetri

DEMETRI OVERHEARD THE CRIME SCENE Unit confirm what McManus had expected: Pervis's body had been mutilated elsewhere then brought to the anatomy lab. The big surprise came after the medical examiner had finished his examination.

"It looks like the patient was still alive when Dr. Edgar Allan Poe carved him up, McManus," he said as he stripped off his latex gloves and mask.

"Say what?"

"I can't be absolutely sure at this juncture—the vomit from the student has obscured the tissue planes; until that gets washed off, it's hard to tell."

McManus's face started to turn green.

"Come on, Pat, you're not going to get sick over a little thing like vomit covering up tissue planes in a head that's been split open and dissected, are you?"

"When you put it that way, Doc, of course not." McManus swallowed and steadied himself by holding onto a chair.

The ME placed his papers in his messenger bag then closed it. "See, if he'd been dead when it happened, the blood loss would have been minimal, and it was anything but. Plus, the core body temperature indicates he died within the last twelve hours."

"So he didn't . . ."

"Die on the operating table yesterday? Unlikely." He got into his down coat. "As for the security guard, he died from near decapitation down by the stage between 2 and 3 A.M. Based on the blood trail up the aisle, he was placed in the rear seat while still bleeding. I'll have some more answers for you tomorrow. One hell of a mess you've got here, McManus."

He started walking down the hall. "Yep. One hell of a mess."

The ME turned away and started walking down the hall, mumbling within McManus's earshot, "Yep. One hell of a mess."

Demetri, sitting behind a pylon still listening in, shook his head in disbelief and knew what he had to do. McManus needed all the help he could get.

20

McManus

THE INSPECTOR LATER ARRIVED TO survey the scene in the lab. "Well, Pat, got anything big for me?" she said as she eyed his crotch.

"Get this, Mary. ME says our boy's brain was cut out while he was still alive."

McCarthy looked McManus in the eye. "That means a shitload of problems. The press is camped outside and blurry pictures of the body are already posted on Bigelow's website. The reporters all know something's up. Plus, the mayor's onto the story, so the commissioner's on his way. He'll need to make a statement."

"Stall. Say that the body was misplaced but has been recovered. No further information until tomorrow when the ME files his report. Mary, you know that the guard's murder complicates things tenfold."

"Yes, I do know, Pat. And you know that you've got less than twenty-four hours to sort the whole thing out."

"Thanks."

"By the way, don't you have a partner?"

"Home with 'the flu.'"

"'The flu?'"

"'The flu.'"

"I'd partner with you any day, Pat. Or any night."

"Would you now?"

The inspector smiled. "Twenty-four hours, Pat." She turned and walked away, more perky than she had any right to.

THE MED SCHOOL DEAN OFFERED McManus half a dozen offices in Academic Affairs to use for interviews. McManus placed Nathan, Pear, Carter, Mortimer, Toll, and Demetri each in a separate room and began taking statements. Most of what he heard was the usual: ass-covering and blame-shifting.

The first three proved the least edifying. Nathan interrupted his texting—to his patients, the doctor said, although McManus assumed he was spilling the facts of the case to his contacts in the media—long enough to give the detective an earful about Pervis: "I loathed him. He was a fat, egocentric pig of a man who didn't care about his fellow human beings one bit except for what they could do for him." Pear tried to smooth-talk his way out of meaningful cooperation: "Please rest assured that I am here to facilitate your investigation in any way I can in order to end this nightmare as soon as possible," which McManus took to mean that he'd sell out his favorite uncle in order to protect his reputation. Carter critiqued the cop's clothing—"Armani, Detective? P. Elliott is so much more timeless."—before claiming an alcohol-and-sex-fueled date as his alibi.

Mortimer, at least, was honest.

The department chair shared little of value to the case, but McManus couldn't help feeling for the guy. Clearly depressed, he said more than once that the Pervis affair "could destroy everything I've worked for, for over thirty years—and I'm helpless to stop it." He could barely look at the detective as they talked. McManus, the Marine, had seen PTSD dozens of times, so he wasn't surprised when Mortimer let slip that he'd been a combat surgeon in Vietnam just after finishing med school.

THE MED STUDENT WOULD BE last. But first, Toll, the only doctor to actually treat the patient that afternoon.

"Is it true you called the deceased an 'asshole' prior to his death?"

"As he was falling asleep, he was leering at one of the nurses and claiming he was 'King of New York.' I think that meets the clinical description of asshole, don't you?"

McManus smiled faintly but said nothing.

"But I didn't kill him for it if that's what you're thinking."

"I'm not thinking anything at the moment, Dr. Toll. Should I be?"

"No, no, I didn't mean . . ."

"When did you realize Pervis was in trouble?"

"After I gave him the IV push of propofol, he crashed immediately. I've never seen anything like it. It's as if the drug acted purposefully to cause cardiac arrest."

McManus read Toll within moments. McManus noted how thin Toll was, as well as several small bruises and needle marks on his left forearm. Toll, noticing McManus's stare, said he'd "had some blood tests done." The detective nodded but had seen enough addicts in his years of police work to know he was looking at one. Toll wouldn't be the first anesthesiologist he'd seen with a monkey on his back; these docs had ready access to drugs street junkies could only dream about.

"Can't any anesthetic cause someone to die if too much of it is given?"

"Well, yes, but it takes a few minutes in a well-oxygenated patient. These drugs don't stop the heart. To induce heart stoppage, the blood oxygen level needs to drop off, and it has to be impossible for the patient to be ventilated artificially. Remember Michael Jackson? The propofol stopped his breathing, and he died from lack of oxygen. The records from this case show Pervis's pO2 was high throughout."

His pO2 was high, thought McManus. *My conclusion exactly.* Someday he'd have to tell these doctors that medical jargon didn't impress him nearly as much as tits on a chicken but it did confuse him.

"How did you obtain the drug? Was it sealed?"

"All our drugs are distributed through a computerized dispenser."

"Because anesthesia doctors abuse them?"

"Uh, yes, that . . . but . . ."

"But?"

"Also to prevent billing fraud."

"Bet there's a lot of that." He stared at Toll. He straightened his tie, then took a sip of bottled water the dean had given him. "So how did the drug come out of the dispenser?"

"In a sealed glass vial with a break top. It's tamper proof."

"Of course, you still have the vial."

"Uhhh . . . no."

"Really? Is that standard procedure, considering there's so much . . . billing fraud?"

"After I aspirated the drug into a syringe, the vial went into the sharps disposal box. I assure you, Detective, that is standard procedure."

"You're sure none of the drug in the vial was left over for other uses?"

Toll eyed McManus and shook his head no.

"Not a drop left in it for any possible other use?"

"No, Detective, although there could be some residue."

"And the vial—it's gone?"

"Well, there is a chance the vial is still in the OR. It depends on whether the orderlies have emptied the box since then."

McManus made a mental note to have Murtaugh find the vial. Then he made another: not to trust this anesthesia doctor as far as he could throw him.

High-tech junkie, he thought.

21

DEMETRI

RITUAL MUTILATION? PSYCHOTIC SCIENCE?
Witchcraft? Waiting in the small room for the detective, Demetri went over what he knew so far. Once he finished with the detective, he planned to do some research: first to visit Medical Records to request the files of the patients murdered years before, then to the library to see what else he could find out.

Could any of those old cases be related to this one?

McManus entered the room.

"Medical student Demetri Makropolis. Have you done any unauthorized dissections in the last few days?"

Demetri's epinephrine spike caused his pupils to dilate, his chest to pound, and his palms to sweat.

"Ease up, kid. A joke."

McManus sat down. The boy looked familiar to him—had he seen him before? That face, that name. "Any relation to Micky Makropolis?"

"He's my dad."

"No shit. The best detective in the department, or so the legend says. But you know that already."

"Thanks, I do."

"All right, son of Mic Mak. What happened here?"

"I think the body was stolen for some nefarious use. I overheard from the ME that he was still alive when the brain was entered so the person who did it had to be sophisticated in the use of drugs—good enough to fool multiple physicians and a medical student. The proof is the sore arms I have from an hour of CPR trying to revive him."

"Go on."

"The perpetrator is most likely a physician, or a Ph.D. in neurophysiology. He has intimate knowledge of the medical center, its workings and its layout. He's powerful enough to kill a sizable guard and likes to grandstand in the way he discards the bodies. True psychopaths are often exceptionally intelligent, with a striking flair for the dramatic."

Demetri held back what he'd learned, from his father and from the Web, about the old body snatchings. The connection was too speculative; he needed to know more before he could put it all together.

"Not bad, son of Mic Mak," said McManus as he got up to leave. "One more thing: What do you know about Murtaugh?"

"I asked my dad about him. He said that Murtaugh was an ass kisser with the intelligence of your average block of wood."

"Couldn't have put it better myself."

IN THE HALLWAY, DEMETRI MET up with Carter, who told him nothing was happening this afternoon that required Demetri's presence. So Demetri was free to play detective.

He walked down the hall to the hospital entrance. He then walked to the main hospital corridor, took the stairs down, and entered the hospital's Health Information Management Office (although everyone still called it the Medical Records Room). A petite brunette was at the counter.

"Yes, Doctor, may I help you?"

Demetri noted a slight accent, which he could not quite place. Spanish, perhaps, or Portuguese. The girl had striking green eyes. "I'm not a doctor . . . not yet, I mean. I'm a student. A student in school." The brunette giggled. *Get it together, Demetri,* he said to himself, as he tried to avoid her eyes. "I'm fourth-year medical student Demetri Makropolis." He reached over the counter, took her hand, and shook it gently. He was surprised by his action: who shook the hand of the clerk in the records room?

"Pleased to meet you, fourth-year medical student Demetri Makropolis. I am health information management administrative assistant Maria Bassias."

Maria, thought Demetri. *The most beautiful sound I ever heard . . . West Side Story* was one of his mother's favorite movies. He felt himself blush. The petite brunette with the green eyes giggled again.

"I assume you didn't come to this office just to introduce yourself."

"Ahhhh, no. I didn't."

She let the silence linger for a few seconds before saying, "Well?"

"Uhh, I need some old patient records."

"How old?"

"From the 1940s. And the '60s.

"Well, all records—"

"And the '80s."

"Yes. All records older than five years go onto microfilm and into a warehouse in New Jersey. How many are we talking about?"

"Just three." He handed her a sheet of paper with names and dates on them.

"The bad news is, records usually take a couple of weeks to arrive. The good news is, I could put a rush on them, maybe get them in a day or two. Of course, I'd need to state a reason. Is there a medical emergency involved?"

"No, but they're for a study. An important study—for Dr. Chief. I mean, Dr. Mortimer." *Deep breath, Demetri.* "He's the orthopedics chief. It's a study of post-morbid obesity causing cardiac arrest." Fibbing like this, he wanted to look away. But he couldn't take his eyes off this girl.

"Oh my, that does sound important. Getting fat after death seems like a rare and dangerous condition. I'll light a fire under our friends in the Garden State. Should I let you know when it arrives?"

"Yes, please."

She looked at him. *She's waiting for something. What? Oh, right.*

He took back the page with the patient names, scribbled his cell number on it, then slid it back across the table.

"I'll call you tomorrow morning, fourth-year medical student Demetri Makropolis. Until then, you know where to reach me."

WITH THE TUNE RATTLING AROUND in his head—*Say it loud and there's music playing*—Demetri walked through the hospital's main lobby then entered the medical school and headed for the library. Inside he removed his laptop from his backpack and sat at one of the tables near the door. Once it booted up, he logged onto the library's secure wireless network.

He started by looking through medical center archives for some basic history. The initial building of the Hospital for the Consumptive was completed in 1855 as a facility for patients with tuberculosis, but during the Civil War, the hospital's mission was expanded as soldiers returned to New York needing care. In 1875, a new wing was opened, doubling the institution's capacity to 200 beds. It was the first hospital in the United States to go to eight-bed wards for the indigent population, although the top floor featured private suites for patients wealthy enough to insist on sick luxury.

The hospital's fortunes took off in 1885 when Frederick Von Hausen joined the board of trustees. Von Hausen's millions came from selling his health elixir, which he called The Blue Cross. Thought to cure consumption, smallpox, pneumonia, the plague, and piles, it was merely grain alcohol mixed with herbs and sugar. Nonetheless, it sold like hotcakes for five cents a bottle, enabling Von Hausen to "give back to the community," just like every other robber baron of the era seeking to soothe his conscience and repair his public image.

Thanks to Von Hausen, the Hospital for the Consumptive developed the largest hospital endowment in the United States, and that was before 1895, when, as chairman of the board, he donated $5 million to once more double capacity and another ten to start the medical school. He declined offers to have the hospital renamed in his honor, opting for a tasteful plaque in the main lobby of what he christened the Eastside Medical Center. He did accept the honor of having the medical school named after him. After his death, the school's board of trustees, most of whom considered the old snake-oil salesman something of an embarrassment, renamed the Frederick Von Hausen School of Medicine simply the Eastside Medical School.

The Lindsey Children's Hospital was completed in 1915; in 1926, the Slade-Kettack Cancer Hospital opened. Thanks to its huge endowment, the center survived the Depression and in the '40s, '50s, and '60s opened a research wing and the Orthopedic Hospital. With its available street footprint maxed out by 1980, the center was forced to demolish some of the older buildings in order to accommodate the newer and much taller Medical Towers.

Fascinating stuff—but not really what Demetri was looking for. Then, looking at some files from the '40s, he found something that caught his attention: apparently there was an intricate network of underground tunnels connecting all parts of the medical center. They had been used heavily during World War II-era blackouts, when street lamps were turned off and buildings were kept dark to protect against the danger of Nazi attack. People could move freely through the tunnels in a way they couldn't above ground.

Demetri often used a couple of the tunnels to get around the center himself but had had no idea how extensive the system was. Was it now as large as it was during the war? Did the several postwar additions connect into the network and make it even larger?

He kept looking, finding floor plans from the '30s showing hundreds of corridors, including some for buildings since demolished. One plan showed a connection between the hospital and a Lexington Avenue Subway station that no longer existed. A plan from the 1890s indicated a rail connection, passing under what were then notorious slums, to the East River docks for direct delivery of coal from barges. What had happened to that passage?

With the development of the neighborhood—not just the medical center, but high-rise apartment buildings and the FDR Drive—how much of the tunnel network survived?

One thing was obvious: if a killer wanted to enter and exit the medical center surreptitiously, he had no shortage of routes to take.

THE FLOOR PLANS ON THE Web server were poor representations: low-resolution and blurred, as though viewed from an airplane at 20,000 feet. He needed the originals, which were housed in the library stacks two and three floors below where he was now. He copied the scans to his hard drive, taking care to make sure he got the exact locations of the documents. All were stored in a locked area of the sub-subbasement. He needed a librarian to get in there.

He walked to the front desk and found a skinny bald man who looked to be about 40, with spectacles, seated with eyes glued to his computer monitor. His left hand rested on the desk. His ID badge said his name was Gus Reinholt.

Demetri didn't speak but merely observed the man's state of heightened concentration and labored breathing, the screen's reflection in his glasses, and the position of his right arm. After two minutes, Demetri finally said, "Excuse me."

"Yes? Is there a problem?" He looked right and left to see if anyone else was watching him.

"I need to get into the secured stacks downstairs."

The man looked back at his screen. "No can do. Doing an important search for the chief of ObGyn."

"Dr. Pear would be disturbed to know that his project was delayed because you were busy surfing porn sites on a hospital computer."

Reinholt hit the escape key and eyed his adversary. "How do I know you're here on Dr. Pear's authority?"

"I'll call his office right now to verify . . ." He reached for the man's phone.

"That won't be necessary."

The librarian turned away for a moment—to tuck himself back in, obviously. "Follow me," he said after Demetri heard the zipping of the man's fly.

They walked to a doorway set between two floor-to-ceiling shelves of books and descended a wooden staircase to the basement stacks. The air immediately changed, filled with the smell of old books and journals, thousands by Demetri's quick eye count. He tried to control the claustrophobia that was setting in from row upon row of filled shelves.

While they were walking, Demetri filled Reinholt in on what he was looking for. "Pear wants to give a talk on the history of the institution." Gus nodded.

A long walk through a narrow confine brought them to another staircase, metal this time, and spiral, enclosed by a metal cage. Reinholt opened the door, and they descended another floor. The spacing between the rows of shelves got, if anything, tighter.

Down another narrow, dimly lit corridor. They stopped at a locked gate.

"No trouble for me with Pear."

"No trouble."

Reinholt unlocked the door, and they went through. "These are the most important archives. To the left," he said as they turned right, "is the climate-controlled room with some real ancient stuff. Manuscripts and scrolls dating back to the Byzantine Empire, or so they tell me. Most of it from Van Hausen's private collection." They came to a room with a large central table. A few books were stacked on it, as well as a couple of document boxes. A large shelf of old journals stood behind it.

"You're asking for the most remote goddamn stuff in the whole goddamn library. I haven't been down here in years; practically everything's been loaded onto the Internet. Once it's all on the servers, this paper will be history."

"So all these old books and journals will be destroyed?"

"My job will be much easier."

Yeah, Demetri thought. *All porn, all the time.*

They approached another tight metal spiral staircase.

"I call this the staircase to hell. Go down the stairs, then walk straight ahead to the shelves with the plans. Can't miss it. It's goddamn hot down there—a Con Ed steam pipe must run nearby. A person could die there from heatstroke. Don't say I didn't warn you."

"You're not coming down?"

"Nope, I have to finish what I was doing."

"Your research on ObGyn."

"Exactly." He turned and headed back. "The light will shut off automatically a few minutes after you leave."

Demetri looked down the stairs. There was absolute silence except for the receding steps of the onanistic librarian. Then they were no longer audible. He faced the staircase to descend and was hit by a blast of hot air emanating from below. *The breath of the dragon,* Demetri thought.

22

McManus

HE FOUND THE TWO ORDERLIES fearful of losing their jobs. McManus assured them they wouldn't, although who knows how many people that asshole Murtaugh would fire to save his own neck?

McManus separated the two men and found their stories virtually identical without seeming rehearsed. They had deposited the body in the morgue, registered it in the log, then turned out the light and locked the door. Neither of them had left the body alone at any time. One of them said he saw the face of the deceased in the body bag because, before leaving the morgue, he saw that the zipper had come partly open. He recalled a strange feeling when he zipped the bag shut: it seemed as though the eyes of the deceased were looking right at him and pleading with him to help.

It was almost 6:00. McManus left the medical center to get some dinner. On the street, he saw at least half a dozen camera crews, with make-up artists touching up the faces of botoxed reporters getting ready to go on the air.

He called the inspector on his cell as he crossed First Avenue.

"Mary, I should bring you up to date. I'll be at the diner across from the emergency room."

He pocketed his phone and pulled up the collar on his coat. The temperature was dropping. He passed an old man with a walker and a bandage on his face who was talking to himself. Probably an escaped inmate from the psych ward, McManus thought. He looked disheveled but not homeless.

It wasn't McManus's job to save everyone in New York.

He sat at the counter and ordered the Greek salad. He looked up at the TV hanging from the ceiling and saw that the 5:00 edition of the local news was about to end. The ex-jock with the Hugo Boss suit and the Rolex was finishing the sports report. As usual, the Knicks were in sad shape. Better luck next season, as always.

The inspector walked in. McManus tried not to leer as she smoothed her tight black skirt before taking a seat next to him.

"Hungry, Mary?

"Nope." She caught the waiter's eye and ordered coffee.

"The interviews are finished. The anesthesia doc's a junkie, the department chief's a head case, and the hospital president is as smooth as they come."

"Pat, I hear things are not going well at home."

Is that what she came to talk about? He had to be careful. A wrong step with the highest-ranking woman in the Detective Division could land him in community affairs doing safety presentations for fifth graders.

"My wife and I are under a lot of stress at the moment."

The inspector slipped her hand across the counter and touched his, ever so lightly, as she readjusted herself on the seat. She and McManus both could see that her skirt was riding up; neither did anything to stop it. McManus noticed that two more buttons than usual were undone on her blouse, exposing cleavage and a generous helping of her fire-engine-red bra.

"I understand what it's like for you, Pat. I want you to know you that I am available for you."

His heart skipped a beat then started racing. Although his marriage was on the rocks, he wasn't ready to give up on it. But neither was he ready to take his eyes off the slit in the center of McCarthy's skirt exposing the tops of her thigh-high stockings.

Her taste in clothing turned him on. He could see that her apparel and her accessories were of a higher grade than his wife's ho-hum wardrobe. Mary was an ABC type: "A" for Abercrombie and Fitch, which supplied her casual clothing; "B" for Bergdorf's and Barneys, where she bought her business outfits, shoes, and bags; and "C" for Cartier, whose line of diamond earrings and 18-karat bracelets she wore with the self-assurance that came from knowing she deserved every bit of the attention men paid her. His wife on the other hand was strictly rated G, for Gap.

He was about to respond—no doubt to say the wrong thing—when he saw a shot of the medical center pop up on the TV screen.

"Waiter, turn up the volume."

The two cops watched as the 6:00 news started: "Shocking new details in the case of the missing body at the Eastside Medical Center."

The anchors threw it to the station's reporter, who was stationed across the street from the diner. McManus got up to look through the window and saw a line of bright lights illuminating coiffed airheads trying to look smart.

Warren Nathan's face appeared on the screen. He was in his office, answering questions. On his face was a big smile.

23

MAKROPOLIS

MICHAEL WAS TIRED. THE DRY-cleaning business was a tough one, and he hated it: the clothes, the chemicals, the clients. He'd been at it all day, sorting, labeling, and carrying large bundles, while his wife dealt with the customers, fielding complaints all day about stains that didn't come out, about missing shirts, about melted buttons. It never ended.

What a way to spend his retirement. Once the younger kids were on their own, he'd move to Florida—he had his eye on a gated community in Tarpon Springs. He'd play golf and tennis during the day, and at night he and his wife would play piripa—a card game resembling gin rummy—with their Greek friends.

He was driving the van on 31st Street near Ditmars Boulevard in Astoria, making deliveries, when he began turning over in his mind the conversation he'd had with his son the night before. Demetri always seemed to get into trouble getting involved in things he shouldn't. Suddenly, Michael was overcome by a feeling of dread: something bad was about to happen. That sixth sense, which was always accompanied by a tingly feeling at the back of his neck, had saved his ass more than once back in the day. So he called Demetri but got no response. As he neared the Triborough Bridge, the feeling intensified. He checked his son's whereabouts on his phone. He had paid extra to have the GPS locator activated on his son's phone but until now had rarely ever used it. Nor had he ever told Demetri about it. Checking the map on the small screen of his phone, he saw that the boy was somewhere in the medical center. His aging eyes strained for more detail but could not deliver. He checked his pocket for his reading glasses—he must have left them at home. He swerved the van around a pylon supporting the elevated N/Q train, gunning the engine as the flimsy vehicle teetered like the Leaning Tower of Pisa, and moved onto the approach to the bridge. The van's nearly bald tires screeched. He recalled his training in high-speed maneuvers at Floyd Bennett Field: "You wants the tires to squeal a little but not too much: like a whore," his instructor had told the class, "but not like a drunken whore. You're after maximal traction and speed." He wove around the tractor trailers and headed for the Manhattan exit.

He pulled out his cellphone and hit Demetri's number. It immediately went to voicemail. He shut the phone. "Shit!"

He got through the tolls. Rather than take Second Avenue with the rest of the commercial traffic, he veered left onto the FDR Drive, passing the sign reading "Passenger Traffic Only. No Commercial Vehicles." At this hour, and with the new subway under construction, it would take forever to get to midtown on Second, while the Drive would be light going south.

As he turned the bend onto the Drive, he came to a standstill. It was a parking lot.

AFTER TEN MINUTES AND FORWARD progress of 50 feet, Makropolis called his son again, with the same result. Up ahead, just past the 106th Street exit, he saw the lights of fire trucks, ambulances, and police cars. He forced his way to the right lane and edged onto the skimpy shoulder. The groan of the van's sheet metal against the guard rail did not slow him down. He slipped out the exit and onto Second. He dodged taxi cabs for twenty minutes and finally reached the hospital with the hairs on the back of his neck standing on end.

He pulled up in front of his son's apartment building, leaving the truck in a no-standing zone. He ran to the front desk. Mic Mak's memory was a steel trap for faces and names. He recognized the security guard as the guy who'd helped his son move in three years ago.

"James, have you seen my son today? Demetri Makropolis."

"I'll ring his room."

The guard picked up the phone and punched in the room number. No answer.

Michael didn't bother to leave a message. He pivoted and headed out the door. As he ran toward the medical school, he saw a traffic cop writing out a ticket for the van. Nonetheless, he didn't break stride. He showed his ID at the main entrance and signed the register. Neither of the guards had seen his son today. They suggested the Student Affairs office.

He ran past the library and saw the sign on the door. He entered without knocking and found two women, one older, behind a desk, with reading glasses on a lanyard and a pencil stuck in her hair, one younger, leaning against a doorpost, with tight jeans and 5-inch heels. He didn't have time to schmooze.

"Have you seen Demetri Makropolis?"

"And you are . . ." said the younger one.

"His father," said the older one, pulling a wisp of hair off her forehead. "I never forget a face."

"He may be in trouble," said Makropolis.

"He was here about two hours ago, Detective. One of your colleagues was in this suite conducting interviews about the missing body of that over-stuffed TV critic."

"And then?"

"After his interview, I heard him talking to a resident." She adjusted the string of pearls around her neck. "Said he was going to medical records. Make a right, then down the hallway, and follow the blue line on the floor."

"Thanks, Gloria. I never forget a face, either, especially one as memorable as yours."

He rushed out with the hair on his neck positively bristling. He made the right turn then followed the blue line on the floor to the Main Hospital. The guard gave him directions to Medical Records.

Down the stairs, then left to the records room. Behind the counter was the prettiest girl he had ever seen.

"May I help you?"

Her radiant green eyes were slowing him down. "Uh . . . I'm looking for someone."

"Do you need the records of a specific patient?"

"No, a medical student who was probably here within the last hour or two."

"Demetri. And you're his father. I didn't expect to meet his parents so soon."

Meet his parents? What else had his son been keeping from him? he wondered.

"I met your son an hour ago. He came here to request some records."

Gotta hand it to the kid, he thought, *he works fast.*

Fast. Right. His neck felt as though it had been wired for 220 volts.

"Pleasure to meet you, but I must find Demetri."

"Long gone from here. He said something about going to the library, though."

"Where's that?"

"My shift doesn't end for half an hour." She looked to either side and saw no one. "But who's counting?"

She grabbed her purse and her coat and scooted under the counter. Grabbing Makropolis by the hand, she led him out the door at a near run.

"So you just met my son?" said Michael as they leapt up the staircase, two steps at a time.

"Yes, but we're right for each other."

Jack the Ripper and now this girl out of a 1940s screwball comedy. One couldn't make this stuff up, thought Makropolis.

After multiple turns—*How does anyone know where he's going in this place?*—they arrived at the library. Makropolis didn't see his son.

He spoke to the bald man behind the desk staring at his computer.

"I'm looking for someone."

No answer.

Makropolis leaned over the desk and saw both what was on the screen and where the man's right hand was. He jabbed the guy by his shoulder.

The librarian looked up. "What's your problem?"

"I'm looking for someone. He's a medical student here."

The librarian tilted his head to the left at the reading room behind him. "Half the people in here are medical students."

"Demetri Makropolis," said Maria.

"Oh, Jimmy the Greek," said the librarian as he returned his gaze to the whips and chains on his screen. "I took him downstairs to the stacks half an hour ago."

"And did Jimmy the Greek come back up?" said Michael.

"How the fuck should I know?"

Makropolis grabbed the librarian under his armpits, lifted him from his seat in one powerful motion, and delivered him to the top of the desk.

"Take us to him. Now."

Maria was as shocked as the librarian at the show of strength. Then she started to giggle at what she saw.

"But first," said Makropolis, "put that back in your pants."

AS THEY REACHED THE SECOND staircase, Mic Mak knelt for a second and reached for his ankle holster, then stood up with a gleaming, stainless Kahr PM9 in his right hand. He pushed ahead of the librarian then turned back to his two companions. He could hear fear in their labored breathing. "NYPD. Follow me."

He headed down the stairs with the gun in ready position. He glanced back to the librarian. "Which way?"

The librarian pointed the way down the gloomy, narrow aisle. Beads of sweat started dripping off the ex-cop's chin.

"Is it always so fucking hot down here?"

"Next time you come, I'll buy a fan," said the librarian.

As they approached the last staircase, the librarian noted that the lights were out below.

"They should be on."

Makropolis stepped to the side of the staircase, craned his neck around, and yelled down, "Demetri, are you there?"

Silence. The hot air billowing from below was far worse than what came out of the exhaust vents from the dryers at the store. It seared his eyeballs and the inside of his lungs as sweat soaked through his shirt.

The librarian commented sarcastically, "It's a dry heat."

"Demetri?"

Michael Makropolis, the best NYPD detective of the last thirty years, then did a most unprofessional thing. He didn't call for back-up; he didn't even call for a flashlight. Instead, deciding to be a good father and not a police officer, he ran down the stairs, blinded not only by the darkness but also by his determination to save his son from his own foolishness.

24

Pear

HE WAS PACING HIS OFFICE yelling multiple expletives at his security chief, who was seated in front of the desk. Murtaugh couldn't get a word in edgewise.

"You asshole. You idiot. I hired you to keep this institution out of the news except when I want it in the news. This is the most royal fuck-up in the last thirty years. Have you forgotten that I gave you your brand-spanking-new detective's shield? If it wasn't for me calling my patient, the commissioner, you'd have been busted down to patrolman and spent the rest of your twenty years pounding a beat in Coney Island."

The buzzer rang at Pear's desk. He walked over and slammed the button.

"It's the detective calling," said his secretary over the intercom. "He says it's urgent."

Pear punched the buttons for the speakerphone and line one. "Detective. What can I do for you?" His security chief was amazed at how Pear could switch the charm on and off at will. The old buzzard was even smiling, as though McManus could see his face through the telephone line.

"Did you happen to catch the local news just now, Channel 4?" said McManus.

"No. Why?"

"It featured an interview of your boy Nathan, big as life. Everything's out in the open now, Doc. That complicates my job. Watch at 11—I'm sure they'll repeat it."

And he hung up.

Pear's smile was gone. He turned red as a cranberry cocktail. Murtaugh thought he was on the verge of popping an aneurysm.

"No more slip-ups," Pear said, narrowing his eyes as he spoke, "No more leaks—especially to that self-promoting bastard Nathan. Find me a freak we can pin this on by tomorrow morning, or you'll spend your golden years checking receipts at Walmart."

Murtaugh knew enough about his boss to know when to keep his mouth shut, but he still didn't know when to leave.

"You're still here because . . ."

The security chief got up and walked out.

Pear stepped over to his office door and locked it. He then walked to the far wall and lifted the painting of his predecessor off its hook, revealing a wall safe. He placed the painting on the floor and dialed the combination. He opened the safe and reached all the way to the back to retrieve an old manila envelope. He took it to his desk and sat down. Staring at the envelope brought back a whole slew of memories he thought he'd forgotten. He undid the metal clasp, opened the envelope, and removed its contents. The first page was a psychiatric report profiling a psychotic murderer, identity unknown.

Pear grimaced and hung his head as he pounded his desk.

25

MAKROPOLIS

AT THE BOTTOM OF THE stairs, the heat was so thick that his sweat was making it hard to grip the Kahr. That and the dark made him keep his finger off the trigger lest he inadvertently shoot his own son. The adrenaline rush had sharpened his vision as it adjusted to the near darkness with only the faint light from the staircase filtering down. His hearing, too, was heightened. He heard the hissing of a steam pipe and the distant rumble of the subway. But most of all he heard the pounding of his own heart.

"Demetri, are you down here? It's me, Dad! Demetri!? . . . Where are the goddamn lights?"

"They should have turned on automatically," said the librarian, standing on the last step with Maria. "The switch is on the righthand wall, 3 or 4 feet ahead of you."

Makropolis edged along the wall. A second later, he found himself off his feet, flying through the air head first, away from the stairs, the darkness punctured by a blinding flash and a deafening crack. It was the Kahr. One shot.

Maria shrieked then began calling for Makropolis and Demetri. When she got no response, she stepped off the staircase carefully, expecting to bump into the librarian. She didn't. She slowly inched her way along the wall until she reached the light switch. When she turned it on, she screamed again.

The librarian was coiled up on the floor, in fetal position, shaking uncontrollably in a puddle of his own urine. On the floor in front of him were

Demetri and his father. Neither was moving. The father lay on top of his son, who was lying in a puddle of blood that was still flowing from a huge gash in his head.

26

THE DOCTOR

HE ENTERED THE STACKS THROUGH a long-unused doorway from a mechanical engineering room. The hiss of steam pipes, from valves opening and closing, was incessant.

The Con Edison steam was forced under great heat and pressure into a subterranean complex of pipes throughout the city. Mechanical rooms were necessary to regulate the pressure so that buildings wouldn't explode. The Doctor found the nearly abandoned underground rooms and corridors, once so integral to the structure and functioning of the medical center, comforting. He could come and go at will and be seen only when he wished.

The temperature in this lowest chamber of the library was at least 120 degrees, but his advanced physical condition gave him the ability to endure extreme environmental conditions—he'd hardly broken a sweat. He smiled as he rounded a support pylon in the deep recesses of the room. The space between the pylon and the hot pipes and conduits was tight for a child, let alone a full-grown adult, but the Doctor had an ability to twist and contort his body and limbs that would make a circus performer blush. He had to crawl through the maze of intersecting pipes, the heat burning the skin of his hands and knees. He felt no pain, however, and knew the skin would heal in hours, not days or weeks like a mere human.

He had kept an eye on the Makropolis student for the last twenty-four hours, noting his every move utilizing Security's own video systems that he'd hacked into years before. He admired the young man's physique as well as his avenue of research. Of course, the Doctor could not allow his own mode of moving throughout the center to be revealed. Such a shame to waste good young stock, but such was the way of the world.

He slithered to the wall near the room's entrance. Just before he flipped the light switch off, the stainless steel in his hand reflected a ray of light in Demetri's direction.

27

CARTER

CARTER COULDN'T REMEMBER A MORNING as strange as this one. After his interrogation by the detective, he returned to normalcy as he finished his floor rounds then scrubbed in to assist on a case with Dr. John Xerses, an old-time fracture specialist. This was the first time Carter had worked with him. The senior residents called Xerses the X Factor, for reasons Carter would soon find out.

The patient, an eighty-year-old man suffering from dementia, had fallen at his nursing home, fracturing his left hip. It required, Carter was told, a simple pinning.

According to his daughter, the patient was "magically" found in bed with a shortened and externally rotated leg. Carter assumed that the nursing home staff was trying to hide the fact that someone had dropped him.

The patient was a delight to talk to before the surgery started. He described the eight-course meal he'd enjoyed with "two dames" at Arturo's Restaurant in Bellrose earlier in the day. He then offered Carter a ride in his chauffeured Cadillac, which was waiting outside. He told his story in exquisite detail, but, according to the daughter, his timing was off by fifty years.

After Toll had sedated the patient and applied the spinal anesthesia, Carter and Xerses placed the patient on the fracture table in the OR. The C-arm fluoroscope showed a displaced subcapital fracture of the hip.

Cater turned to Xerses. "Since it's a displaced fracture, shouldn't it be replaced rather than pinned?"

"Well, Carpenter, it's . . ."

"It's Carter, sir."

"It's what?"

"My name is Carter, Dr. Xerses. Not Carpenter."

"What I'm trying to say, Dr. Carter, if you'll shut up and listen, is that the patient is demented. Add that to possibly severe heart disease, and he'll probably dislocate a hip replacement the first day home from the hospital. Pinning is much safer."

Though only a junior resident, Carter knew Xerses was bullshitting him. "Right, but since he's demented, he probably won't follow instructions. So he'll put weight on the leg, displace the fracture, and still need a hip replacement. That's why hip replacement is considered the gold standard for these fractures. Plus, the incidence of avascular necrosis of the hip is so high in this setting, wouldn't it make more sense to replace it now so he doesn't need more surgery?" What Carter really thought was that Xerses wanted to do the quick procedure because he was no good at hip replacements.

Toll, at the head of the table, looked up from the patient's chart.

"Look, son," said Xerses, "I've been doing this type of surgery since before you were born. Watch, listen, and learn. Now put the leg in traction."

Carter did as he was told and said nothing more. Xerses made small stab incisions in the skin then inserted the pins. From start to finish, his part in the case took seven minutes.

"Another day, another dollar," he said as he exited the room, leaving Carter to finish.

"I should have warned you," said Toll.

Carter looked up from suturing the patient's skin. "Huh?"

"I should have warned you to keep quiet. Everyone knows he selects his cases purely for how fast he can get them done."

"This guy needs a new hip. What's Xerses's problem?"

"He's a chain smoker and a caffeine addict with a prostate the size of a basketball. Once he leaves, he hits the bathroom then lights up a cigarette and chugs a Coke."

Carter put the dressing on. "But the whole hospital is no-smoking."

Toll laughed. "Well, why don't you tell him that? Okay, one, two, three, lift." The two doctors placed the patient on the gurney then wheeled him to the recovery room. As they entered, the patient lifted his head and said, "Double scotch for me, whiskey sours for the girls."

Toll pushed the man's head back down. "Easy, boy. You've had too much to drink already."

28

McManus

MCMANUS LEFT THE INSPECTOR AND her 3-inch gray Manolo Blahniks at the diner. He crossed the street and entered the hospital. The security guard directed him to Nathan's office on the eighth floor.

The door was open. No one was in the waiting room except for a janitor vacuuming the carpet.

"Is Dr. Nathan here?"

The middle-aged man looked up. "Over there," he said in a heavy Russian accent while motioning with his head.

McManus walked into the back office and saw Nathan putting on his overcoat. The doctor stepped back in surprise then put a grin on his face. "Detective. What a pleasant surprise," he said as he extended his gloved hand.

McManus breezed past the hand and took a seat in front of Nathan's flimsy faux-wood desk. He looked around and noted photo after photo of the doc next to an actor, athlete, or politician, all autographed by the celebrity in the picture. The doc craves attention, McManus concluded.

"Please sit down, Dr. Nathan," he said.

Nathan continued to stand. He fidgeted with his gloves. "I have a dinner engagement, Detective. Perhaps we could talk in the morning?"

"Oh, we will talk in the morning. But first, let me make sure you get a good night's sleep. We're going down to the precinct." McManus stood up directly in front of Nathan. Nathan's jaw dropped like the New York Stock Exchange in 2008. "It was obvious from the television interview that you know more than you've been telling us. Let's see if a change in surroundings encourages you to speak freely."

"I've told you all I know. What are you charging me with?"

"I'm not. I'm bringing you in as a material witness. When and if you are charged, I will read you the Miranda."

"I want to call my attorney."

"You may not believe it, Doctor, but we do have a telephone at the station."

"There will be repercussions for this, McManus."

"Dr. Nathan, are you threatening a peace officer?"

Nathan held his tongue. His eyes, however, made clear his contempt for the highhanded cop, whose salary after years on the force was less than what Nathan had made in his first month in private practice.

"I don't think you want me to lead you out of here in cuffs, Dr. Nathan. The cameras are still outside."

"Let's go," said the doctor.

THE SMELL OF GENERATIONS OF people in fear permeated the station house; the strongest detergents could not eliminate it. Nathan felt nauseated as he entered. McManus noticed but made no mention. The desk officer grinned as the two men approached.

"Now what do we have here, Detective? Is that the pedophile we've been hunting?"

"Nope," said McManus, "the serial homosexual rapist from the West Village." He took a moment to enjoy Nathan's ashen appearance before continuing. "He's a material witness in the medical center case. Interrogation room one?"

"One's busy. Use two."

"Damn, two's where the audiovisual recorders are broken." He turned to Nathan, "Room one would have been safer for you. Anything can happen to you in two, and no one would ever know." McManus was enjoying giving Nathan a lesson in police tactics.

Nathan nodded as he tried hard to swallow.

A patrolman accompanied the detective and the doctor upstairs to the windowless room. Nathan sat in the metal chair and pulled out his cellphone.

The patrolman snatched it from his hand. "No electronic devices allowed. It will be returned to you when you leave."

"But I have the right to contact my attorney."

"You will have the right to contact your attorney in a bit," said McManus.

"I'll be right back. In the meantime, Officer Pulio will keep you company." He smiled at the patrolman and left.

I've always liked the way that door slams, the detective thought.

He stopped and checked the time, figuring he'd let Nathan stew for an hour or two before calling back to set him free. A taste of jail often helped a witness see the benefit of full cooperation with the authorities. Plus, Nathan was a sniveling little snit who needed to be taught a lesson.

He walked up another flight of stairs to the locker room and into the bathroom. After using the urinal, he washed then checked himself in the mirror. He straightened his tie and smoothed his coat. He noticed a sprig of hair out of place and straightened it with some water from the faucet.

He walked down to the front desk and asked for the executive officer. A moment later, the XO, Feder, was rushing past him.

"Trouble at the medical center, Pat. Come on, you're on the case there."

McManus followed and got into the back seat of the XO's RMP. The car was already moving when he slammed the door.

"What is it, Jake?"

The sergeant behind the wheel gunned the engine as it took off down Lexington Avenue. Feder, riding shotgun, was shaking his head. "There's been an attack in the hospital library. One possible homicide. One serious injury, apparently PD. Every available RMP has responded. Expect chaos."

29

McManus

THE SCENE IN FRONT OF the hospital was something out of *Law and Order*. There were twenty-five RMPs and two Emergency Service vehicles, including a Hercules Unit and an overhead chopper. Every officer was looking for an excuse to arrest or shoot someone—nothing like the call "officer down" to bring out the finest in New York's Finest.

McManus hopped out of the XO's RMP and ran through the medical school entrance and into the library. Seeing commotion by the stairs, he bolted down the flight with his coat floating like Zorro's cape. One flight, two, three—he kept going down, toward the voices. As he descended, the shelves of books felt to him as though they angled in, progressively restricting the air he was breathing. The weight and space of the printed matter reflecting the medical wisdom of the ages was crushing. He hadn't been in a library in ages and now remembered why: years of arduous study to get his bachelor's degree.

The bedlam that awaited him was no more than what he expected. The room was packed wall to wall with officers, some with heavy weapons, and EMS personnel with three stretchers. Murtaugh was there, shouting into his walkie-talkie. In the center of the wall of blue were five people: one young woman standing, one man sitting against a support column, another sitting against the wall, and four people, two EMTs, and two women wearing long white coats, stooped over a bloodied body.

McManus pushed through the throng.

"What's going on?" he asked the sergeant.

"The two white coats over the body are doctors from the medical center. They heard screams and came down."

McManus looked at the body lying prone. The head was in the center of a large pool of congealed blood. The victim's short white coat was soaked in crimson. The doctors and the EMTs were fastening a cervical collar on him. An IV-line had already been started.

When the collar was secure, the doctor at the victim's head, a fortyish blonde, called out, "On three, turn. One, two, three." They turned the body in unison onto the stretcher.

It was the Makropolis kid. "Is he still alive?" said McManus.

"He is," the blonde doctor responded. McManus couldn't help himself: he checked her hands for a wedding ring. He didn't see one. He made a mental note to catch up with her again. "Nasty gash across his forehead. He didn't get it running into a wall."

"Where's the injured officer?"

"The injured *ex*-officer—apparently whoever called 911 mistook him for an MOS. He's the woozy one against the column. Seems to have hit his head as he tripped over the body in the dark. He's the kid's father; he was looking for his son, and this is how he found him. The bald one against the wall is the librarian who led him here. Afraid he's in shock."

Mic Mak and Son of Mic Mak? thought McManus. *What the fuck?*

He walked over to the dazed older man. "Detective Makropolis, Detective McManus. We'll help your son any way we can."

Makropolis looked up with an empty expression on his face. "My son?" At that moment, McManus felt a touch on his shoulder. He looked up and saw the young woman, in tears.

"I'm afraid he hit his head in the fall—he seems out of it. Also, I think he may have shot his son in the dark."

"Shot his son?" McManus turned to face the sergeant. "Shots were fired?"

"Yes, sir. One 9mm jacketed hollow point, Corbon, from this small Kahr, his and registered, at close range."

"You didn't tell me when I got here? You think I wouldn't be interested?"

The sergeant said nothing.

"Anything else?"

"The lady said the former detective knew his son was in trouble and pulled out the semiauto when he was walking down the stairs. She says it was pitch black when they got down here. He was looking for the light switch when his gun went off."

"Doctor, is there a gunshot wound?"

The blonde shrugged. "Hard to tell without a CT scan. Head wounds bleed like a stuck pig, even if it didn't penetrate the cranium."

McManus was speechless. A complete clusterfuck.

As the EMTs were carrying Demetri out, McManus asked his newly favorite blonde, "Will he be okay?"

"As I said before, it's hard to say. He has at least a bad concussion and has lost a fair amount of blood, but he's still breathing. We'll know more once he's in the ER."

The doctors left with the kid. EMTs took the victim's father and the shocked librarian out on stretchers; the young woman walked out, accompanied by two patrolmen.

"The victim is a key witness in the body-snatching case," McManus said to the sergeant. "He needs to be protected." As the room started to empty, the sergeant barked out orders for the kid to be protected by officers at all times.

The Crime Scene team arrived. They marked where the Kahr was found, then bagged it. They took samples from the blood puddle.

McManus turned to find Feder behind him. "This is related to the body-snatching case, isn't it?" said the XO.

"It sure as shit is. What a fucking mess. No suspect, and now this." Suddenly, McManus had the urge to call the inspector and take her up on her offer. "Can you give me a lift back to the precinct?"

"Sure."

"Now, how did he get that cut on his forehead? My pension says he wasn't grazed by a bullet."

30

CARTER

AFTER SHARING A PIZZA DINNER, Carter and Tony Mindalo, another resident, entered the apartment building they both lived in. Tony got off the elevator on the fifth floor, where he was greeted by his two small twin boys and his wife, Elaine, a former floor nurse who'd hitched a ride on the orthopedic-surgeon express, never to look back. A good looker, thought Carter, who got fat fast but pregnant faster. Carter would steer clear of the marriage dung heap for the time being. His next stop after his residency would be a spine fellowship. He wanted to do the huge front and back spinal-fusion deformity cases that net $50K to $60K per.

He unlocked his door and threw his white coat on the sofa. He grabbed a bag of chips and a soda and sat down in front of his laptop to check lacrosse scores.

Leaning over to his right, he grabbed the remote for his B&O and turned it on. Amy Winehouse was belting out her song. His Internet browser retrieved the day's sports news, and there it was: Hobart, his alma mater, 3, Cornell 2. David had slain the Goliath across the lake.

He was about to log off when he noted a news clip: Shooting at Eastside Medical Center Library.

Huh? He'd had no idea. He clicked and began to read: "Medical student injured at Eastside Medical Center library. . . . stable but guarded condition . . . doing research . . . name being withheld . . . may be related to the Pervis body snatching. . . ."

He spilled the chips all over the floor on his way to the door.

31

MAKROPOLIS

SOPHIA MAKROPOLIS WAS ANGRY. HER husband, out on a routine delivery, had disappeared without a trace and wasn't answering his cellphone. The dry-cleaning store had gone from total boredom to a crush of customers fifteen minutes before closing. It took almost two hours to catch up with the work after she locked the doors.

Eight forty-five and still no word from Michael. He'd done this before, disappearing for hours, hanging with his buddies at one of the pubs near Jackson Avenue. She could swear, if he wasn't Greek, he was definitely Irish. Well, she couldn't wait at the store any longer—she was tired and had a long drive to Glen Cove, where they had their new home.

Well, not exactly new. A sixty-five-year-old cape, it was located on a small cul de sac off of First Street, near St. Rocco's Roman Catholic Church in a predominantly Italian neighborhood. The Greek Orthodox Church that used to be a couple of blocks away had just moved to Brookville, ten minutes away by car but too expensive for the family of an honest ex-cop. The Glen Cove home wasn't luxurious but was better than the attached home they'd occupied off Ditmars Boulevard in Astoria for the last twenty-five years. Better except when the roof leaked or the furnace stopped working, which was often.

She got into her ten-year-old beater sedan. As she pulled out of the parking lot behind the store, she didn't see the NYPD RMP pulling up in front. Traffic on the Grand Central was light, but there was an accident on the eastbound LIE; it took ninety minutes to reach the Glen Cove exit. Needing to wake at 5 A.M. to get to the store in time to open at 7, she figured she might as well have slept on a cot in the rear of the store, but she wanted to check on the kids and on her mother, Yia Yia. She wondered how much longer she could leave the kids in the care of her mother, who had just turned eighty-eight. She did know they'd be well-fed, however—her mother was still a spectacular cook. Her specialty was homemade breads, including tsoureki, the sweet holiday bread revered by family and friends. Sophia was a good cook in her own right. She rolled out her own phyllo dough for her tiropita, the flaky, feta cheese–filled concoction butchered by most restaurants and catering halls.

As she reached her home, she was surprised to find an NYPD RMP in front and an officer talking to her kids. As the spouse of a cop, she knew all too well what could be signified by an RMP that's not your husband's parked in front of your house. As she anxiously exited her car, she was met on the sidewalk by a sergeant who explained the situation.

"No. No, not both. Please, God, no."

She collapsed into the arms of the sergeant, who then helped her into the back of the RMP. She cleared her throat and yelled out to George, Demetri's fifteen-year-old brother, who was standing on the sidewalk, "Get your sisters back inside and don't tell Yia Yia a thing until I get back."

The sergeant turned on the flashing lights and the siren. He floored the accelerator as he pulled out, heading to the westbound LIE and the East Side of Manhattan.

32

CARTER

HE RAN LIKE A LACROSSE midfielder through the emergency entrance and toward the trauma room. Turning the corner, he ran right into Beth, practically pinning her back against the wall.

"Whoa, baby!" she said. "I know we had a good time the other night, but tackle football is not my thing."

"Sorry, I'm in a rush."

"You weren't the other night."

"I'm looking for the medical student who got hurt. Demetri Makropolis."

"I think they took him to CT scan. You can't get in there now; the police have blocked it off." She then fingered the lapel to his white coat as she whispered, "Since you have a few minutes, perhaps we can slip into a closet somewhere."

Carter hesitated for a moment, weighing the alternatives. "The ER is packed with people. Besides, didn't you get into trouble down here once before?"

"That was months ago. I've been a good little girl since then." She looked both ways and copped a feel of his rock-hard member. "Wellll?"

Carter hated what he was about to do. "Can't, Beth. I want to look in on Demetri."

"Don't worry, Mr. Boy Scout. I saw the chairman of neurosurgery in there."

"Ransom—he's the best there is."

"His penile implant certainly is," she said, giggling, as she turned and walked away. Carter, speechless, had a good idea how she'd come by that information. He looked wistfully at her swaying ass as she moved down the hallway and turned a corner. I'll attend to that later, he thought.

HE RAN DOWN THE HALL to radiology, dodging people, wheelchairs, stretchers, and carts as if still on the lacrosse field. The waiting area was packed with the usual mix of humanity awaiting their turn for a radiograph and then, hopefully, a pat on the back from the ER doc, a simple prescription, and a quick exit from the hospital. Scanning the room, Carter was fascinated at how easily he could tell who needed to be in the ER and who needed to visit a general practitioner. What a waste of medical resources.

Carter slid past the front desk into the back, where the techs did most of their work. He reached the CT control room and found it eerily empty and quiet. Strange, he thought, it's always manned at this hour. Well, perhaps the staff are in the scan room setting up. He peered through the window into the scan room expecting to see as many as four people: the tech and the radiologist, plus a nurse and an anesthesiologist working the ventilator. Instead the room was packed to the gills with maybe twenty physicians and nurses. Demetri was obscured by the crowd, but the fact that all these people were just standing there doing nothing could only mean one thing: Demetri had gone into cardiac arrest, the code was called, and Demetri was dead.

Carter slumped into the empty technologist's chair and began to sob.

33

DEMETRI

CARTER EVENTUALLY LOOKED UP TO see Dr. Mortimer among the crowd, motioning for him to come into the room. The resident wiped his tears and stood up slowly. Worried about what the ghoul who'd cut up Pervis might have done to his friend, the last thing he wanted was to see the corpse. He walked into the room. Everyone was talking—the mood was altogether too cheerful considering that a colleague had just died.

"Hi, Tom."

The voice emanated from someone sitting up on the CT stretcher with a bandage on his head. He sounded and looked vaguely like Demetri. Carter's only response was stupefaction.

"Tom, what's wrong? You look like you've seen a ghost."

"You should be at least brain dead from what I heard," Carter said as he plopped down on a nearby stool, weak in the knees. Everyone in the room laughed, except for Mortimer, whose flat expression didn't change. Carter got up and smiled. He grabbed Demetri by the shoulders to make sure it wasn't a trick.

"You jerk!" Carter said as he kept his grip on Demetri's shoulders.. "You look like shit!"

Ransom, the neurosurgeon, stepped up. "While in the scanner, he wakes up and pulls himself out. I've never seen anything like it. He's got a substantial cut, especially for bumping his head all by himself . . ."

"But I wasn't alone."

Everyone turned to face the patient.

"I was doing research in the lower stacks and heard a noise," Demetri continued. "I turned to look for the source, and the lights went out. I yelled to see if anyone was there, but no response other than the sound of steps. Like an idiot, I got up to look for the lights, got spooked, and ran straight into a beam. That's the last thing I remember."

The trauma surgeon, G. Thomas Waits, spoke. "The ER nurse said there was a huge pool of blood at the scene, and your H&H were pretty low."

"Head lacerations can bleed badly," said Ransom. "Plus, he's had some concussion. Let's keep him in the Neuro ICU overnight for observation."

Demetri reached up and felt the blood-soaked bandage. "Boy, my head aches."

Pear entered the room. "Your dad is going to be okay," he told Demetri.

"My dad? What about him? Was he here?"

"Yeah, he's in the ER with a concussion. Hit his head looking for you, but he's doing fine now."

"That's strange. How'd he know?"

DEMETRI WAS PUT BACK ON a gurney and wheeled to the emergency room. Carter and the police officer assigned to Demetri accompanied him.

"I'll check up on you in the NICU," Carter said when they got there. Then he left—he had some unfinished business to attend to with a nurse named Beth.

The chief of plastic surgery, Margolies, was in the emergency room to close the wound on Demetri's forehead. The job needed sixty sutures.

"Nasty knife wound. Went right down to the cranium with some degloving. You were nearly scalped."

"But I hit my head against a beam."

"Maybe you did, maybe you didn't, but this laceration was made by a very sharp knife. You're lucky you have a hard head."

Demetri was then whisked upstairs to the Neuro ICU, where he was poked and prodded by the ICU resident taking the admission history and administering a physical exam, then subjected to a thoroughly embarrassing sponge bath by the ICU nurse, an elderly behemoth by the name of Nurse Waldheim. She spared no effort in scrubbing off all the dried blood from head to toe and everywhere in between. Her demeanor and heavy accent came straight out of *Stalag 17*.

Cleaned, dressed in one of those awful hospital gowns that offer no privacy, Demetri lay back on the bed, noting the officer sitting outside his room by the door. He tried to recall the moments before his concussion. His head was still hurting, and the laceration was burning like a son of bitch, but the memory and the realism and fear came back to him with a vengeance.

The document room was quiet when he was down there, aside from the hiss of the steam pipes. The heat was stifling. The shelves were jammed with rolls of floor and construction plans dating back to the medical center's founding. It took him twenty minutes to find the plans he was looking for. They chronicled the hospital expansion of the 1940s and '50s. He noted some hallways and tunnels around the morgue area that no longer existed—they must have either been closed off or eliminated during later construction. Just as he was about to take the documents to the Xerox machine upstairs, he thought he heard steps. He looked about the room. Although most of it was cast in shadows, he was sure someone was there.

"Hello?" The response was the hiss of the pipe. "Anyone?" Nothing.

He calmed himself, turned back, and continued to collect the plans he wanted off the desk. He heard the steps again and whirled about. Again, no one was there.

"Not funny. Is anybody there?" The hiss continued, but he thought he heard a low voice in the background—so low, in fact, he thought it might be his imagination. What the voice said, he could not remember. He stepped forward toward the center of the room, both hands full of blueprints almost as tall as he was. Then the room went dark just after the lash of steel by the exit door. What followed probably took less than five seconds but seemed like an eternity.

"Who turned off the lights? What is this?" The steps again, only louder and right in front of him. As Demetri's adrenal glands pumped enough epinephrine into his bloodstream to kill a cardiac patient, his eyes tried to accommodate to the low light. But even with his pupils dilated to maximum, he couldn't see his bundle in front of his face, let alone the exit. He tried to recall where the door was and made a mad dash for it. He bumped into someone big and solid then dropped the blueprints as he felt a strong hand grab him by the arm. He heard—no, felt—a ripping against his forehead, followed by a feeling of warmth flowing down his face. He broke free and ran—maybe toward the exit, maybe not—and hit a support beam at full speed. He heard the clunk of his head against steel before he blacked out.

What was it he'd heard the person say? Demetri tried to reach into the recesses of his memory. "I'm your d—" The word was *doctor.* "I'm your doctor," the voice said as it grabbed him with a grip so powerful he could not resist. He saw someone hovering over him, his face out of focus but his white lab coat distinguishable. The glint of steel in his hand illuminated the room.

"Doctor. Doctor! *DOCTOR!*" Demetri thrashed about as he screamed. Nurse Waldheim took hold of his arms.

"Calm down. It's a dream. You're having a nightmare. It's okay."

34

THE DOCTOR

HE WAS ROYALLY PEEVED. SO close to achieving his objective only to be interrupted by some idiot with a gun.

That Makropolis kid was strong but not strong enough. He was fast but not fast enough. He was smart but not smart enough.

But he was erratic, and that's what saved him.

After shutting the lights, the Doctor had expected the kid to head for the exit or, at the very least, the light switch.

But no, he picked up his papers and backpack then headed in the wrong direction. The Doctor was on him in a flash, his left hand gripping Demetri's arm in a vise of muscle and sinew, the papers and backpack slipping from Demetri's grasp. The Doctor's other hand slashed across with his precision blade, aiming for the carotids and windpipe.

Instead of the boy trying to pull away, he dipped down to grab his falling papers. What an idiot, thought the Doctor. But the move was brilliant in retrospect. Instead of steel slicing through soft tissue and cartilage, it merely hit skin and bone.

He reversed his arm's motion to attempt a backhand kill. That was when his prey reversed direction again, against all instincts, and slammed into a beam. The Doctor's blade hit air where Demetri had stood.

Then came the voices and footsteps from above. The first intruder was big and armed with a handgun—an uncouth weapon, in the Doctor's opinion. The Doctor stepped aside to let the intruder pass, then shoved him in the small of his back. The shove sent him flying over the prone student's body and into the same beam that had found the boy's head.

The Doctor leaned over to finish the job he'd started when more people came down the stairs.

As he backstepped into the recesses of the room, the big man, dazed on the floor from his collision with the beam, lifted his weapon and fired toward the Doctor. The bullet pierced his lab coat and penetrated the back wall, missing his torso by millimeters. Too close for comfort, he thought. He headed for the steampipes and a safe exit.

35

MAKROPOLIS

HE AWOKE IN A STRANGE bed, in a strange room, with a pretty girl seated at his bedside. He must be dreaming, but if so, it was a nightmare, because his wife was standing behind the girl, and, boy, did she look mad.

"Hi, honey." Was it directed toward his wife or the pretty girl? He wasn't sure, and at this point, with a fog still enveloping his brain, he didn't care.

"I should hit you in the head," Sophia told her husband in Greek. "Perhaps it would knock some sense into you. Didn't you learn anything on the police force all those years? Keep your finger off the trigger until you really plan to shoot. *Vlaka!*" The Greek word for "idiot" was one she often resorted to when angry with someone, particularly her husband.

The girl looked at both of them and smiled, seemingly oblivious to the tirade. Sophia ran over and hugged her husband until he was nearly asphyxiated. As his brain kicked into gear, he sat up in a start. "My God, Demetri! Is he okay?"

"He's all right, Mr. Makropolis. I just stuck around until he and you were awake," said the girl. "When your gun went off in the dark and then we saw both of you on the floor, we all thought you'd shot him. But he'd just hit his head in the dark, and you tripped over him in the dark, and your gun went off. Boy, I was scared that you shot my future husband."

Maria turned toward Demetri's mom and stuck out her hand. "Hi, I'm Maria Bassias."

Sophia took the girl's hand, in mute shock to hear of her son's engagement. She glanced toward her husband, who shrugged his shoulders and whispered to her in Greek, "I'll explain it to you later."

"Demetri is in the Neuro ICU for observation," said Maria. "They're keeping him overnight. They want to keep you overnight as well, Mr. Makropolis. Well, I have to go. Perhaps I'll see you tomorrow."

Maria exited the emergency room, seemingly elated at meeting her future in-laws.

At least that seemed like the plan to Michael Makropolis, an expert in solving puzzles.

36

McManus

HE ARRIVED HOME AFTER 9 P.M. He walked the dog, ordered in Chinese, washed it down with three or four beers, and drifted off on the couch halfway through Letterman. He awoke the next morning with cottonmouth and a headache. He got up and headed toward the bathroom. His body ached from the night on the sofa. His knee creaked as usual.

He noted Marcia's door was closed. He had no doubt that she had tucked the blanket over him. He hesitated for a moment, smiled, and entered the bathroom.

After he showered and shaved, he went into his closet and selected a gray pinstripe Hickey Freeman with a white Ike Behar shirt and yellow Hermès tie with penguins on it. He put on Ferragamo black wingtips and walked to the kitchen, where Angus awaited him. McManus took the dog out for a quick walk then got into his unmarked car. It was just after sunrise, and cool, 40 degrees at most.

He drove down Utopia Parkway to Northern Boulevard. He parked in the bus stop in front of the Utopia Diner and took a seat at the counter.

The waiter set his usual in front of him: bacon and eggs, hash browns, dry wheat toast, coffee. All the morning papers were lying on the counter. The medical center case was front-page news on each one. He read the sports pages instead.

He paid the tab and left. He grabbed the parking ticket off his windshield and put it in the glove compartment with the others. He headed to the Grand Central Parkway since the radio was reporting a multicar pileup on the LIE. The Grand Central was moving at ten miles an hour, but at least it was moving.

He stopped off at the Highway Division just before the 188th Street exit. The CO, D'Agostino, had been his partner in the 34th precinct years ago. He'd moved farther and faster up the ladder than McManus had—unlike McManus, he knew how to follow orders and execute protocol. And he had the ambition McManus lacked. McManus had missed the grade for sergeant by a point after losing his Acosta Challenge to an exam question. But even though he knew the department's answer to the question was incorrect, he never bothered to retake the test.

D'Agostino warned McManus that the scuttlebutt coming out of One Police Plaza was that the high-profile case he was handling would end either with the perpetrator's arrest or with McManus permanently assigned to the VIPER Squad, where he would spend the rest of his police career monitoring video feeds along with the department's drunks, derelicts, and chronically ill. Or maybe yardstick punishment would be in order: reassignment to a precinct at the farthest reaches of Staten Island, with a two-hour commute each way.

Back in his car, he called his partner. He didn't bother leaving a voice-mail. A text arrived a minute later: "In bed. 104 fvr."

The Grand Central Parkway was jammed. He got off and navigated side streets to Queens Boulevard. It was easy to see why the papers called it the "Boulevard of Death." The road was wide, the cars were fast, and the pedestrians crossed the street with all the speed of a turtle, either too old to move faster or too preoccupied with their cellphones and iPads to see the light changing. Short of building pedestrian bridges to span it, the death toll on the boulevard was sure to keep rising.

The boulevard allowed him to get his speed all the way up to 25, but with the stoplights, the detour didn't save him any time. It was 8:30 by the time he hit the 59th Street Bridge.

As he made a left onto Second Avenue, he called the medical examiner's office. He hated voice menus. Pretending he had a rotary phone, he waited for an operator to pick up. He identified himself and asked for the ME, Dr. Peter Winter.

"Detective?"

"Is the autopsy done?"

"It is. And it was . . . interesting. Too interesting to talk about over the phone."

"Be there in fifteen minutes."

What, McManus thought, could be so interesting?

He parked in the bus stop in front of the ME's office and went inside. He walked straight to Winter's office but found it empty, so he headed to the autopsy room. Winter was there, standing over the now-dissected remains of Mr. F. J. Pervis III. He was discussing the case with half a dozen assistant MEs and residents. McManus held back and listened.

"He was declared dead on Tuesday," said one of the assistants, "but the forensic evidence indicates he didn't die until Wednesday morning."

"All the forensic evidence is in agreement," said Winter. "Only the declared time of death on Tuesday afternoon doesn't jibe. The code was called in the OR at 5:45 P.M., and asystole was noted with only a rare occasional beat—not uncommon just after death. The EKG documented it."

A resident chimed in. "Perhaps someone resuscitated the body in the hospital morgue. We know that the body was clinically alive when the craniotomy was performed—we've got the epinephrine and cortisol levels in the blood showing that the brain sensed the surgical stress. Maybe he was even conscious during the procedure."

"That's preposterous!" laughed another.

"I don't think it's preposterous," said Winter. "Neurosurgeons do plenty of surgery with patients fully awake. The craniotomy was savagely but expertly done; the dissector knew what he was doing and knew he needed to do it quickly. The heart was still beating when he reached the brainstem. He obviously wanted the tissue well perfused. He basically scooped and threw out the cerebrum to get to the much deeper brainstem, so the victim had to fall unconscious at some point after the craniotomy."

Winter spotted McManus and held up a finger to indicate he'd be done with the teaching rounds in a minute.

Winter turned to one of the residents. "Was the patient anesthetized during the dissection?"

"Apparently not. The toxicology screen showed no significant levels of any known anesthetics. Just some small residuals from the surgery the day before. The local wound did show lidocaine about the craniotomy site in the skin and soft tissues."

"Very good, Doctor. Now why?"

"Well, if the patient was conscious and if the dissector needed the brainstem tissue well perfused and intact, he used local to numb the skin and periosteum to keep the patient still. The calvarium itself has few or no nerve endings. Some neurosurgeons can manipulate brain tissue with the patient awake to determine function."

"Exactly!" said Winter. "He needed the patient still but not anesthetized. Okay, you're on a roll. This is *CSI: New York*—give it your best shot. Why was it so important to avoid anesthesia?"

The resident began to sweat. She thought for a few seconds before responding. "General anesthesia affects the brain in many ways. It essentially blocks and/or accentuates certain neural pathways. Therefore, it affects the tissue itself."

"You're on the right path. Continue."

"The dissector needed the brainstem tissue not only well perfused and oxygenated but also in as normal a state as possible."

"Excellent! The dissector wanted normal, living, unmedicated brainstem tissue. Now why a psychotic killer would want that, our tests can't answer." Winter turned to McManus. "That's your job, Detective."

He spoke again to his group. "That's all for now. I want all of you to figure out how the patient's death was faked and how he was resuscitated after the code team was unsuccessful. I want any theory, no matter how ridiculous. E-mail your thoughts to me by tomorrow morning."

The group broke up. Winter motioned for McManus to follow him.

"How much of that did you catch?" the pathologist said as they entered his office. They remained standing as they talked.

"I was here for most of it. And maybe I even understood most of it, too. Pervis's brain was ripped out of him while he was awake by someone who knows enough about medicine to know exactly what he was doing."

Winter smiled. "A+, Pat. I'm impressed."

"My brain hasn't been scooped out yet. It only seems that way from time to time."

McManus shook the ME's hand and started to leave, but Winter stopped him.

"Wait. There's something else. The cardiac arrest rhythm—the pattern of those few irregular beats—was highly unusual, but I know I've seen it before. I just can't put my finger on when it was. It must have had something to do with the feigned cardiac arrest."

"The medication vials and discarded IV bags from the time of the surgery —anything from them?"

"We're running the toxicology on them now. We'll have an answer to-morrow. Until then, remember, whoever did this is smart, determined, and ruthless. Be careful, Pat."

"Don't worry, Pete. My colleagues tell me I have the hardest head they've ever seen. No maniac is going to cut it open."

As he walked to his car, the wind whipped his coat about him. He removed the parking ticket from the windshield and got in. After he turned the key, he called the inspector.

"It's McManus. Big break in the case. Meet me in front of the ER in an hour."

37

Mortimer

FRIDAY MORNING'S CONFERENCE WAS MORTALITY
and Morbidity, also known as Death and Donuts. Its purpose was to review
complications so as to avoid them in the future if possible.

Many of the complications presented each month were routine and
unavoidable complications, such as total hip dislocations due to noncompliant
patients, and spine surgery infections, a common problem and hard to eliminate. These cases prompted little discussion. But every so often, a complication arose that was so outrageous that the normally genteel orthopedists
became like hyenas turning on their own as they excoriated the attending
who made the error. If that physician was smart, he stayed away from that
month's meeting.

As usual, one of the chief residents, Warshauer, presented the cases this day.

"A compartment syndrome and gangrene occurred within twenty-four
hours after foot surgery. The patient expired twelve hours later."

The normally quiet Dr. Patel, an accomplished spine surgeon, turned to
the hapless foot-and-ankle surgeon, Dr. DeMartin, and blurted out, "After
eight hours of tourniquet and surgical time to fix a bunion, you might as well
have put a gun to the poor patient's head and shot her!"

Mortimer stood and, over the microphone, said, "Dr. Patel, please. Dr.
DeMartin, can you explain the unusually long surgical and tourniquet time?"

DeMartin stood, placed a hand on his rotund belly, and faced his peers.
"This was a complicated case to begin with and was further complicated by

interoperative findings that were unexpected, resulting in loss of fixation followed by an inadvertent nerve injury, all caused by the resident's ineptness at retracting . . ."

Patel stood and faced DeMartin. "To blame it on the junior resident when you were doing the wrong procedure—and doing it poorly—shows you don't even belong on this faculty. Are you even board-certified?"

DeMartin was seventy-five years old and most certainly not board-certified, having failed his board exams on multiple occasions. Every department had a klinker, and DeMartin was it for this one.

Mortimer tried to defuse the situation. "Next time, Dr. DeMartin, perhaps a senior resident should assist you."

Mortimer scanned the room and saw that Nathan was not present. He then checked the time, declared the M&M conference to be over, and left the room.

38

THE DOCTOR

THE RENEWAL PROCESS HEIGHTENED NOT only his senses but also his appetite for conquest, and that appetite was far from sated. What appeased it was the death of others. He did not, after all these years, understand why, but then again, he didn't care about the pitiful lives of other people. His superiority was absolute, and other humans were no more valuable than the hamsters he'd used in his labs for decades. If only he'd published his research, the profession would be celebrating him, not hunting him as though he were a mad dog.

He checked the video monitors in his lab deep below the medical center. He had access to not only the center's security feeds but also the feeds from the nearby subway station. The rush-hour crowd was swelling on the platform. Several screens were scrolling through the station cameras when he noted a thin station worker walking toward the end of the platform, onto the track, and into the tunnel to check a light. From the worker's walk, he knew she was female.

"Excellent," he murmured. He ran the sleeve of his white lab coat under his chin, realizing he was salivating. He ran out the lab door and down the corridor.

He loved the thrill of the hunt.

39

CARTER

TODAY WAS CLINIC—THAT IS, his day to work the ambulatory care center. As much as he hated the slowness of Eastside's clinic, he enjoyed not wearing surgical scrubs, as well as actually getting to talk to and examine patients. The clinic at the VA, on the other hand, was nothing but fun: the alcoholic, chain-smoking veterans were always interesting, if only because he got to manage them directly, with minimal supervision. By far the worst clinic he worked was at City Hospital, down Second Avenue, where every time slot was triple-booked and waits averaged two hours. Patients were irate by the time they were seen—for five minutes, by an intern or resident, with oversight by attending surgeons in name only. It could take six months and as many visits to diagnose and treat a patient for a minor problem that could be wrapped up in a visit or two at Eastside.

After last night's emotionally draining events with Demetri, and a bodily draining later with Beth, Carter was looking forward to an ordinary day. He had on a pink oxford-cloth shirt with a yellow-and-blue dotted tie, khaki pants, and black penny loafers. His short white coat completed the picture. He couldn't believe that, in English hospitals, physicians were no longer allowed to wear white coats, street clothes, or even a tie, instead doing everything in scrubs. The idea was to reduce the risk of infection. Didn't anyone there ever wash their clothes? Carter figured that he and his ilk were rapidly becoming the only ones left to carry on the tradition of civilized English haberdashery.

Before going to the clinic, he'd stop in at the Neuro ICU. He found his friend dressed and getting ready to leave the hospital.

"Can't stand it anymore, Tom. Last night, they woke me up every hour with a penlight in my eyes. At this point, my only problem is a bad headache. Besides, my dad stayed in the ER overnight, and I want to get him home."

"Have you seen what you look like? It's like someone took a baseball bat to your head."

"Appearances deceive, friend. I'm a paragon of health. Plus, I need to speak to that detective. I have information about the case."

"So are you going to tell me?"

"I could swear someone was watching me down there in the stacks. I can't be sure, but I think he identified himself as my doctor."

"I think you have irreversible brain damage and need some good Greek chicken soup—what do you call it, avgolemeno?"

"The very same. I'm outta here. See you Monday."

"Stay safe." Carter turned and left.

Demetri bent over to grab his backpack, which held the books and plans, bloodstained but readable, from the library. However, leaning over made him lightheaded. The room started to spin and a wave of nausea hit him. He grabbed the bed's handrail to steady himself as Nurse Brunhilde came running over.

"You should stay at least a few more hours. Your signing out of the hospital against medical advice is not a good idea."

"Thanks, but I'll be fine." He recovered his bearings and stood straight.

"Vell," the nurse said, "doctors always know the vorst vay of taking care of themselves. I guess students are no different. You're not as healthy as you think, you know. My God, last night, when you started screaming and climbing the bed's side rails, I don't think I could have kept you in bed if that doctor had not happened to be in the room."

Demetri felt his heart pound. "Doctor? What doctor?"

"I've seen him before, but he's not a regular on the floor. I don't know vat his name is."

The man from the stacks, Demetri thought. It had to be. A chill ran up his spine.

Meanwhile, Carter left Demetri and headed for the clinic. As he walked through the jam-packed waiting room, he noted a man getting around with a walker. He had a gauze patch on his cheek and was talking to himself. Carter had seen him around before. The gauze was always in the same spot on his cheek. He remembered seeing Demetri, the day of Pervis's death, helping him across the street.

The man looked old but, up close, was not. Just above the man's collar

Carter saw a glint of aluminum foil, no doubt to ward off gamma rays. He'd seen the foil thing in paranoid schizophrenics since medical school. Carter smiled his set of chiclets, a brilliant idea having flashed before him. Fishing McManus's card out of his pocket, he walked up to the nurse's station, picked up a phone, and dialed. He got the detective's voicemail and whispered into the receiver, "Detective, this is Dr. Carter at the medical center. I have someone here in the clinic area who seems mentally deranged. I would consider him a 'person of interest' in this case." He'd heard the phrase on *CSI: Miami.* "It's 8:30 A.M. I'm in the Red Clinic area, third floor, main hospital. I'll keep him here as long as possible." He gave McManus his pager number then hung up.

Carter figured he could stall the patient with the walker for two hours at least. He turned to the head nurse. "Mary, the patient with foil ascot, where's his chart?"

"He's a regular. Nothing wrong with him, but he always uses a walker. I think he comes for the company."

"Schizophrenic?"

"Absolutely, but harmless." She handed him the chart. Carter looked at the cover: Charles Waxman. He tucked the 3-inch-thick medical record under his arm and then placed it in the house officer's desk for safekeeping.

"Please assign him to me to see today."

40

THE DOCTOR

HUMANS WERE THE MOST PLEASURABLE prey the Doctor could think of. Pursuing them in such a manner as to make sure the public never found out only added to the thrill.

The underground labyrinth of Manhattan was ideal. Years had gone by before some of his victims were found, devoid of flesh. The island's flourishing population of rats made rapid work of the corpses, leaving skeletal remains of what was obviously a homeless person who'd died of exposure or disease. At least that was how the police reports would be altered by superiors eager to keep crime stats low—if a report was filed at all.

The knife was the Doctor's favorite instrument, especially his long and utterly sharp amputation scalpels, all many decades old. Today he picked his 10-inch blade, specifically used for amputations at the hip.

He pranced silently along the darkened tracks like a leopard stalking a zebra. Knife in hand, he spied a moving light about a hundred yards ahead—undoubtedly the track worker. As he neared, he noted her narrow waist and her wide bottom, over which was suspended her work belt full of tools.

"Excellent," he murmured.

The worker turned, her light flashing across the tracks.

"Hello, anyone there?" She removed up her radio from her belt. "Chris, is there anyone else supposed to be down here?"

"Negative, Sandy," the receiver squawked.

"Track 10 is shut down until I effect the repair on the broken signal?"

"Affirmative."

"Out."

She took a quick look around. She was annoyed being here by herself, but budget cuts necessitated her union's agreeing to the change in work rules. No one to watch your back for trains or rats. Seeing nothing, she walked up to the broken signal and took out a screwdriver to open the casing. After trying to turn one of the screws with no luck, she took out a small can of WD-40 and sprayed the box to loosen up the years of caked-on oxidation. Checking her watch, she figured about three to four minutes should do the job, so she sat near the wall, on an old cinder block, and whipped out a candy bar. The area quickly was illuminated with staccato lights as a train passed by on another track, temporarily blinding her. She took another bite of her Snickers and tossed the rest down the tracks.

Seeing his chance, the Doctor advanced. Rats scurried along his feet in their quest for the candy. Another train passed, with lights again blinding the worker. The conductor and passengers did not notice the flash of the blade.

As the worker's life flowed slowly from her eye, through which the blade had penetrated her brain before slashing across the inside of her cranium, instantly doing away with her consciousness, the Doctor quickly removed her belt and dropped her pants and penetrated her. With explosive force, he deposited his seed inside her nearly lifeless form, sating his monstrous desire, if only for a bit. He then re-dressed her. He arranged the tool belt just as he had found it.

He carried the body a few feet then placed it perpendicular to the currently running track, laying the head directly over the outside rail.

THE CONDUCTOR WAS JUST ABOUT to start braking for the station when he felt a bump. Not large, but enough to derail a train if not fixed. He called it in and was told someone was in the vicinity working on a signal and would be asked to check it out.

"Sandy, it's Chris. Can you check Track 11 for debris reported by a conductor at marker 21.5?"

The receiver squawked on the tool belt belonging to the now headless body lying perpendicular to Track 11, marker 21.5.

41

PEAR

AT LEAST THIS MORNING WAS not as bad as the previous two. The student was alive and well, and no more missing or dead bodies had been reported—although, at this point, nothing would surprise him.

Enough of this. He was the one whose job it was to steer the ship clear of the shoals. If he had to sacrifice a few members of the crew to save the ship, he wouldn't hesitate for a second. That, he thought, was leadership. He opened the drawer to his desk and pulled out an old newspaper clipping he'd taken from his safe. He hadn't looked at it in over thirty years. He thought back to the 1980s, before he'd been appointed CEO, a boy wonder, the perfect combination of medical acumen, administrative ability, and ice water for blood. The article, no more than 3 column inches in length, was headlined "Homeless Man's Body Goes Missing After Death at Eastside Center." As he scanned it, the names Pear and Murtaugh flashed across his retinas. He reached to his left, grabbed his cigar lighter, placed the clipping in the ashtray, and lit it afire. Why he kept the clipping so long he could not fathom, but he'd always figured that someday this scourge would return to haunt him.

This time around, he planned to eliminate that scourge forever. He had decided then and there that he would hunt the killer down, back to his lair in the catacombs below the medical center. He dropped his head into his hands as his face felt the heat from the flame.

He got up and went into his private bathroom to compose himself. He felt confident that the spin that had worked so well in the '80s would work again today to alleviate some of the negative press. Pear knew that nothing changes, not even names. Only dates.

After washing and drying his face, he exited the washroom. The phone on his desk buzzed. He tapped the intercom. "Yes?"

"The Chief of Security is here with that detective."

"Send them in. I'm ready."

Ready for anything, he thought. He slipped on his lab coat and sat in the leather chair behind his desk. In came Murtaugh and McManus.

"Well, gentlemen, it was a relief to find that our student was alive and well and not shot by a former police officer who happened to be his father. A simple bump on the head—not much to the story after all."

"Not much at all," said McManus, with not a hint of sincerity. He walked to the front of Pear's desk and fingered the humidor. "You're a cigar smoker, Dr. Pear?"

"Only on special occasions."

McManus opened the humidor. "Cubans."

"A gift from the ambassador of France."

"Mind if I take a couple?" The detective didn't wait for an answer before helping himself to half a dozen and placing them in his breast pocket. "You know, I've never come across a cigar that smells like burnt paper."

"The wrapper caught fire when I put the match in the ashtray."

"I see." McManus picked up Pear's sterling silver lighter, felt its heat, then laid it back on the desk. He put his hand in his pocket and felt the cigars there—none had wrappers. He looked at the ashtray—no match.

"Well, Detective, I'm sure you didn't come up here to talk cigars."

"Can't put one over on you, can I, Doc?" The smile he gave Pear was so cold a cadaver's radiated warmth by comparison. "I have news about the autopsy. The media will get their hands on the report soon enough; I thought you should know before. I suggest you prepare yourself."

"Prepare myself? A pervert stole and mangled the body. Period, paragraph. I can't imagine what the autopsy would add."

"How about this? Our boy Pervis was not, repeat not, dead when your hospital personnel stuck him in the Ziploc baggie and wheeled him to the morgue."

"Detective McManus, he was declared dead by the code team, all trained physicians and nurses. The EKG record showed no evidence of a life-sustainable rhythm. With all due respect, Detective, you're not a doctor. What you're saying is medically impossible."

"Call the ME if you don't believe me. The death was feigned so that, with all due respect, even the hotshots you have working in your operating rooms couldn't tell the difference. And here's the kicker: he was alive when Dr. Doom scooped the brains out of his skull like so much Jell-o. And not only alive. Awake."

McManus paused to let the news sink in. It did, rendering Pear ashen and silent. Satisfied that he'd one-upped the pompous ass, McManus continued.

"The ME's running toxicology tests on the discarded IV tubes and drug containers and on what's left of the patient. No doubt your security guard came upon the culprit and became a victim as well."

Pear thought back to the early '80s when another patient's body had disappeared shortly after death. That one was never recovered. It was a homeless man, not a minor celebrity like Pervis, so the papers dropped the story after a day or two. He looked at Murtaugh, who stared back with mindless eyes. Murtaugh was essential in making the prior case disappear. Pear saw to it that Murtaugh was rewarded with his current position after he retired from the PD.

This was history he didn't want revisited—in the press or by this half-cocked Popeye Doyle. He put his game face back on.

"I appreciate the heads-up, Detective McManus. I'm confident this one-time incident, perpetrated by a deranged mind, will not happen at this hospital again."

"I'm sure you're confident, too. I'm also sure you'll continue to provide the hospital's full cooperation in the investigation."

McManus walked toward the door. Halfway out he turned, patted his breast pocket, and said, "Thanks for the Cubans. Don't get them often on a detective's salary."

When McManus was gone Murtaugh took a seat opposite Pear.

"Doc, everyone in the department hates McManus. He's a loser and a lone wolf."

"Don't worry. He's not as smart as he thinks he is. In the wild, lone wolves starve and die."

"So do you think this case is related to the last one?"

"Not only am I positive that it is, my feeble-minded security chief, I'm also sure it's related to an even older case. One I never told you about . . ."

42

TOLL

HIS MORNING WAS AS ROUTINE as it could be. Up at 6, shower, breakfast with his wife, kiss the kids, out the door at 7, at the OR by 7:15, surgery scheduled for 7:30. In the holding area was the first patient, a fifty-four-year-old male, there for gastric bypass surgery performed by Dr. Meyers.

Toll never liked giving anesthesia for those procedures. The patients were morbidly obese, making the rate of complication high: blood loss, fluid shifts, cardiopulmonary events. After introducing himself to the patient and reviewing the man's history, he gave his usual boilerplate about potential risks. He tried not to scare the poor guy, so he didn't tell him what concerned him most: not only was the guy short and squat, with a barely perceptible neck that by itself made intubation a nightmare, he also had had prior cervical-spine surgery, with lingering pinched-nerve symptoms. Toll was sure to be blamed if the patient woke up with his symptoms worse than before.

Finished with his spiel, he handed the patient a pen to sign the informed-consent form. But then Meyers popped his head through the curtains.

"Ah, Dr. Toll. All set?" Toll nodded as Meyers whipped out a marker, yanked the patient's gown aside, and wrote his initials on the man's abdomen, as required by all ORs to prevent wrong-site surgery. If only they could figure out how to prevent wrong-surgeon surgery, thought Toll. Meyers looked at the patient and asked, "Any questions?" He waited a millisecond before saying, "Great, see you in the OR," and was gone, on his way to the locker room, leaving Toll to wonder how surgeons got away with barely knowing their patients.

Once the patient signed the form, Toll headed to the Pyxis medication dispenser. New to the hospital, the system was supposed to track all anesthesia drugs used, returned, and billed for each patient and each anesthesiologist. It was supposed to eliminate waste, theft, and drug abuse by anesthesiologists. But it was easily circumvented.

Toll had the machine dispense a bottle of inhalation anesthetic for use on this case, plus vials of propofol, Versed, and Fentanyl. He opened his briefcase, which contained his laptop, journals, and iPod, and dropped all the drugs in except for the Fentanyl. He placed that vial in the breast pocket of his surgical scrubs. It's been a rough week, he thought. I need something special today.

In the OR, Toll used the propofol and Versed to sedate the patient while he performed the nasotracheal intubation that was finally required after the patient's short neck had caused the attempt at regular intubation to fail. It took forty-five minutes to get the patient asleep and ready for the surgery. It took another twenty-five for the circulating nurse to find Meyers. He'd gone to the floors to do rounds.

Trailed by the assistant surgeon, he finally swept into the room. "Ah, asleep already. Another magnificent job, Toll. Well, let's get going." The pair went into the scrub room, neither one showing any remorse for the delay. After a few minutes, they returned and began prepping and draping the patient's abdomen. While they were occupied, Toll removed the vial of Fentanyl from his pocket and drew the liquid up into a syringe, which, out of habit, he then labeled with the drug's name—standard operating procedure in the anesthesia business. He liked going by the book whenever he administered anesthesia, even to himself. After capping the needle, he placed the syringe in his pocket.

The record showed that entire vials of propofol, Versed, and Fentanyl were administered, followed by the inhalation anesthetic. This was meticulously documented on the anesthesia sheet by the attending anesthesiologist, Gregory Toll, MD, as the abdominal incision was made.

43

Demetri

HE WALKED TO THE EMERGENCY room, where his parents were waiting. "You look terrible," said his mom, hugging him. "You look like . . ."

". . . someone hit me with a baseball bat? Yeah, I know, Ma, but I feel fine. And how do you feel, Dad?"

"Like I got hit in the balls with a basketball except they're inside my head. But I've had hangovers that were worse."

"You mean you feel the way you do after I've whacked you with the back of my hand," his wife said as she elbowed him. "Which, by the way, I should do more of."

They left the building and saw the dry-cleaning van, which sat, illegally parked, where Michael had left it the day before. Three parking tickets were on the windshield, and another was in progress. The traffic officer's handheld spewed out a ticket, which she handed to Makropolis. He collected the others and unlocked the vehicle.

"I'm driving," said his wife, taking the keys. Her husband got in the passenger side. Demetri sat on a jumpseat in the back.

Sophia drove toward the 59th Street Bridge—Demetri knew she hated paying tolls, even if a route saved time. The traffic in Queens was heavy, but the LIE was moving. Once she took her usual spot in the middle lane, she could contain herself no more.

"So who is this woman?"

"What woman?" said Demetri, contorting his face in confusion.

As she always did when she was annoyed, she switched to Greek. "Demetri, don't give me a hard time. I've had a rough night thanks to you and your *vlaka* father. Now, who is this Maria?"

Demetri was still puzzled. Then it dawned on him. "Do you mean that girl from Medical Records?"

"Don't deny it!"

"Deny what?" Demetri knew he had a concussion, but something more than a clouded brain was going on here.

His dad joined the attack. "That she is your fiancée."

"My fiancée? I only met her yesterday!"

His mother reasserted her position as lead interrogator. Demetri had seen it before: good cop/bad cop. "I met this Maria in the emergency room last night, and she said you were going to get married."

"Ma, I just met her yesterday. I spoke to her for ten minutes. I mean, she's attractive, but I haven't even asked her out."

"Ah, so she's attractive. The attractive girls are the ones to stay away from."

"Dad, help me out."

"Sophia, honey. She's a pretty girl, she helped me find Demetri, and she likes him. What's wrong? Demetri, do me a favor. On Monday, when you get back to school, bring her a flower and tell her you want to get to know her."

His wife whacked her already concussed husband in the head with the back of her right hand as she steadied the wheel with her left. "Greek men! You're all handsome hunks with roving eyes."

As they pulled into their driveway, the front door burst open, and the entire family—siblings, Yia Yia, aunts, uncles, and cousins—came pouring out to embrace each of the van's occupants. Hugs and kisses all around. The scene might have gone on for hours had not a cousin reminded everyone that the two heroes had just come home from the hospital and might need to rest. The extended family said goodbye, and the immediate family went inside.

In the entrance foyer, Yia Yia started to cry. At 5 feet 1 inch tall, and shrinking every year, the white-haired, black-garbed grandmother kept saying, "Demetri! Demetri! What's happened? Where have you been all these years?" It was clear she was talking about her long-departed husband, Demetri's grandfather and namesake.

"*Stamata.* Stop, Yia Yia. I'm fine," Demetri said as he took her hand and seated her in the living room.

"Demetri!" It was his thirteen-year-old sister, Elena. "Tell us about the body snatcher and the fight you had with him."

"Yeah!" This was George, his fifteen-year-old brother. "Did he carry a big knife?"

Demetri shook his head and did his best impression of Charlie Brown. "Good grief," he said as he turned and walked into the kitchen.

George looked at Elena and then his parents. "What did I say?"

"As usual," said his dad, "the wrong thing." He turned to his wife and announced, "I'm going to take a nap," then went upstairs to their bedroom.

Sophia looked at her two youngest with a glare that would cause a hardened convict to cringe in fear, but Elena and George merely giggled. She went to the kitchen, finding Demetri. He was seated, rubbing his temples. "Demetri, are you hungry?"

The boy's head popped up and his eyes brightened. "French toast?"

His mom smiled as she opened the refrigerator to get the milk and eggs. Although her recipe for the toast was conventional, she had her own concoction for the syrup: Golden Blossom honey diluted with water, with sugar added for extra sweetness, then heated until smooth. Fifteen minutes later, Demetri had finished off eight slices.

"Ma?"

"Yes, sweetie?" she said as she was washing the dishes.

"How did Dad show up in the library yesterday?"

"He got the tingles about you." She let out a breath. "Your father and his tingles."

Demetri wanted to know more but decided he was better off getting the story from his father. He opened his bag and started to spread out the hospital blueprints on the kitchen table.

"What's that?" asked Sophia.

"A project I'm working on. About the history of the medical center."

"Sounds interesting." She placed the last dish on the drying rack, wiped her hands, and exited the kitchen.

Demetri leaned over one of the floor plans, following with his finger the path of the walkways and conduits.

"Yes, very interesting."

44

NATHAN

HE WAS RELEASED, WITHOUT CHARGES or an explanation, at 3 A.M. He was questioned for hours about his private life, his whereabouts for the last several days, and his personal habits. Somehow he'd been able to avoid divulging his taste for pornography involving "mature" women.

He'd take up the matter of this police harassment with his attorney.

Four hours later, he was back in the operating room; by 8:30, he was finishing his second knee arthroscopy. The patient was a forty-nine-year-old male, a self-identified "athlete," although at least 20 pounds overweight. His left knee had a degenerative meniscal tear. Nathan had suspected the knee was also arthritic—the condition didn't show up on the pre-op tests but was confirmed during the procedure. Although the débridement went well, Nathan knew that the benefit from the surgery would be minimal. He considered it stage one of a two-stage process, the next step being a total knee replacement in six months or a year when the patient realized he'd not improved. By then, Nathan would have taken the course on partial replacements at the Mayo Clinic and would be able to offer the guy a partial, which would save him the pain of full replacement. Then, if Nathan was lucky, the partial replacement would fail before the patient reached sixty-five and Nathan would perform a full replacement in time to avoid doing it for the peanuts paid by Medicare. Nathan had become adept at maximizing his rate of return per patient.

Nathan's phone vibrated. A text message from Bigelow: "Ur ofc. 30 min."

He had a shoulder scope scheduled for that time, but surgeons at this hospital were late so often it almost seemed mandatory. He headed to the locker room. He punched in the three-digit code—3-5-1—on the door. He remembered the code by thinking of Cleveland—not the city but the 351 Cleveland automobile engine used by muscle cars of a certain era. He didn't pull down enough to be a serious car collector yet, but that would change as his workload expanded to include more, and more remunerative, procedures.

He opened his locker—half-height, since senior surgeons hogged all the full lockers. Nathan would have to wait for thirteen more of those dinosaurs to die off or retire before he got his own full locker. But if he played the Pervis game correctly, he would insist on a full locker immediately, perhaps even Mortimer's. Yeah, that sounded good.

He changed clothes and headed to deposit his surgical scrubs in the vending machine that also dispensed them. If he didn't leave a set, he'd be out of credit for a clean one. He punched in his initials and placed his index finger on the biometric scanner. An error code came up: "Identification error. Please resubmit." "Fuck you!" he shouted at the machine as he tried again, then again, appalled that the hospital didn't trust its own doctors not to steal scrubs—as though they were items of great value. "Fuck you! Fuck you! And fuck me!" Then he remembered what that Greek medical student had told him: "Wipe your finger on your forehead to get some skin oils on it." He did, and this time the machine clicked open. Shouting "Fuck you all!" he tossed in the soiled garments.

On his way out, he spied an open locker and looked inside. He found two sets of clean scrubs. He tucked them under his lab coat and left, smiling like a Cheshire cat.

BIGELOW WAS SITTING IN NATHAN'S office when he got there. Nathan tossed his purloined sets of scrubs on the desk and closed the door.

"How about this, Warren? Pervis was still alive when his brain was removed."

"What?"

"His death in the OR was a fake."

"Are you sure?"

"Straight from the horse's mouth, a resident in the ME's office who likes to watch Knicks game from the press area. Our mad scientist put one over on you."

"Jesus Christ."

"Yep, almost fooled Him, too."

Nathan couldn't help himself—he felt admiration for whoever had masterminded the grisly theft. He had to be a medical genius to fool the entire code team, unless . . . unless the perpetrator was a member of the code team. He'd never liked Toll—maybe he did it, although he hardly seemed smart enough. Whoever had done it, Nathan had one concern and one concern only: keeping clear of the shitstorm.

Fortunately, Bigelow was thinking along the same lines.

"Help me out here, Warren. We need to pin this on the hospital in general and Pear in particular. That pompous jackass has hated my guts for years." Indeed, Bigelow had once almost lost his job when Pear called the paper's metro editor to lodge a complaint about the reporter's "unorthodox" methods.

"Hmm." Nathan looked at the wall as he thought. The light bulb turned on after only a few seconds. "Okay. Let's say that the attending surgeon suspected foul play from the beginning and tried to keep the code going longer. The powers that be, however, had him outnumbered and outgunned and were deliberate in their plan to make him the scapegoat. Fortunately, though, Warren Nathan, brave and true, had the fortitude to fight the system. Patients come first for the noble man of medicine, even at the risk of losing his position at the hospital."

"Impressive. You just thought of that?"

"I think of a lot of things."

Bigelow phoned his editor and filled him in. Then the conversation seemed to go to another subject. Bigelow listened for a few moments then said, "Forget it. Who cares?" and ended the call.

"Who cares about what?" asked Nathan.

"Accidental death of a subway worker, apparently by a passing train."

"Right. Who cares?"

45

PEAR

THE BOARD OF TRUSTEES, CALLED by Pear to an emergency meeting, was seated around the long mahogany table. Pear sat at the head. At the opposite end sat the board chairman, Nigel Gord III, whose ancestors came over on the Mayflower. On the wall behind him was a glass-and-wood case filled with surgical instruments from the nineteenth century. Along the sides of the table were shelves holding first editions of medical books going as far back as 1750, including the anatomical prints of Vesalius's muscle men. Copies of the prints had been seen by millions of people. Pear knew that most of the anatomy detailed by Vesalius was learned from corpses stolen out of the shallow graves of Venetia. Grave robbers—the fitting complement to this morning's discussion.

"Good morning, ladies and gentlemen," said Pear. "The meeting is brought to order."

"Dr. Pear," said Gord in his Mainline Philadelphia accent, "if you would be so kind as to explicate why this meeting is so urgent."

Pear heard his voice quiver as began to speak. It had never done so at a board meeting before.

"My apologies for calling you together on such short notice. A circumstance has occurred which may rock the foundations of this institution. As you're all well aware, the media have been at our doorstep the last several days, like wolves waiting to devour us should we show weakness. It all stems from the death of Mr. Pervis."

Gord interrupted him. "Apologies accepted, Fred, but we all read the papers."

"What you haven't read is the coroner's report. It won't be released until Monday."

The mouths of the normally unflappable captains of industry and doyennes of society hung open as Pear described the medical examiner's bizarre findings.

"The near-decapitation of one of our security guards," Pear continued, "who apparently happened upon the murderer, presents an added complication. When this news hits the streets, ladies and gentlemen, patients will leave the center en masse. We will face serious financial and legal difficulties and a public-relations nightmare. You all know that hospitals in New York are in worse financial condition than those anywhere else in the country. This fiscal year, we have been running a projected 20 million in the red, and this will quadruple the losses this year, and that doesn't include the millions, if not billions, lost due to the inevitable avalanche of lawsuits. Throw in some criminal investigations, and we've got a catastrophe of biblical proportions."

"Fred, Gladys Jones." The hospital CFO was participating by telephone from the Cayman Islands, where, for tax purposes, the hospital parked most of its endowment. *"Surely, the financial picture is not so bleak. We simply hire more physicians who have contracts with managed-care companies in order to increase our volume."*

Pear and Gord winced in tandem. Neither liked the CFO, whose answer to every hospital problem was to find ways to attract more "customers—and we're talking quantity, not quality." At that moment, both Gord and Pear, without so much as a nod to each other, knew it was time to fire the gold-plated ninny.

"Thank you, Gladys," said Gord. "You're as helpful as you always are." Deftly, without anyone else noticing, he disconnected the phone cord running from the jack on the wall by his chair to the speaker phone on the table. Addressing the board, he continued, "I think I speak for all assembled when I say that, although this matter will certainly leave a serious blot on the center's magnificent reputation, murder by a psychotic individual cannot be blamed on the institution. Our PR people ought to be able to spin this."

"I'm not so sure they can, Nigel," said Pear. "There is an old medical saying that goes, 'You can't make chicken salad out of chicken shit.' And chicken shit is what we have here, especially since this isn't the first case of such murders in the hospital's history."

The board members stared at Pear in total silence for several seconds before Gord, despite the laws and customs forbidding it, pulled a cigarette from his pocket and lit it. He took a deep, deliberate draw. "Explain," he said as he exhaled.

Pear gathered himself as he prepared to share a secret he'd kept for over thirty years. "It began when, as a young medical attending, I noted the loss of a homeless man's body. I did a little homework and discovered that this was what could reasonably be called a regular incident at our institution, occurring every twenty-five years or so. The victims were always homeless and without families. The last was in the 1980s as far as I can tell, when Murtaugh, then of the NYPD, and I tracked and thought we got rid of the murderer "

"Obviously," said Gord, "you were mistaken."

46

McManus

AFTER LEAVING PEAR'S OFFICE, MCMANUS headed to the diner by the emergency room. He had only ten minutes before his 9:00 with the inspector, but he'd had only three cups of coffee this morning and needed more.

He took a seat at the counter and ordered. Then he felt his phone vibrate in his pocket. He looked: a voicemail. He dialed to get the message. It was from Carter, the orthopedic resident. He listened, downed his coffee, threw some money on the table, and got up. Outside he saw McCarthy's car pull up across the street. He checked his watch: 8:57. McManus liked women who came on time.

She stepped out the passenger-side door, her walk and attire all business. McManus waved her toward the ER entrance. They met in the vestibule. McManus flashed his badge, and they were buzzed into the back.

"Blow me away, big boy."

"With pleasure." He loved a woman in a business suit. "ME says Pervis did not die on the operating table. It was a fake. He was alive—and awake —the next morning when his brain was lifted from his skull."

"Wow."

"Yeah, wow."

"In eighteen years on the force, I've seen some sick fucks, but this . . ."

"Yeah, this. My first guess would be it's someone on the code team. But the resident who was at the surgery just called me, says he has a 'person of interest' up in the clinic area right now."

"'Person of interest?' Who and why?"

"Hell should I know. I'm on my way up now. Join me?"

"With pleasure."

THE WAITING ROOM IN THE red zone was a sea of humanity, with every person using a cane, crutches, a walker, or a wheelchair. There was a prison inmate wearing an orange jumpsuit and shackles. A correction officer sat on either side of him.

McManus walked to the front desk, "Is Dr. Carter here?"

"Do you have an appointment?"

He flashed his badge. "My appointment slip." McManus had seen that look of surprise and fear a thousand times and always got a kick out of it.

"This way." As she wheeled around the counter, McManus realized she was sitting on a motorized wheelchair. Her two legs were withered, and she used her abnormally small left arm to manipulate the joystick. McManus felt a touch of guilt for the act he'd just pulled, but it passed quickly. He and McCarthy followed the clerk into the examining area. It was expansive, well-appointed, and well-staffed. Not like the decrepit outpatient clinics at City Hospital, the municipal facility he was most familiar with.

Carter, who was making some notations on a chart, spotted McManus. "Detective, in here." He led them into an empty examination room.

The room was large by most standards, with an examining table, two high chairs used for total-joint-replacement patients, and a wheeled stool.

"Inspector McCarthy, NYPD," said Mary, holding her hand out to the young doctor.

"The person of interest is in room two. I've interviewed and examined him. He acts like he's disabled but isn't; he's also not as old as he appears to be. He's diagnosed as a paranoid schizophrenic— he hears voices. The nurses tell me he hangs around the hospital all the time. I remember seeing him the day of Pervis's surgery; he was just outside the medical center after the code was called."

McManus eyed Carter and didn't speak. He considered all the physicians involved to be suspects, even the P. Elliott model standing before him.

Carter continued. "He walks with a walker or crutch and wears a bandage on his face. Always in the same spot: left cheek."

"So why is he a 'person of interest'? You've given me practically nothing to go on."

"I know it's circumstantial. No jury would convict without evidentiary corroboration," said Carter, using language he'd heard on *Hawaii Five-O.* McManus and McCarthy rolled their eyes at each another, recognizing the TV reference. "But how about this?" Carter took the thick folder from under his arm and plopped it on the table. "This is volume six of his chart. He used to be a medical student here so he has medical knowledge and knows the layout of the institution very, very well.

"You've already got motive—he's crazy—and this gives you opportunity. I like this guy for the murders," he said, quoting more TV cops—this time from *NYPD Blue.*

The two real cops could only shake their heads.

47

MORTIMER

THE HIP REPLACEMENT WAS SUPPOSED to be routine. The patient was a fifty-five-year-old male with osteoarthritis caused by impingement of the hip, a developmental deformity that in all likelihood had a strong genetic component, considering that he reported a strong family history of hip arthritis.

Two years prior, the patient had undergone a hip arthroscopy in Park City, Utah, by Dr. Steve Pachmeyer. Known internationally as the hip specialist to the stars, especially dozens of pro athletes, Pachmeyer was, technically, a poor arthroscopist whose procedures took hours. On the CT Mortimer had received earlier, he'd seen that Pachmeyer had removed bone from the femoral head and neck in an attempt to eliminate the impingement. Review of Pachmeyer's operative notes revealed that he knew, pre-op, that the patient had arthritis, making clear to Mortimer that the hip specialist to the stars had been too gung-ho. The Utah surgery was a waste, because it would not prevent progression. In fact, it was worse than a waste: the hip's femoral neck was now so notched that a surface replacement was no longer possible. A conventional hip replacement was the only option.

Mortimer sighed as he reviewed the CT scan on the view board in the operating room while Toll administered regional anesthesia. Mortimer was still depressed over the entire Pervis mess. Nathan was being subversive, and Pear wanted only to cover it all up. Mortimer was becoming less and less interested in running his department, let alone practicing orthopedic surgery. He thought of the approaching weekend he'd planned weeks before with his wife: two nights at a bed and breakfast in the Berkshires. His wife was set on going so he had no choice, but he didn't have the energy to relax. He sighed again.

"Yes, Dr. Mortimer?" It was the circulating nurse.

"Nothing, Amanda. I was just thinking I may need the Midas for this case. The neck area is pretty sclerotic."

"I'll set it up."

Mortimer looked over the nurse's shoulder and saw the patient prepped and draped. He walked to the scrub room and donned his headset. It featured a built-in spotlight and fans to circulate the air in the "spacesuit" that was *de rigeur* for joint replacements and laminar-flow operating rooms. Once he attached the battery, the familiar hum of the fans started up.

Minutes later, he was standing over the patient. Knife in hand, Mortimer paused as Amanda called the time out. All present agreed on the patient, the side, and the procedure.

He began by making a 3-inch incision angling forward from the trochanter of the hip. The senior resident asked, "So this is an anterior approach?"

Mortimer stopped at the fascia. He looked at the resident and at Calvin, his surgical tech for the last fifteen years. "It is now."

He stared at the wound. *What is* wrong *with me?* He'd planned on a posterior approach and a straight stem component. Now that had to change.

"Amanda, please open the anterior instruments. Also, we need the broaches and implants for the curved micro prosthesis."

"But you had that prosthesis and those instruments removed from the inventory last month when the company refused to meet the prices of the other vendors."

Mortimer knew he was between a rock and a hard place: Struggle with this small anterior incision using suboptimal instruments and the wrong implant, or extend the incision by at least 12 inches to allow the longer implant to fit more easily, in a patient who was expecting a tiny cut and a quick exit from the hospital.

He'd later realize that, of the two choices, he made the wrong one.

"We can make do with what we have," he said to the team. "It shouldn't be much more difficult."

What should have been a routine one-hour procedure took over three times that long after he inadvertently cracked the femur while trying to insert the straight stem implant into the medullary canal. The repair took four cables, a strut graft, and a 16-inch incision. Once he'd closed the fascia, he handed the suturing off to the resident. "I'm exhausted. Please finish."

Mortimer removed his hood and gown, left the OR, and headed to the chiefs' locker room.

Thankfully, it was empty. He sat on the bench and began to cry.

48

Bassias

SHE ENTERED THE MAIN ENTRANCE of the hospital at a near run. She was late for work because the Long Island Railroad had had switching problems at Jamaica Station, adding twenty minutes to her commute from her parents' home in Mineola.

She flashed her ID at the security desk and walked through the central lobby. As she turned the corner, she felt she was being leered at. A pretty girl in New York City, she'd developed a sixth sense to detect ogling. This time, however, it felt different, malevolent somehow. She felt cold and scared, as if the person eyeing her meant her harm. She looked around to determine where it was coming from, but all she saw was a mass of white coats. But then, between the rushing bodies of the residents and students, she caught a glimpse of a face locked in concentration on her.

As quickly as she saw it, the face was gone. She did not recognize the man but would not soon forget the intensity of the dark, hard eyes. She shivered as she took the staircase down to the record room.

She went to work, filing and cataloguing. She tried to write off the incident to natural New York paranoia.

But those eyes.

49

DEMETRI

AFTER PORING OVER THE PLANS for several hours, he thought he'd discovered how the perpetrator moved around. Near the morgue, adjacent to the kitchens, was a sealed hallway that led to a staircase and an abandoned dumb-waiter shaft. The staircase led to lower levels with corridors that led to all the main areas of the hospital. Used for moving supplies from a light-rail line that connected the hospital to the coal and supply barges on the East River, these passageways were far below the sub-subbasement, below even most of the East Side subway and MetroNorth commuter lines. Demetri surmised that they had been closed down once the medical center both abandoned coal for steam heat and got its supplies brought in by truck.

He looked up from the kitchen table and realized he was alone. The siblings had finally gone off to school, his mother to the dry cleaners. Yia Yia was asleep on the living room couch, and he could tell his father was asleep upstairs—his snoring was causing the ceiling to vibrate.

His headache was gone, but he needed some air. He grabbed his backpack, took the old Jeep Renegade out of the garage, and started to drive along the North Shore. It was sunny but cool and windy. He wanted to clean out the cobwebs.

The Pervis death consumed him. He'd never wanted to be a police detective but this case was making him understand why the old man worked on cases 24/7. Demetri took local streets to Piping Rock Road then found himself driving through Locust Valley, with its preppy clothing shops that catered to Carter and other members of the horsey set. Continuing north, he arrived at the two massive stone pillars that marked the entrance to The Lattingtown Club, one of the most exclusive country clubs in the United States. The club's golf course, which winds down to the edge of Long Island Sound, offers views as spectacular as those at any course in America.

Demetri took a left through the pillars, figuring that, at this time of year, the gate would be unguarded. His hunch was correct—the whole place looked deserted. He drove along a tree-lined road that made a beeline to the shore. The massive beach house and outdoor Olympic-size pool were closed for the season, so he parked, grabbed his backpack, and took the walkway toward the water. To his right, he saw the ninth green, surrounded by wetlands and accessible only by a small footbridge. Although he planned on someday taking up golf—it was, after all, the official sport of orthopedists—he imagined he'd never be able to afford a club like this. Heck, the place was so exclusive it had rejected an offer to host the U.S. Open not once but twice.

He walked along the beach into a biting wind until he reached a path that angled back into the wetlands and toward the golf course. As he walked the path, he could see hundreds of birds—gulls, ducks, geese, cormorants, herons. Back on the mainland, he came upon an old cemetery with headstones dating back as far as the 1780s. The names were illegible, worn by time and the Nor'easters that pound the area each winter, year after year.

He sat down on a large rock, took his laptop from his backpack, turned it on, and plugged in his broadband wireless card. Reading the news of a subway worker found beheaded by a train not far from the medical center, he pondered its connection to the Pervis case then dismissed the idea. Logging into the archives of the *New York Times,* he began to investigate the stories he'd heard from his dad. He found only a brief mention of the homeless man whose body went missing from the Medical Center in 1986.

He Googled for more on the story, and two names kept popping up: Pear and Murtaugh. He also found something else: the homeless man wasn't the only bizarre death in Manhattan at that time. Within a week of the hospital's losing the body, several bizarre murders were reported. For some reason, the police and the press didn't link them to the homeless man's disappearance. All involved young, good-looking men and women who were sexually attacked, had their throats slashed, and/or were mutilated in one way or another. After that one week of murders, the papers became quiet, and no additional news surfaced. He would ask his dad what he remembered.

He logged on to the hospital's website and began searching the archives, recently made available online. He was looking for missing corpses. His first search was for all deaths in the 1980s. The list was enormous. Even after multiple modifications of the search terms, he could not hone the list down to manageable size.

At that moment, he heard a hawk's shrill cry overhead and decided to take a break. He lay down on the ground, leaned against the rock, and looked across the Sound. A large commercial vessel was slowly making its way east, the low vibration of its engines echoing for miles across the water. A sailboat flew in the opposite direction, heading for Westchester. He let his mind drift—and then he realized: he'd never find what he was looking for by searching through thousands of individual patient records. No, he would search hospital reports, specifically those of mortality and morbidity conferences and the quality-assurance committee, cross-referencing the names of Pear and Murtaugh.

He resumed work on his laptop, and . . . bingo!

At the time of the homeless man's death, Pear chaired the quality-assurance committee, which reviewed the case. The patient was an alcoholic found by the police under the 59th Street Bridge during a January cold spell, with temperatures in the single digits. Today he'd be taken to a homeless shelter, but at that time, cops routinely brought such people to hospitals. Aside from his addiction and hypothermia, he was healthy and was admitted as a Medical Service patient under Pear's authority—Pear was on call for medical service admissions in the ER at the time. Two days later, in his hospital bed, the man was found not breathing. A code was called, but he could not be resuscitated, and so the body was taken to the morgue. Then it disappeared and was never found. Pear surmised at the committee meeting that the patient died from an overdose of drugs he had smuggled in. The committee made no recommendations in the case. No mention of it was made in any subsequent reports.

Demetri looked up and saw that the tide was starting to recede. He checked the time. He'd spent over two hours at the cemetery, and it was getting cold.

He packed his laptop and followed the path, thinking it led back to the golf course. Soon, however, he was in a deep thicket of bittersweet and evergreens. Startled by a large red fox that darted past him, he stepped into something soft and gooey. He looked down to find himself ankle deep in horseshit.

He was standing in a bridle path. Goddamn horsey set.

McManus

IT WAS TOO NEAT AND clean—he'd been a detective too long to believe it. As he sat behind the podium at One Police Plaza, he knew this news conference was a colossal mistake.

He sat next to McCarthy, close enough for their thighs to touch—which she made sure they did with regularity. On his other side was the chief of detectives, whose thigh he hoped never to touch. Past the chief were Pear and Murtaugh, both looking like boys who'd just looked up the skirt of their smokin' hot teacher. They were hiding something. But what?

The event was scheduled for 1 P.M.—it was now a quarter after. They were waiting for the commissioner.

McManus and McCarthy had interviewed the suspect only a couple of hours before. Pear must have called his undergraduate classmate, now known as Hizzoner the Mayor of the City of New York, who must have ordered the commissioner to announce that a suspect was in custody.

It was all happening too fast.

EVERYTHING TOLD MCMANUS that Charles Waxman was not the murderer. A paranoid schizophrenic who'd dropped out halfway through his first semester of med school, then spent the next twenty years sleeping in cardboard boxes on the steps of Temple Emanu-El yards from Central Park? No way. Pervis had been murdered by an evil genius, not a schizo charity case.

McCarthy, however, had gotten the idea that the killer had been caught, and dismissed every word he said to the contrary.

Her only evidence was a confession—if you could call it that.

"So you stopped taking your medication a few weeks ago?" she'd asked the poor schnook in the interrogation just hours earlier.

"I was told to," the poor schnook replied.

"By whom?"

Waxman pointed upward, then whispered, "It's them." He leaned forward and opened his shirt to reveal a layer of aluminum foil. "This gives some protection, but you're not really safe unless you cover your head. I have a helmet at home. I sleep with it but can't wear it outside."

"Why's that?"

"Because they'll see it and recognize me as a resistance fighter. Isn't that obvious?" He looked around as he rebuttoned his shirt. Mary, unfazed by the Martians looking over her shoulder, continued.

"Do you know anything about the deaths that occurred the other day, Mr. Waxman?"

"Deaths? It's what they want for all of us. In my defense, I only kill perverts."

Perverts? Pervis? Oh, jeez, thought McManus, Mary had a fetish for Freudian slips when interviewing suspects. Often he wanted to shout at her, "Sometimes a cigar is just a cigar."

Waxman spoke again. "You have to eat the brain. Otherwise they reawaken and suck your soul out of you."

Mary's eyes widened. "Did you eat Pervis's brain, Mr. Waxman?"

"While his heart was still pumping. That is the key."

Game, set, match. Mary had her man, even though he was a lamentable nut job whose competence barely reached to brushing his teeth, not a criminal mastermind capable of planning and executing a brilliant medical atrocity.

Mary cuffed the suspect herself then read him his rights.

McManus knew better than to argue with her.

Meanwhile, Murtaugh, who'd shown up late, whipped out his cellphone, grinning from ear to ear as he left the room, "Boss? We got the fucker . . ."

THE COMMISSIONER ARRIVED. AFTER THE mandatory glad handing, he took the podium at One Police Plaza.

"Good afternoon. We're here to talk about the recent death of F. J. Pervis at the Eastside Medical Center. The medical examiner has determined that Mr. Pervis was murdered and that the time of death was approximately twenty-four hours after what doctors perceived to be his cardiac arrest in the operating room. In addition, a security guard was murdered the following day, after a chance encounter, it is thought, with the killer as he was trying to dispose of Mr. Pervis's body." There were gasps in the room followed by a flurry of photographs. "Today we can announce with some certainty that we've solved the case. The suspect in custody is a former student of the Eastside School of Medicine with a history of mental illness. He has intimate knowledge of human anatomy and of the layout of the center, where he is frequently seen. Questions?"

"Jack Bigelow, *Metropolitan Post.* Commissioner, is it true that the suspect is a paranoid schizophrenic who is now undergoing psychiatric examination?"

"It is."

"Is it not also true that a physician treating the suspect detained him in an exam room under false pretenses until the police could arrive and arrest him?"

"I can't comment on that."

"And didn't the police review his medical records without a warrant?"

"No comment."

"And since the psychiatric evaluation is still in progress, isn't it premature to anoint him as the suspect when half a dozen prior examinations, conducted over the space of twenty years, have concluded he can barely remember the day of the week, let alone the anatomy of the brain?"

"I have no comment."

"And didn't he give a confession in which he talked about aliens from outer space?"

By this time, the other reporters were all shouting their own questions. The department spokesman stepped to the podium and spoke over the din. "That will conclude this conference. Thank you all."

As the hacks continued shouting questions, the commissioner led the way out, with McManus and the rest following. Now Pear and Murtaugh looked like boys who'd just seen their dog run over by a garbage truck. Once out of earshot of the press, Pear abruptly turned and stared up at the much taller Murtaugh. "Boss, we got the fucker . . . my ass!"

Before the security chief could respond, Pear turned again and headed straight to the exit. "Imbeciles!" he shouted, flapping his arms. "I'm surrounded by imbeciles!" Murtaugh nodded in agreement, infuriating Pear further.

Once out of the press room McCarthy turned to McManus. "Gee, Pat, that went real well."

"I fucking told you so," McManus felt like saying, but said, "Yeah, sorry" instead.

"I need to go do damage control with the brass. But I'll need consoling later on. A Guinness at Clancy's? Half past seven?"

She didn't wait for a reply but took off after the chief and the commissioner. McManus had no doubt that she would blame one P. McManus, Detective First Class, for the massive embarrassment to the department, the commissioner, and the mayor. She didn't become the youngest female inspector on the force only by fucking her way up the ladder, although she did a bit of that. Others had tried that method also, but she succeeded where they failed because she was shrewd, calculating, and remorseless.

Nor had he any doubt that, after *figuratively* screwing him in One Police Plaza this afternoon, she would want to make up for it by *literally* screwing him in a hotel bedroom later on.

51

The Doctor

IT HAD BEEN YEARS SINCE he felt this much vigor and power, both physical and mental. As he walked the main lobby of the hospital, his predatory senses were alive, taking in every detail. His eyesight was exceptional. Twenty feet away, a woman was reading the *Times*—he could make out the fine print of the restaurant review: "lifeless, soggy summer terrine." Through the windows on either side of the main entrance, he noted a flock of house finches perched on the bare limbs of a London planetree. In less than a second, he counted thirty-three birds. His hearing was no less phenomenal. From 30 feet, he heard a mobile-phone conversation conducted in hushed tones via Bluetooth. The twenty-something man holding the newest hi-tech smartphone was nodding, saying, "Okay, okay" between sips of coffee. On the other end of the call, a man was complaining about a case of genital warts. "I can't believe you did this to me," the voice said. The coffee drinker pressed the screen to end the call, then put the phone in his pocket, muttering under his breath, "Asshole."

He and the Doctor passed each other moments later. They exchanged smiles.

His sense of smell rivaled that of a bloodhound. The twenty-something man was drinking something strong, either Kona French roast or Jamaican Mountain—what a shame that he'd diluted it with skim milk and sugar. As a gaggle of students walked by, he could make out their drinks, all from the lobby Starbucks: Four lattes, one of them decaf; one black Pike Place blend. One student had cocaine on her breath, another was menstruating—he could tell despite her pad and a vinegar douche. The scent made him start to salivate.

A pretty, petite young woman entered the lobby and rushed toward the back—late for work, no doubt. She had green eyes and shoulder-length jet-black hair that smelled of the rose-scented shampoo she'd used this morning. Her body odor was consistent with her being in the middle of her menstrual cycle, at or near ovulation. "Ripe," he whispered to himself. He stared at her through the mass of white coats. She turned and looked at him. He let her see him for a moment then moved back and to his left, lost to her in the lobby's bustle.

His predatory impulse was taking over. He looked forward to more conquests—male or female, it didn't matter. The encounters would not end well for the partners he chose, but then again, that was what made the thrill of the couplings so intense.

But first, there were things to do. He had to ensure that his lab was secure. Then he had a few errands to run in the operating room and the orthopedic clinic. The nosy medical student was out of the way temporarily, but not finished off and harvested as intended. He needed another specimen. The infusion from the obese theater critic had reinvigorated him but didn't possess the potency of prior doses. He hoped the problem was the poor quality of the donor but feared that his own body was developing resistance to the treatment. His last infusion, done only twenty-five years ago, had worn off earlier and more abruptly than those before, which typically lasted twenty to twenty-five years at full strength and tapered down slowly over a period of several more years. His heightened need had forced him to act rashly, risking exposure when he sacrificed a two-bit celebrity, not a nameless street dweller.

A young, healthy specimen was definitely on the menu for the near future. After all, 120 years of success was not nearly long enough.

52

JOHANNES

FRANÇOIS JOHANNES FINISHED MOPPING THE floor in the OR nurses' lounge. He emptied the trash can and checked to make sure the coffee machine was stocked. After twenty-three years on the job, he was still disgusted at how the nurses and the doctors left their lounges. Opened containers of food were commonplace; half-empty cups of coffee were all over. More often than not, there was coffee or soda spilled on the floor with no attempt made to clean it up. "The porter will take care of it," he was sure they said. He hoped they were cleaner in the operating rooms.

He'd never been in any of the ORs. His job was to clean nonsterile areas on the tenth floor: hallways, lounges, bathrooms, locker rooms, and the family waiting room. He hated doing the waiting room, because patients' family members would ask him to check on their loved ones. He would often shake his head and, in broken English with a Haitian accent, say that he was not allowed.

As expected, the doctors' locker room was a mess. There were wire hangers on the floor, overfilled garbage cans, and the smell of sweat, blood, and pus from the soiled scrubs, both those tossed in the lockers and those strewn across the floor. He always wore rubber gloves for this room.

He usually did the chiefs' locker room next. The door was closed so he knocked and heard a muffled "Just a minute" in reply. He'd come back. In the meantime, he'd take care of the doctors' men's room. He saw no one inside, but the faucet in one of the sinks was running full tilt, the drain barely keeping it from overflowing. Why should the doctors care? "The porter will take care of it." He shut the faucet but still heard water running.

It was one of the toilets continually flushing, probably the automated flusher stuck again—another doctor's mess for him to take care of. He opened the near stall and found nothing. Likewise for the middle stall. He went to open the far stall, but the door was locked from the inside. He looked underneath and saw a pair of feet in a set of clogs. He knocked on the door. "Please, *docteur,* open the door. The toilet will flood."

No answer.

"Please, sir, open."

Again no answer, and the door wouldn't budge. He entered the middle stall, stood on the commode, and looked over the divider.

"Noooo!"

He saw a doctor, unconscious, with his skin tinted blue, leaning back against the flush button. He remembered the voice in the chiefs' locker room. He jumped off the toilet and ran. He pounded on the chief's door.

"*Docteur!* Emergency! Come quickly!" Mortimer came out half-dressed, looking haggard.

"Come! *Docteur* in toilet. Very sick."

Johannes led Mortimer to the men's room. "Door is locked. Stand here and look," he said, showing Mortimer the middle toilet. Mortimer stepped up and saw the lifeless anesthesiologist.

"Toll! Can you hear me? Toll!"

Getting no response, he jumped down. "The cart," he said to the porter. "We have to break down the door!"

Together, the two men grabbed the cart, then pushed it forward, hard, at the stall. The door started to come off its hinges. They rammed it again. This time the lock gave, and the door slammed open.

Mortimer grabbed Toll's wrists. He found a pulse, but it was faint. Toll was anoxic—missing oxygen. He turned to Johannes. "Get help! Call 5454. Say 'Code blue, OR doctors' men's room.' Go!"

He grabbed Toll by his scrub shirt, pulled him off the toilet, and laid him on the bathroom floor. He saw an elastic band around Toll's upper left arm, with a syringe in the antecubital fossa of the elbow. He yanked out the syringe and commenced CPR. After two minutes, he checked for spontaneous breathing—none, although the pulse felt stronger and he looked less blue. Johannes returned and assisted Mortimer in pulling Toll out into the open area of the bathroom. Mortimer showed Johannes how to do chest compressions while he gave the respirations. They continued the artificial respiration until the Code Blue team arrived. Dr. Zayal, the anesthesiologist on the team, intubated Toll, and Dr. Reislinger, the surgical resident, started a central line and then injected a dose of Narcan. Within seconds, he started to breathe on his own, although he did not awaken.

While the team was working, Mortimer called the chief of anesthesia, Rizzuto, who quickly arrived on the scene. Mortimer took him off to the side and handed him the syringe. "I found this in his arm," he whispered.

Rizzuto grabbed the syringe and read the label: "Fentanyl." He shook his head at the stupidity of it. Anesthesiologists are more prone to drug abuse than doctors in any other specialty, he knew that. But here it was in one of his own. Toll had seemed preoccupied and remote the last few months. Even Rizzuto's wife mentioned it to her husband at a departmental cocktail party. How could he have missed the signs?

"He's a trained anesthesiologist," said Mortimer. "Could it possibly be an accidental overdose? Or was it attempted suicide?"

"Fentanyl is the most potent narcotic known to man. It's easy to overdose on it—even for a trained anesthesiologist. Either way, he's through in my department."

As Rizzuto and Mortimer walked out of the bathroom, the code team was moving Toll onto a stretcher and toward the ICU.

53

CARTER

AFTER THE POLICE HUSTLED WAXMAN away in cuffs, Carter had felt terrible. He feared he'd made a big mistake. After seeing the news conference on television, his feeling was more like panic: would he even have a job on Monday? Seated alone at a table in the doctors' section of the cafeteria, he tried to eat his sandwich, but couldn't.

He didn't have long to wallow in his self-pity. His pager went off: A multi-trauma case in the emergency room.

Carter took the stairs—faster than the elevator, especially taking two steps at a time. He got to the trauma room as the general surgery resident was placing a central line and administering anesthesia. The patient was intubated and in a cervical collar.

"What do we have?" said Carter.

"Twenty-two–year–old bike messenger, male," said the surgery resident, "struck by motor vehicle. Loss of consciousness, bilateral probable punctured lungs with multiple rib fractures, possible pelvis fracture, definite humerus grade-two open, and degloving of right ankle. Radiographs done; should be ready in a minute. BP low but stable. Running Ringer's Lactate. Blood on the way."

Carter looked first at the leg, with the skin ripped off the patient's ankle down to the tendons and muscle, and then at the bones sticking out of a definite grade-three wound, the worst type, in the upper left arm—a huge spike of humerus bone was protruding through. The orthopedics of this case, he realized, was far in excess of what he could deal with alone. The orthopedic chief resident and the trauma fellow, as well as the attending, would be needed when they took the guy to the OR. But before Carter called in the troops, he would need to see the radiographs—he wanted to know exactly what to report to them on the phone so he wouldn't look like an incompetent moron.

"Anything I can do at this point?"

"The surgery resident could use a hand putting in the chest tubes. Look at the chest X-ray." Jeffrey Strauss, the ER doc who had just stepped in the room, pointed to the monitor on the opposite wall.

Carter looked at the display. Strauss, the Physician in Charge, was right: two punctured lungs with at least four ribs fractured on each side. Next the PIC and Carter looked at the shots of the cervical spine: no fracture or dislocation seen. The humerus, however, had a comminuted midshaft fracture with, as Carter had seen with his naked eye, a big spike sticking out through the soft tissue. In addition, the pelvis showed a displaced acetabular fracture. Carter would need Judet X-ray views and a CT scan before surgical decisions could be made. The ankle had no fracture, so at least he wouldn't have to deal with it—he'd leave it to the plastic surgeons, who would have a field day with it.

Bad but, overall, not as bad as he'd expected.

As for helping the general surgery resident, forget it: Carter now had the X-rays to work with and thus could get started on the dealing with the fractures. He walked over and checked the arm—road dirt was embedded in the exposed spike. He put on a pair of sterile gloves and removed the feeble dressing. Before cleaning the bone and wound, he took a swab for culture—it would guide the doctors should a bone infection set in later despite the administration of antibiotics, which the PIC was about to begin. He placed the culturette in the pocket of his white coat then débrided the clothing and dirt fragments from the bone spike before irrigating the area with copious amounts of saline solution. Considering the pain the patient would be in were he conscious, it was fortunate he wasn't. However, until he woke up, Carter couldn't check nerve function in the arm.

At least the hand was warm, pink in color, and had a pulse. Once Carter had thoroughly cleaned the wound, he grabbed the arm and pulled on it to reduce the spike back under the skin. Then he applied a new sterile dressing to cover the wound until the patient got to the OR. Next he went to the sink and grabbed two rolls of Gypsona plaster, with which he created a splint. After dunking the splint in water, he wrapped it in Webril, then placed it over the patient's arm in a U shape, under the elbow and over the medial and lateral side of the upper arm. He then wrapped the arm in Ace bandages.

Once the splint had hardened, Carter looked up to see the general surgery resident standing over him, looking annoyed.

"Are you done? Strauss told you five minutes ago to help me with chest tubes. I need to get one in on this side."

Carter stepped aside to allow the surgeon access but made no effort to assist. He was pleased that he'd acted to get the arm stabilized for the time being. Although the pelvis fracture could wait a few days before being repaired, the humerus and the ankle soft-tissue injury would need attention tonight, right after the neurosurgeons got their head CT to see if the patient needed evacuation of a subdural hematoma.

Carter checked the leg with the fractured acetabulum: it was shortened due to the fracture and rotated outward but, like the arm, was warm and with a pulse. The patient would need a traction pin placed just above the knee to stabilize the leg until definitive surgery was done, but Carter decided to wait until they got to the operating room to do it.

The general surgeon awaited the abdominal CT scan. The urologist had already gotten a retrograde urethrogram, which allowed him to insert a urinary catheter. The chest surgeon arrived only to declare that he wasn't needed. "Chest tubes and time are needed to fix the patient's chest," he said, "provided he doesn't develop adult respiratory distress syndrome." He was about to leave, then added, "Although, with this much chest trauma, ARDS is likely."

Carter knew that this patient could die from any number of problems: ARDS, pulmonary embolus, cardiac contusion, subdural hematoma, sepsis, or blood loss, to name but a few. If he survived, the poor guy would have lifelong disabilities and need multiple additional surgeries.

As he stood watching the nurse and PIC take the patient to the CT room, Carter's beeper went off again: "Report to Dr. Mortimer's office, asap." He sighed and checked his watch: 5:47. He called the chief orthopedic resident to update him on the bike messenger, adding that Mortimer had pulled him off the case. He entered the orders for the patient on the Clinisys Computer System: humerus post-reduction radiographs, CT scan, and Judet views of the fractured acetabulum.

He then ran for the elevators. He was pleased with his work on the messenger, thinking, "Not a bad case to close out my medical career."

54

MORTIMER

EXHAUSTED PHYSICALLY AND MENTALLY FROM his efforts to resuscitate Toll, Mortimer awaited his junior resident. He'd just gotten off the phone with Pear, who demanded Carter's firing. Shit, Mortimer knew, always rolls downhill.

Mortimer sighed. He decided, before even hearing Carter's side of the story, that he would not blame the kid for the police bungle. Mortimer always supported his house staff, even when they were wrong. Residents were doctors, yes, but still in need of guidance, education, and training. They needed his protection. He'd think of something to tell Pear.

A few minutes later, Carter arrived at the waiting area, and Peabody waved him into Mortimer's office. As Carter walked in, he noticed that the chairman was blowing his nose and, it seemed, wiping tearful eyes. Mortimer looked up at him, then, at the older man's direction, motioned for Carter to sit.

Mortimer noticed Carter's right leg bouncing up and down on the ball of his foot, a nervous tick he'd never been able to get rid of. He had Carter wait while Mortimer shuffled some papers on his desk.

Finally Mortimer peered over his reading glasses at Carter.

"Well, Dr. Carter, do you know what this is about?"

"Mr. Waxman?"

"The head of the hospital wants you fired."

"But I was told to cooperate with the police. I didn't . . ."

Mortimer interrupted him. "I know what happened, and as far as I am concerned, the matter is over."

"But . . ."

"Maybe you did not hear me, Doctor. The matter is over. Now get back to your patient in the ER."

Mortimer reburied his head in his papers. Ten seconds later, Carter got up wordlessly. He bowed slightly toward Mortimer in appreciation of the chief's mercy and backed out of the room, practically bowing in reverence all the way out.

MORTIMER WAITED UNTIL CARTER HAD left before giving up the pretense of reading the printed matter on his desk. For a long few moments, he stared out his twentieth-floor window at the dimming sky. He was beginning to hate the dark—his spirits sank with the setting sun, plunging him, each night, further into the depths of depression. He felt helpless to fight it. Telling anyone endangered his chairmanship. No, he thought, he had to go this alone.

He opened the bottom drawer of his desk and pulled out an ancient black-and-white photograph. It was creased and faded, with a small coffee stain in the upper right corner. It was a picture of his grandfather, Hyman Mortimer Levenberg, taken in Lvov, Poland, in 1901, shortly before he left for America. He looked at the shot, then at the photo on the wall of his home in Maine. He tried to remember a few lines from the prayers he'd said as a boy standing next to Zeyde in synagogue, but could summon up nothing.

He'd come a long way from Sheepshead Bay, Brooklyn, where he grew up. He'd changed his name while an undergraduate at City College, before he transferred to Princeton. Eastside Medical School was famous for not accepting Jews; had he not changed his name, corrected his accent, and remade himself as a Westchester WASP, he'd never have gotten in. He'd cut off ties with his family—he hadn't seen his father in twenty years before attending the old man's funeral. Whenever anyone told a "Jew joke" in his presence, he laughed; he even told a few himself from time to time. Even his loving wife didn't know the full truth about him, thinking he was without family.

But what was the point of it all? He'd never been much of a doctor, more like a mediocre carpenter in a white coat. He'd admitted it to himself years ago, but never to anyone else. He'd gotten the chairmanship through connections: the previous chairman's sister owned a house across the lake from his in Maine.

Somehow he'd managed to play hospital politics deftly enough to survive as chairman. He went to the cocktail parties and drank the martinis. What else was the house in Maine if not a prop for the role he'd been playing the last forty years? It was a role he no longer had the stomach for.

His entire adult life, he thought, had been one massive charade.

55

NATHAN

HE WAS JUBILANT AFTER WATCHING the press conference on the TV in his office. When he'd heard that the cops had taken Waxman away in cuffs, he knew immediately that they had the wrong man.

That suited him just fine.

Nathan had had enough dealings with Waxman to know the guy wouldn't hurt a fly, even if he was a raving lunatic. Nathan had briefly been Waxman's doctor about five years ago. At the time, Nathan had an understanding with the disabled clerk in the clinic. The clerk, at $50 per, steered patients to Nathan—patients with private insurance, that is. Waxman was one of those for whom Nathan acted as a "private doctor"—until the crazy prick lost his job and his coverage. Medicaid patients weren't worth Nathan's time, so the next time Waxman called, Nathan routed him back to the clinic.

The arrest of Waxman had to set the Pervis investigation back a few days, at least. Nathan hoped the case wouldn't be solved for another week, even two. Every extra day meant more airtime and press attention for a certain up-and-coming orthopedic surgeon. Bigelow had promised Nathan at least a full paragraph of glowing praise on the front page of Saturday's paper. If things fell the right way, that article would be just the beginning.

As he rose and put on his overcoat, a sudden feeling came over him: something was amiss. He knew that the entire unit—half a floor—was empty, as was typical for an early Friday evening, but he nevertheless had a strange feeling that he was not alone. He froze for a moment while a chill ran up his spine. As the epinephrine rush hit his brain, his breathing deepened and his forehead and palms started to sweat. He turned the doorknob and peeked out toward the reception desks. They were in dark shadows, accentuated by the low light emanating from the exit signs. The air felt unusually still.

"Hello, is anyone there?" he said.

No one answered. He saw nothing, he heard nothing, he smelled nothing —but he couldn't shake the feeling of menace. *Creepy* was the word that came to mind. He needed to get out of there. He turned and started to walk briskly toward the elevator. And then he heard a loud crash behind him.

He started running. Five feet in front of the elevator, he slammed into Murtaugh, who was approaching from another corridor.

"Whoa! Is there a problem, Dr. Nathan?"

"I heard a crash in the examination area."

"Let's have a look."

"I'm sure it was nothing. No doubt one of the cleaning people."

"No doubt. But just in case, why don't you show me where the sound came from?"

"But . . ."

Murtaugh grabbed Nathan's left arm at a pressure point just above the elbow and squeezed, just hard enough for Nathan to feel some pain.

"Where to, Doctor?"

Murtaugh relaxed, but did not remove, his grip as Nathan led him back to the exam area. Nothing seemed disturbed, but Murtaugh noticed what appeared to be stains on the floor leading to Exam Room 3.

The security chief tried the door and found it locked. He grabbed the bulky keychain on his belt and searched until he found his master key. He unlocked the door, opened it, and flipped on the light switch. He then realized his hand was wet. With his eyes now adjusted to the light, he saw what the liquid was: thick blood. It covered the light switch, it was all over the floor.

Nathan, behind Murtaugh, staggered. He grabbed at Murtaugh's shirt in a failed attempt to remain upright. Murtaugh reflexively shoved Nathan aside with his elbow, and the doctor fell to the floor.

Murtaugh looked at the room and started retching.

56

THE DOCTOR

ALL THINGS COME TO HIM who waits, he thought. And he hadn't had to wait long.

The young gentleman so distraught over his genital warts needed a shoulder to cry on. In fact, the fellow figured, that was just what the doctor ordered. He'd recognized the smile he'd gotten in the lobby from the virile young physician—it was a smile he'd seen from countless men before.

Even so, this doctor was different. There was something special about him, something extra. His muscular body betrayed the habits of a body builder. He had long, swept-back blond hair. And most of all: those eyes. Those eyes, even more than the smile, were what had caught the clerk's attention when the two men first passed.

Moments after arriving at his fifth-floor desk job in human resources, he decided to go back to the lobby, hoping that the fine physical specimen would be waiting for him.

He was.

The doctor knew of a quiet exam area that had finished seeing patients. Once they entered Exam Room 3, the physician closed the door. "I'm your doctor," he said. "It's time for your examination."

The clerk was enchanted by the tone of command mixed with raw, animal seductiveness.

"No names," the doctor said. "Strict HIPAA rules. Ready, patient?"

"What type of doctor are you?"

"Why, I'm a rectal specialist, of course." The clerk's loins quivered with anticipation. "Just drop your pants and bend over the exam table. This won't hurt a bit."

Seconds later, a gloved hand inspected the clerk's genitals and anal sphincter. Although the doctor noted genital warts, he was not fazed by them. He knew his enhanced physical state made him immune to this and a thousand other normally communicable maladies.

"Someone's been a bad boy," he said.

"I was going to tell you . . ."

"On the contrary, I like bad boys." He shoved his fingers, and gradually his entire right hand into the clerk's rectum as he clenched the clerk's hip with his left. The action was rougher than the clerk was used to, but he didn't mind. The feeling of the doctor's hand was electric. The clerk applied his own hand to his penis, stroking vigorously as the doctor probed ever deeper into his internal organs. Then the clerk felt two hands on his hips as something granite-hard and enormous invaded his lower intestine and seemed about to thrust itself through his abdominal wall.

The clerk tried to hold back, but the feeling was too intense, and he soon felt a titanic orgasm building—he knew it would be the best he'd had in years. The doctor was about to climax, too—the clerk could tell by the quickening speed of the breaths he felt on the back of his neck.

It was the last thing he noticed before his throat was slashed down to his vertebrae with a number-10 scalpel.

57

McManus

AFTER THE PRESS CONFERENCE, MCMANUS checked his voicemail. There was a message from the ME.

"Saw the circus on TV. I'll be damned if you didn't look like you were enjoying it. Get your Irish ass down here. I have mind-blowing news."

Half an hour later, McManus was sitting across from Winter, listening as the ME provided details that sent the already bizarre case hurtling into the Twilight Zone. Winter was twirling a jar containing what looked like a human eyeball.

"The toxicology tests show no drugs of any kind in Pervis's system," said Winter as he took off his reading glasses, "which is, to say the least, strange, because most anesthetics, including propofol, normally linger in the bloodstream in one form or another for two to three days post-dosing. And they stay in the fat cells even longer. And there's something else: a used vial from the OR, labeled as propofol, contained at least two unknown chemical substances."

"Unknown?"

"One is similar to some neurotransmitters; the other appears to be like curare. That's all I know. In fact, that's all I may ever know."

"So you're saying these are drugs you can't test for?"

"I'm saying that they may be drugs no one has ever *seen* before. And there wasn't much of them left in the vial, so we can assume they were administered." He put the jar with the putative eyeball down, then took a bottle of Auchentoshan eighteen-year-old Scotch and two glasses from a file drawer.

"Do you know that I could have retired last year at full pension?" He poured the whiskey and handed a glass to McManus. He then lit up a cigarette; McManus watched the smoke waft past the "Absolutely No Smoking" poster on the wall behind Winter's head. "To psychotic killers," McManus said, and lifted his glass. Winter nodded, raising both his glass and the jar. "Here's looking at ya," he said, convincing McManus that the jar did, in fact, contain an eyeball.

They clinked, then both threw back their heads and emptied their glasses in a single gulp.

"Where was I?" said Winter.

"Drugs no one's seen."

"I finished first in my class in med school, McManus, but this sonofabitch leaves me in the dust."

"So are these never-to-be-known substances the drugs that simulated Pervis's death?"

"Probably. The opening of the glass vial was scored twice, meaning it was opened and resealed before it was opened again for use. P.S.: It has Toll's fingerprints all over it."

McManus was not surprised. He made it a habit never to trust junkies.

"It will take another couple of days for answers." Winter went on, "if we get them at all, for chrissakes. Whoever did this is expert in medicine, anesthesia, and, especially, neurosurgery." He paused for a moment, swirling the eyeball, waiting for McManus. Seeing the detective wasn't biting, Winter continued, "Why especially neurosurgery? I was hoping you'd ask. Because although much of the anterior cerebrum was destroyed by the murderer, he was meticulous in removing what lay behind it, the hypothalamus."

"The hypothalamus, of course. Know it well. Just one question: what the fuck is it?"

"One of the most primitive parts of the brain—so primitive even your friend Murtaugh has one. Many of its functions are basic to life: it controls many organ systems, like the pituitary gland, for example, and the autonomic nervous system, which regulates breathing and body temperature. In fact, at one point in our evolution, when we were not even mammals, the hypothalamus ran the show the way the cerebral cortex does now."

"So let me get this straight. You're telling me that the killer tore through the more sophisticated parts of Pervis's brain just to get to this piece that goes back to the primordial ooze?"

"More like when we were fish or amphibians, Patrick, but yes, behind the savagery of the mutilation was a very specific and delicate target. As to why—well, how the fuck should I know? Here's how unheard of this all is: if you told me that the guy was an alien from another planet, I'd ask, 'Which galaxy?'"

At that moment, McManus's phone rang. He answered and was told there had been another murder at the hospital, this time in an examination room on the eighth floor. Victim a white male, mid twenties, a desk jockey in the HR department. Pants and undershorts around his ankles. Rectal bruising. Head barely connected to body.

"Pete, you're gonna love this."

58

DEMETRI

THE SMELL OF HORSESHIT ON his shoe pervaded the car's interior as he drove home so he opened all his windows. He was freezing, but at least he could breathe.

He was turning over in his mind the ton of information he'd discovered about the hospital while sitting in the cemetery, trying to link it with the blueprints he'd taken from the library: hallways and stairwells, many sealed and/or unused for decades, that must have allowed the perp to travel unimpeded. A variety of murders and supposed medical deaths that may have been murders. The involvement of Pear and Murtaugh in some way. It was all there; he just had to get the puzzle pieces to fit. In some ways, the head injury gave Demetri time to think this through, but the free time the chairman gave him was not enough. He needed some help.

Dad. He needed to run it by Dad.

He parked in the garage and got out. His father was sitting at his workbench, tinkering with an old radio. His dad always loved vintage audio stuff.

"The prodigal son returns. Where were you, mucking out a stable for some side dough?"

"No, Dad, I just stepped in—it's a long story."

"It always is. Do me a favor: next time you disappear, tell someone where you're going."

"Sorry, Dad, you were asleep, and Yia Yia would not have remembered."

"There's a new invention out: the pen. You apply it to paper to write a note."

"Okay, Dad."

"And if you're going to blame it on your old man and your grandma, the least you can do is wash out the Jeep."

"I will, Dad."

His father was silent for a moment while Demetri didn't move. Michael spoke again.

"The pail's over there."

"Got it, Dad. But look, I need your help."

"My help? You got that girl in trouble, didn't you?"

"What girl? . . . No, of course not."

"We'll figure it out. Don't tell your mother."

"Dad, will you stop already? It's the murder at the hospital. I saw online that they arrested someone, but it doesn't add up."

"Remember the last time you played detective?"

"Yeah, I remember." Five years ago, there were several thefts of clothing from the dry-cleaning store, and Demetri was determined to find the culprit. He found trouble instead. He accused an elderly woman based on circumstantial evidence. The evidence turned out to be wrong, and the elderly woman turned out to be a New York State Supreme Court judge. It cost his parents six months' worth of free dry cleaning to mollify the angry jurist.

"So what do you have?" Michael asked. Demetri, even in the darkness of the garage, knew his dad was smiling.

Demetri switched on the light and shut the garage door. Michael had a shiner that made Demetri's head ache to look at. "Dad, that looks bad."

"You think *I* look bad? Have you looked in the mirror lately? I'm surprised Maria still wants to be in your vicinity." Demetri sighed and removed his backpack from the Jeep, spread out his papers on the workbench, opened up his laptop, and sat down.

"So, Dad, do you believe me when I say I was not alone in that library room?"

"I wouldn't have been in that room with my gun drawn if the prickly feeling weren't overwhelming me. I don't know much of what happened down there, but one thing I do know: I did not trip over you. It wasn't the first time something like that ever happened to me, so I know what I'm talking about. I was hit in the back of the head, then pushed to the floor. I also know it was a very powerful man who pushed me. Based on where he placed his hand on my back, he was at least my height, maybe a bit taller."

"Guess what, Dad? I got the prickles down in the library, too."

"So you finally believe in them? They're an old Makropolis trait, passed down for generations since our family lived in Pontos when the Ottomans ruled us. It kept our family from being killed off many times by Ottoman spies."

Demetri joined in on the last two sentences. He'd heard them a thousand times before.

"Okay, Dad. Here's what I have."

59

PEAR

IT KEPT GETTING WORSE. A third murder, whether or not related to the first two, was going to be hell for the hospital's bottom line. The one-percent profit margin would quickly become a several-percentage-point drop into the red.

How could this be happening again so many years later? A quarter-century ago, this maniac had murdered not only a homeless patient at the hospital but who knows how many others in the city. Why was he back? Why was he murdering again in the hospital? Christ, couldn't he find someplace—and somebody—else to terrorize? Why couldn't he just die of old age?

Pear realized he'd made some big mistakes back then, but letting the killer get away was his biggest. He and a young Detective Murtaugh had followed a trail of blood that ended in cool dust and ash deep within the bowels of the building. When Murtaugh had the perp in his gun sights, Pear purposely bumped him, knowing that at the other end of the hall was a fellow physician—psychotic, yes, but with a store of knowledge that may be beneficial. He wanted the man wounded and captured, not killed, so that his treasure trove of information could be mined for the sake of medical science. He told Murtaugh it was an accident. Unfortunately, the shot missed completely, and the murderer escaped, not to be heard from again—until now.

Pear knew then that the body snatcher had struck before, in the early '60s, when Pear was still a student at the medical school. Missing bodies and bizarre murders all somehow connected to the medical center. A recurring pattern of crime every twenty-five years or so—it was déjà vu all over again. Too similar to dismiss as happenstance but far enough apart in time for detectives investigating the case to age and retire. But this guy didn't, and Pear, like an elephant with its long memory, wanted to know how. He'd instituted a cover-up twenty-five years ago by offering Murtaugh the position of security chief if he let the case fade away, because it was the only way to end the news barrage. Fortunately, several other crime waves in the city overshadowed the hospital's so-called missing body. He connected a cluster of other murders to the corpse that disappeared from the morgue, but the police and the press never caught on.

The discovery of the homeless man's body in that dark sub-subbasement conduit had led Pear to wall off the passageway permanently. He now had Murtaugh check to ensure it was still closed. It was. So was the maniac operating in a different area of the hospital? He realized he'd been foolhardy to think he solved anything by bricking up that entrance. There had to be other routes to the now abandoned lower levels.

What was it all about? Why was he murdering people all over the campus? Was it even the same man after all these years of quiet? He would be at least Pear's age by now.

Of course, deep down, Pear knew it was the same man.

How could it not be? The pattern was identical: young healthy individuals were murdered. The first had his brain removed. The rest had their throats sliced open, usually after sexual contact.

Pear knew the murderer was just getting started.

60

CARTER

CARTER NEEDED TO FORGET THIS unforgettable day, so he called Beth. What a looker. Nothing like what his fraternity brothers called a "double bagger": a good body to fuck but so ugly you need not only a paper bag for her head but one for your own in case hers fell off.

Back at his apartment, he put on the uniform: khakis, a navy blue blazer with brass buttons, black penny loafers, no socks, white oxford shirt, and a medical school–emblazoned blue-and-yellow tie. The forecast was for low temperatures so he grabbed his camel-hair overcoat.

At the elevator, he saw Roy Kohl, his neighbor and a third-year general surgery resident, with his pregnant wife, Joan, a former ICU nurse.

"Hey, Carter," said Kohl. "Heard you had an exciting day."

"And you have an exciting night to come," said Joan.

"News travels fast," said Carter, as the doors opened.

Gossip traveled quickly indeed among the nursing corps. Joan probably knew not just his social calendar but also the size of his penis and the sound he made during climax.

To end the conversation, Carter took out his BlackBerry and fiddled with it all the way down to the garage. He waved goodbye, walked toward his Mini, and got in.

After a quick stop at CVS for condoms, he pulled up in front of Beth's building and called to tell her he'd arrived. She told him she'd be a minute; it took thirty, but it was worth it. When she got in, her mink coat fell open, and Carter could see her clothes: a white blouse with a plunging neckline that featured a bit of see-through over her substantial cleavage; a skin-tight, short black skirt; and 4-inch platform pumps.

"Can you dance in those?" he said, pointing to the shoes.

"Do you like them?" She lifted her foot and placed it on the dash, the shoe and dark satin stockings shimmering in the street light. "Christian Louboutin, very comfortable."

"Dinner at Pastis?"

"Go for it, cowboy."

"We have reservations for 7:30. After dinner, I thought we'd go to Bleecker. There's a new dance club that just opened: cool jazz till 10, then technopop until dawn."

Ten minutes later, they were at the restaurant. The crowd was ten thick out the door, with at least a dozen SUVs and limos double-parked in front. Carter spied a sliver of unoccupied curb a few stores down—too small for most cars but just right for a Mini. He parked, carefully, between the Ferrari 458 up front and the Aston Martin DBS in back.

"You sure can wedge into tight spaces," said Beth. She waited as Carter had to go around the Ferrari to get to her side of the car and open the door for her. They ambled up to the restaurant, where Carter caught the eye of the young woman in charge of the list. Beth made her as an emaciated actress-model wannabe, with perfect hair and nails and a barely-there dress, who was counting on being discovered by one of the producers who patronized the place.

"We have a reservation for 7:30. The name is Carter."

"*Dr.* Carter," said Beth, smiling as she placed her arm in his.

The girl barely looked up. She checked her screen and then her watch. "You're five minutes early. We can seat you in forty-five minutes."

"Our reservation is for 7:30."

"Forty-five minutes. The bar is over there. Please stand aside, sir."

A thin, fiftyish man and his silicone escort walked up to the door. "Right on time, Mr. Dopolov," said the girl with the list. "Your table for two is ready."

Beth held Carter's hand and led him away.

"I can't believe this . . ."

"Relax, Tom."

"She seats that Russian gangster—"

"—who probably owns half the Meatpacking District. Let's go somewhere else. I'm famished."

"I defer to your diplomatic instincts. Where to, boss?"

"Since we're in a froggy mood tonight, how about a nice dark French restaurant on Prince Street in SoHo called Raoul's?"

They hopped back into the Mini, and this time Carter worked quickly, tapping both cars just hard enough to set off their alarms as he maneuvered his way out of the parking spot. He gunned the accelerator and sped away, smiling his wicked preppy smile as the Russian gangster came running out of the restaurant.

61

THE DOCTOR

HE WAS JUST GETTING STARTED. Big brains had a big appetite. Long life fed on the short-lived. It was the way nature intended—nature, at least, as the Doctor warped it.

He was looking for a cute brunette. The nurses' housing was always a good place to start. The building was only an avenue from the emergency entrance. The long block in between was overshadowed by the medical center's supply and maintenance building. That structure contained the center's emergency generators and its main loading docks. At 4 A.M., the block was desolate, with most partying nurses snuggled up for bed or sex or both. But by 6, it would be teeming with truckers standing by as their eighteen-wheelers were unloaded. The Doctor would watch them as they harassed each nurse, of every shape, size, and color, headed to the hospital for her morning shift. Truckers had no class, the Doctor lamented.

Then he spied her. She was getting out of a Mini Cooper. As the Doctor expected, the uncouth house officer behind the wheel left her off just around the corner from the main entrance to the nurses' building, probably to avoid scrutiny. Rather than watch her reach the entrance, the boorish driver sped off, no doubt to his apartment building a few blocks away.

The perky young woman walked briskly along the deserted loading docks, shooting quick glances to the dark recesses of each loading door. She was nearing the corner.

"Hello, Beth."

She was startled by the voice but instantly calmed by the sound of her name. She looked in the direction of the voice.

He stepped out of the shadows. She saw the white lab coat and the smiling face. She smiled back. "Do I know you?" He did look familiar.

He smiled as he slithered in her direction. "But of course, Beth. I am disappointed you don't remember me, but then again, you have had so many."

She was embarrassed. He was another one-night stand. "Sure, I remember you, now that I have a good look at you. But I need to . . ." She pointed to the lights at the entrance to her building.

He put his left arm around her, squeezing her shoulder with a powerful hand.

His eyes were mesmerizing.

As was the glint of the blade he held in his right hand.

62

Bassias

SHE WAS DOG TIRED AS the end of her shift approached—she was pulling a double because the evening clerk had called in sick. She hated working nights because it meant traveling home late: despite the mayor's proclamation that New York was the safest big city in the world, she knew better. She had checked the incoming charts all day for those Demetri had ordered, but they hadn't arrived. She thought of calling him to let him know but decided to let him recover from his head injury in peace.

When 11:00 came, she shooed the last of the male interns out—some of the least attractive people at the medical center, all with extreme cases of acne, dawdled there during her shift, ostensibly to sign some old oral orders in patients' charts, as the hospital required, but really to ogle her. She threw on her wool overcoat, picked up her handbag, and switched off the lights, locking the doors behind her as she left. If someone needed a medical record after 11, they would need to contact security to get in.

The basement hallway was empty at this hour. She paused to reach into her bag and feel for the reassuring cylinder of her pepper spray. She placed her index finger over the button. This was not her normal practice, but these were not normal times at the Eastside Medical Center. The story of a third murder on the premises had spread like wild fire—by 8 P.M., everyone knew the intricate details.

She looked both ways and headed for the elevator bank. She was too tired to take the stairs, even for one flight. Besides, the elevator had to be safer than the stairs at this hour. If she was lucky, she'd be home in an hour and a half.

AFTER THIRTY SECONDS, THE ELEVATOR chimed as it arrived. The doors opened. The car was empty.

She pressed the button for the main floor. The green up arrow was illuminated as the doors slid closed, but after thirty seconds, the car hadn't moved. She once more pressed the button for the main floor. Still, nothing.

"These elevators are pitiful," she said to herself as she hit the "open doors" button three times.

Finally, the elevator bucked then started moving. Down.

"Unbelievable." The lights atop the door indicated that the car was going down past the subbasement toward the sub-subbasement. Then the lights went off, but the elevator continued its descent.

"What the . . . ?" Now she was talking out loud.

Squeezing the pepper spray canister even harder, she was about to press the alarm button when the elevator at last came to a stop. The door opened to a hallway, well lit but empty. She pressed the first-floor button again, repeatedly, but the elevator did not respond.

She decided to get off and take a different elevator, or even the stairs, rather than subject herself to another crazy ride. Once she exited, the doors closed behind her. She pivoted to look for the button to call the next elevator, but there was none. There was only a lone key hole, meaning the elevators could be summoned by authorized personnel only.

"Shit!"

She looked down the hallway for the stairs and saw nothing but unmarked doors and overhead pipes and conduits. She saw no signs. She had never been to the lower basement floors—they were as foreboding as she could have imagined. She heard the steam pipes periodically releasing pressure through valves.

"There must be some stairs somewhere."

The vibration of heavy machinery nearby was interrupted by the occasional rumble of what felt and sounded like trains. She figured she was hearing the Lexington Avenue subway or the commuter trains from Grand Central.

As those sounds faded, she became acutely aware of how alone she was. The hallway stretched in both directions for what seemed like hundreds of yards. The walls were composed of a dark cinderblock material that, despite the bright lighting, reflected little light. She saw that the floor was clean and the halls devoid of equipment as she scanned both ends for signs of a janitor or engineer.

"Hello, anybody here?"

Echoes, then silence interrupted by the steam valves.

She pulled out her older model cellphone and flipped it open; no service.

"I'm fucked."

She started trying to open various doors. Each one was locked. She checked her phone again and found a flickering single signal bar.

As she looked up, the hallway seemed to be getting shorter at both ends. She quickly realized that the lights were going out, sequentially and slowly, from the far ends of the hallway toward her.

"This can't be happening! Hey, anybody! The lights!"

All she heard was silence, punctuated by the cadence of her heart.

"Help! Help me! Please!"

As the darkness continued to close in, she backed up against the elevator doors. Then she heard soft footsteps approaching along with the ever-encroaching darkness

"Hello? Who's there?"

She was answered by a sinister chuckle. In desperation, she typed a text message for help to Demetri, whose number was still on the screen where she entered it, on the remote chance that one signal bar was enough for it to get through. As she hit send, the last light, directly overhead, went out. She was left in pitch darkness except for the glow from her cellphone.

She realized immediately that the tiny screen both illuminated her in the dark and blinded her to what was lurking. It was now no more than a few feet away.

63

McManus

WHEN HE PULLED UP IN front of his house, the lights were on—it was Marcia's night off. He walked up the steps to the front door and heard loud snorting on the other side punctuated by the recurring "thwack!" of a certain dog's tail as it kept hitting the walls of the entrance foyer. McManus smiled. As he turned the key and cracked the door open, a black snout wedged itself into the space and forced the door open all the way. Next thing McManus knew, he was pinned on his back on the front lawn as a large, wet tongue was hovering over his face, and drool was dripping over his shirt and tie.

"Angus! Off!" he said, and the dog proceeded to sit on his groin. Mustering all his strength, McManus pushed the big mush off of him. Angus responded by going into his whirling dervish dance. His owner sat up and took stock of his suit. His dry-cleaning bills were astronomical.

After a moment, McManus heard someone laughing and noticed a figure standing in the doorway. At first, he thought it was Marcia, but this woman was shorter and more voluptuous than his wife. The figure moved forward.

"Hi, Mr. McManus. Need a hand?" It was Diane, one of the neighbor's daughters.

"No, thanks," he said, although he could have used help getting back to his feet. The Auchentoshan had gone straight to his head. "So, Diane, were you dog sitting tonight?"

"Your wife had to go in. Someone called in sick. It was a last minute thing."

McManus checked his watch; it was 11:30 P.M. Although Diane said she was eighteen, if McManus were her father, she'd be in bed by now and not in a place to be fantasized about by off-duty cops coming home late while their wives were at work because someone had called in sick. Then McManus remembered her dad was an avid hunter, and put a stop to that line of thinking.

McManus stood up and brushed off the leaves and dirt. His coat was a mess, too; another item for the cleaners.

HE WENT TO GO INSIDE, but for some reason, Diane was continuing to stand in the doorway. As he squeezed past the girl and her ample breasts, he noticed that her nipples were erect in the cold autumn air.

Suddenly they were both knocked into the living room as Angus plowed back into the house.

"Sorry, Diane. Angus thinks he's still a puppy."

"No problem. I love big dogs, especially yours. Angus, shake."

And the dog did. *Why,* thought McManus, *didn't he ever obey me?* "Angus is fond of you, too, I see."

He took off his coat and tossed it onto the recliner. He and the girl looked at each other for a few moments. He couldn't help himself—her come-hither look was giving him a hard-on.

"It's getting late, Diane. You're probably expected home soon."

"Oh, no. My parents went away for the weekend, and my sisters are away at school. I'm all alone tonight."

She sat on the couch and curled her slim legs under her. Her skintight jeans were nearly bursting at the seams.

"I'm watching *Lolita* on DVD. Care to watch with me?"

Lolita? Was this kid for real? McManus didn't know what to say. After a long, hard day, he was ill prepared for an energetic coed intent on screwing a police detective.

"I need to take Angus out." A safe move, he thought.

"Done. And fed, too. Look, he's already asleep." Indeed, McManus saw that Angus was already in dreamland, snoring up a storm. So much for Angus protecting his master from predators.

"Diane, I'd love to stay up, but I'm beat. I need to go to bed."

"My feeling exactly," she said, and started unbuttoning her blouse.

64

PEAR

THE DINNER WAS RUSHED, AS was usually the case with these pre-theater meals. Considering this was a benefit function set to raise $550,000 for the hospital's burn unit, Pear had no choice but to suffer through it.

Although most participants took the provided luxury bus from the restaurant to the theater, Pear and his wife were driven in their car by their driver. Pear's wife, Helen, a socialite from the Stanhope family of Park Avenue and Greenwich, hadn't ridden in a bus her entire life and was not about to start now. The closest she'd ever come to riding public transportation was two days in a luxury suite on the Orient Express.

"Darling?" she said. "Darling?" Pear continued to look out the window at the lights of Times Square. "Darling!"

"Sorry."

"You haven't been yourself for days."

"I haven't been myself? Do you think it might be connected to the fact that three people have been murdered at the medical center? Did that ever occur to you?"

"Don't snap at me."

"The medical center will suffer. Do you seriously think that my nearly fifty years of service to the institution will keep the board from booting me out in disgrace?"

"Come on, Fred. You made the medical center what it is. They know that."

"Did you see them at dinner? They looked like they couldn't wait to put me out to pasture."

"You're imagining things, Fred."

"And now we're going to the play Pervis savaged in his review last month."

"Look, the board isn't going to hold you responsible for the murders. Just keep smiling at them and keeping their glasses filled. Let's just hope the old buzzards don't start snoring in the second act."

The car pulled up to the theater and they got out. Pear's driver knew the drill: keep circling the block should they decide to duck out of the play early. Pear and his wife waited at the entrance for the bus and their guests, who by now were intoxicated on the wine at dinner and the martinis served on the bus.

The bus turned off Seventh Avenue and stopped. The doors opened.

"Fred! Have you met Inga?"

It was Andrew Feld, a plastic surgeon, 5 foot 2 with an Amazon armpiece half his age and twice his height. Pear wondered what escort service Feld was using this time.

"Inga. So nice to meet you," he said while shaking her hand and staring at her breasts. They looked as though they were about to burst and start shooting darts of silicone. Helen dug a high heel into Pear's toe, and then they walked into the theater, followed by the usual assortment of physicians, corporate types, socialites, and trophy wives.

They made it to their seats with less than a minute to spare. Pear looked around. Every face he saw seemed lit with excitement—or was it gin—as the play was about to begin.

He didn't see the face of the man directly behind him. Seated among the hospital benefactors, between a former CEO whose golden parachute had cushioned his escape from his company's collapse and an arms dealer whose donations to hospitals bought him respectability, was a young, physically fit man with long blond hair. The man didn't take his eyes off of the back of Pear's head for the entire first act.

Having seen all he came to see, he left the theater as the first-act curtain fell. Pear and his wife made their exit a few minutes later, just as intermission was about to end. Pervis had been right. The play was a dud.

65

TOLL

THE BAR FEATURED VODKA LACED with Fentanyl. Oddly, all the patrons wore hospital gowns, except Toll. He was in his surgical scrubs. A tall, gaunt woman caught his eye. Her hospital gown was on backwards, exposing her pubis and breasts. She smiled and walked up to him with a drink in each hand.

"You're new here, aren't you?" she said in a seductive European accent he did not recognize.

Not sure what to say, Toll took the drink she offered. "Where are we?"

The woman eyed him and his outfit from top to bottom.

"You're different from the rest. How do you like Club Fentanyl?"

"I don't really belong here. I'm a doctor."

"We all belong here, and most of us never leave. We like it here." She started to nuzzle up to him, brushing her exposed breasts on his arm. Toll practically felt an electric shock shoot through his arm. His heart began racing, and he developed an immediate hard-on. Then his suspicion made him try to back off, but his path was blocked by several other drinkers gathered behind him, busy chatting in several languages. Eurotrash, Toll surmised.

Toll looked at his glass. "Try it," the woman said. "Fentanyl martinis are divine."

Toll knew better but couldn't resist. He took a sip.

"Not bad."

"It's addictive, darling. You can't have just one." She downed her entire drink all at once and reached for another at the bar. Toll started to feel a rush as the Fentanyl martini began to do its work. He asked the woman for another, then finished his drink. As he did, he noticed broken glass at the bottom of the glass and a scratchy feel at the back of his throat.

"Bartender! There's broken glass in here. Bartender!" The robotic barman looked at him, then continued to pour drinks.

The gaunt woman returned with another full glass for Toll and one for herself.

"Mademoiselle, there is broken glass at the bottom of these drinks."

"But of course! Here you must always take the good with the bad. It hurts a little going down, but Fentanyl makes it all better, n'est-ce pas?"

Toll began to cough and found himself spewing blood all over his scrubs. Panic began to set in as the Fentanyl began to drag his consciousness down.

The gaunt woman placed her drink on a nearby table and stepped over to Toll as she stripped off her hospital gown. The nipples on her lemon-sized breasts were rock hard, but her body appeared malnourished and extremely pale. She cradled Toll's head in her hands as she told him, "Let me help you." She looked into his eyes as she drew his face to hers. She kissed him, lightly at first then progressively harder. Toll began to respond in kind. He grabbed her buttocks and ground her pubis against his hardened penis. Soon she was pressing her tongue down his throat. She pulled his scrub pants down to his thighs, took hold of his shoulders, and mounted him in front of all the patrons at the bar, but he didn't care. As he penetrated her, she wrapped her legs around his waist.

After fifteen seconds, he tried to pull away for a breath of air, but the woman only held him tighter. His face was plastered against hers, and her tongue probed even further down his windpipe to his larynx. Toll began to gag and forcibly tried to pull his face from hers but could not. He tried to disengage his swollen penis from her vagina but found it firmly locked by hard rings of muscle strangling the glans to the point of rupture. He couldn't get air past her tongue into his trachea and began to feel an extreme craving for oxygen. His eyes wandered to see the other patrons of the bar laughing and carrying on as if he weren't there. Seconds later, the room began to spin. Darkness overcame him as her tongue pressed ever further down his throat.

TOLL WAS COMATOSE FOR ALMOST twelve hours, during which he had no dreams, just blackness. As his level of consciousness rose, a series of vivid dreams began, none of them making any sense but all

deeply disturbing. As his mind began to focus on things external rather than internal, he noted he was supine with something large in his throat. He soon realized it was an endotracheal tube and that a respirator was breathing for him. He tried to reach up to pull it out but was immobile. Although his eyes were still closed, he realized he'd been chemically paralyzed so that he wouldn't fight the respirator. He was in the hospital, probably the ICU, after stupidly overdosing on the Fentanyl. His mind, although still foggy, began to race through what had happened and what the future might hold. He realized his career was in jeopardy; his heart rate bumped up ever so slightly at the thought. If only he could open his eyes!

After what seemed hours but was more likely minutes, he heard someone next to his bed.

"I'm awake!" he yelled in his mind. "Extubate me! I'm awake!" But he knew the hospital personnel could not hear. Suddenly, with great effort, his right eyelid opened—that meant the drug was wearing off. Looking up, Toll could see that he was in the Neuro ICU and that a doctor was standing next to him administering some medication through the IV.

"He's reversing the induced paralysis," Toll reasoned.

He felt a burn in his arm and seconds later felt horrific palpitations. His open eye turned to see the doctor who faced him. Toll did not know this physician, who stared back at him with a wicked smile and mesmerizing but malevolent eyes while holding an empty vial up for Toll to see. Toll squinted his one open eye to read the label: potassium chloride. In small amounts, it stabilizes the heart, but in massive bolus dosing, it kills, almost instantaneously.

"Noooooo!" Toll yelled. But no one could hear as the doctor pocketed the vial and walked away into the shadows.

The cardiac monitor and pulse oximeter alarms went off simultaneously twenty seconds later.

Ten seconds after that, Nurse Waldheim called the code blue.

An hour later, Dr. Gregory M. Toll was pronounced dead.

Cause of death was described as cardiac arrest secondary to drug overdose and ischemic brain injury.

The Doctor wished it could have been a throat slashing, but in life, one can't have everything one wants.

66

DEMETRI

AFTER DINNER—ROASTED LAMB AND potatoes, stewed to-
matoes, green beans—Demetri sat in the living room with his dad while his
mother did the dishes. His grandmother had gone to bed; his siblings were at
the mall with their friends.

"So run this by me again," said his father. "You found evidence of similar
murders and body disappearances about twenty-five years ago."

"Yes, Dad."

"And then about twenty-five years before that."

"Yes, Dad."

"So you're saying they were all committed by the same guy?"

"Looks like it, Dad."

Michael turned his head sideways as he studied his son, the way a dog
does when he doesn't know what the hell its owner is talking about. "You
may know medicine, kid, but as a detective, you're all mental *malakias*,"
he said, using the Greek word for masturbation. He was always straight up
with his son.

"Dad, listen."

"It's impossible."

"Dad . . ."

"Twenty-five and twenty-five equals fifty. Did they teach you that in medical school?"

"They did, Dad."

"That means the murderer would be at least seventy or seventy-five by now. Guess how many cases I came across where someone committed murders like this over fifty years."

"Dad . . ."

"Guess."

"Come on, Dad . . ."

"Guess." The first two utterances of the word were invitations. This one was a command.

"None?"

"I've raised a genius. Now guess how many cases like this there are in the history of law enforcement, going all the way back to the world's first sheriff —a man in a cave, wearing a bearskin, packing a stone club."

"Okay, Dad, okay. Zero again."

"You're on a hot streak, kid, and you learn fast."

"Dad, listen. It's all in the files. I found a record of bodies missing from the hospital going back to the '60s. And around the same time, there would be a string of gruesome murders, not just at the medical center but also in the surrounding neighborhood. Each block of deaths was separated by about twenty-five years of quiet. And, Dad, here's the thing: it may even go back farther—to before World War II. Maybe even farther than that."

"So now our seventy-five-year-old murderer is pushing ninety? Don't tell me: he holds onto his walker with one hand while he uses the other to wield the knife.

"Dad."

"Wait, it goes back even farther—he's 115. He's 140. He's immortal. Of course. Why didn't I see it sooner?"

"I can't explain it, Dad, but the facts are the facts. Maybe it's a cult doing it."

"Or maybe it's a coven of witches. I can explain it: coincidence, pure and simple, worked over by my son's overactive imagination."

"In the oft-repeated words of one Michael Makropolis: coincidence is providence for the uninitiated and knowledge for the experienced."

"I said that? One or both of us must have been drunk at the time."

"There's a saying in orthopedics that says it simpler: the eye sees what the mind knows."

After a brief pause, they both started laughing uncontrollably.

His dad stopped first. "Jesus."

He thought back to the mid '80s. The city was a jungle back then, but there was one week that stood out in his mind: ten murders in six days. All different, with no apparent connection to one another except savagery he'd never seen in all his years on the job and never saw again. He realized that that was the week the homeless man's body had disappeared from the hospital.

"Dad?"

"Kyrie Eleison."

Just then Sophia came rushing in from the kitchen. "The radio just announced another murder at the hospital. A man's throat was slashed."

Michael closed his eyes and slowly shook his head.

"You stay home for the weekend, Demetri," said Sophia.

"Yes, Mom."

"And you're not going back there until it's safe."

If a look could turn one to stone, his mother was now Medusa, hair of snakes and all.

Demetri paused, frozen in time as he measured his response. "Yes, Mom," he said, looking straight into her glacial eyes, "I heard you. I won't go back."

She nodded and smiled.

Demetri bade his parents good night. He needed to get to the medical center early in the morning.

67

FELD

THIRTY MINUTES AFTER THE SHOW had ended, Feld and Inga sat near the famous bar in the famous East Side café with the famous painted murals in the famous hotel that has housed presidents, dignitaries, and their mistresses. The pre-theater meal for the fundraiser had featured the usual rubber chicken, so both were famished—Feld because he needed to fuel his short, blimpish body; Inga because she allowed herself only one substantial meal per day in order to maintain the statuesque figure that prompted trolls like Feld to pay top dollar for her company and affections.

Inga had been Feld's escort for a dozen evenings by now. Although technically she was off the clock at 11, she allowed Feld to continue lavishing his attentions on her and, for a price, often responded by putting in some "overtime." Since he'd divorced his third wife, Inga was the only woman who catered to his every whim. The fact that he paid for the privilege was, to him, immaterial.

"Jean-Claude," he said to the waiter, "the Puligny-Montrachet, Les Pucelles, 2004, please, and not too cold."

"You remembered, Andrew. Thank you."

After the waiter returned with the wine, they ordered. "The mesclun salad," said Inga, "followed by that curry dish you do so well here."

"The foie gras," said Feld, "then the wild salmon, mustard sauce on the side."

As Jean-Claude walked away, Inga could see Feld's lip turning downward. She knew instantly what was wrong. He'd never taken Inga here, but it was now obvious that she'd dined here before many times. One of the golden rules of being an escort was to not let a customer know he was one of many. A veteran at her business, she'd made a rookie mistake. However, her recovery was flawless. "I had that dish a month ago when I was here with my mother. We'd gone to a Wednesday matinee."

Feld brightened. He knew she was lying but didn't care. He appreciated the superb work of a consummate professional.

TWO HOURS LATER, INGA AND Feld lingered over glasses of Chateau Rieussec Sauternes after their dessert of crème brûlée and espresso. The crowd had thinned out to a handful of diehards as the wait staff counted down till closing. Feld noted an oddly familiar man at the bar. He was tall and muscular, wearing a tuxedo, and periodically looked Feld's way. Feld had seen him and those eyes of his before—but where?

"A quick visit to the ladies room," said Inga, "and then you can show me your etchings. You do etch, don't you?" she added over her shoulder as she walked to the rear of the restaurant. She glanced at the stranger at the bar, smiling as she passed.

Feld caught the eye of his waiter, raised his hand, and flailed it in a scribble—the international sign for "Check, please." When it arrived, Feld looked it over, pulled out his billfold, and removed his American Express Black Card. What a ripoff it was. Not only did he have to spend 250 grand each year using it, but he had to pay an initiation fee of $5,000. All for a card whose benefits were at best minimally better than his old green card. But he liked the heft of the titanium card, and it made him a big man. The waiter took it and returned a minute later with the printout for Feld to sign, which Feld did, adding exactly 15 percent to the total, not including the wine, for which he added $10.

Feld saw that the coat-check girl had his coat and Inga's ready at the door. The man at the bar was gone. Feld checked his watch and noted it was 1:15 A.M.—the staff wanted to go home. Feld did, too. He popped a Viagra, washed it down with the last of his Sauternes, then went to retrieve the coats.

He took his black overcoat and Inga's mink and handed the girl $2. He looked toward the ladies room and checked his watch again: 1:20. He asked the coat-check girl to go into the bathroom and check up on Inga.

At 1:21, he heard the screams. As Feld and the waiters ran toward the ladies room, the coat-check girl bolted out the door and kept running. She slipped and fell into some chairs, hitting her head on the edge of a table. She remained sitting on the floor, screaming and crying, as blood poured from her face.

The waiters were frozen, waiting for Feld to enter the ladies room first. He willed his legs to move in that direction. With a wildly shaking hand, he reached for the doorknob on the dark, solid wood door. Thirty years a plastic surgeon with steady hands, five years before that in the Army as a trauma surgeon, and he could barely get his hand to grasp the brass knob. His heart was pounding, and his senses were so tunneled in on the door that he no longer heard the girl's screams or the waiters yelling behind him. He heard only the metallic creak of the knob as he turned it.

Moving slowly, carefully, he opened the door and stepped inside. His feet stepped into a puddle as his eyes swept the room from the sinks on the left towards the two toilet stalls on the right. The puddle felt familiar in its consistency, but he couldn't place it right away. As he stepped toward the stalls, it hit him: he'd stepped in puddles of blood hundreds of time in the operating room. He looked down: congealing blood. It was time to end the slow motion.

He kicked open the left stall: nothing. He placed his hand on the door of the righthand stall. The sound he heard from behind it was an unintelligible gurgle.

He opened the door. Inga was there, naked, hanging by her arms, which were tied to the heating pipes above with her stockings. The gurgling was the sound of her last air bubbles escaping from her open windpipe through clotting blood. Her eyes were lifeless. The only thing connecting her head to her torso were her exposed, bone-white vertebrae and beef-red paraspinal muscles.

As soon as Feld stepped back, the heaves began, with foie gras, salmon, Les Pucelles 2004, crème brûlée, espresso, Sauternes, and Viagra all cascading onto the floor. Feld had spent two years in Vietnam dealing with traumatic amputations and sucking chest wounds. But even in Saigon, he'd never felt such shock and revulsion.

68

McManus

HE AWOKE WITH THE STALE breath of an alcoholic as his stiff body refused to budge. He was on the couch again.

The evening's events were a total blur: he remembered running to the kitchen for a beer to escape the nymphomaniac in the living room, and downing six. After that, he remembered nothing.

He raised his aching head slowly. The only light in the room came from the streetlamp outside the picture window. The room swirled for a moment then steadied. He found himself unable to move his legs, which were numb from the knees down. Looking down at his feet, he found them smothered by 200-plus pounds of sleeping mastiff. McManus had no clothes on; he was covered by only a light blanket.

Was he alone?

He propped himself up on his elbows and looked around. He saw no one until his focus turned to the floor next to the couch. Diane was there, sound asleep, wrapped in a blanket of her own. Her clothes were strewn over the easy chair in the corner. His eyes widened as the cogs of his brain started to function. Panic set in. He quietly and slowly pulled his paralyzed legs from under Angus, who stirred but did not wake up. The blood rushed into them; his skin and nerves burned and tingled as the legs slowly came to life. He sat on the couch for several minutes as he rubbed his feet, being careful not to wake the wild thing.

Once he felt his legs would hold his weight, he stood up. The wood floor creaked ever so slightly, but Diane continued to breathe slowly and deeply. McManus could see her nipples outlined by the blanket that covered her. What happened McManus did not know and did not want to know. If sex had occurred while he was blacked out, did it count as cheating? Was Diane really of legal age to give consent? Had he committed statutory rape? Surely he was not responsible for his actions: surely the sober partner could be held liable for performing sex without lawful consent from the drunk partner.

He figured that McManus's wife, with her service Glock, or Diane's dad, with his Beretta shotgun, would not wait to hear this nuanced explanation before firing if they happened to walk in.

McManus checked his watch: 6:15. The sun and his wife would not arrive for an hour. He collected his clothes as Angus watched him with one eye open. He snuck into his bedroom, closed the door, and placed his hairy, slobber-stained suit into a bag for dry cleaning. His underwear looked clean, but what did that mean?

He entered the bathroom and showered, the warm water helping to relieve his aching body. Then he shaved and got dressed. Although this was a Saturday, he had a lot of work to do to on these murders. Today called for a white shirt with his yellow-and-orange Indian headdress–patterned Hermès tie, one of his favorites for fall. The suit was a three-button gray houndstooth. His shoes were brown wing tips. He slipped his Glock into a Galco inside-the-waistband holster on his strong-side hip. Although he liked his suits tailored for a snug fit, carrying a gun meant either a looser fit in the jacket or leaving it unbuttoned. As he finished, he realized he still hadn't figured out what to do about Diane. She needed to be out of the house by the time his wife arrived.

He opened the door of his bedroom and was startled to find Diane standing there in his overcoat. "Oh, hi. Can I use your bathroom to freshen up?"

"Uhhh, yeah. The towels are on the rack."

"Great!" She was too perky for this early in the morning. She slipped past him, her breasts brushing against his chest.

McManus sighed as she entered the bathroom. If he played this right, she could be out of there before 7 with no one the wiser. He entered the kitchen, collected the empty beer cans, ten in all, and placed them into the recycling bin just outside the back door. Ten beers? That was a lot, even for Patrick McManus. He remembered only six. Had he drunk the other four, or had she helped? He grabbed the instant coffee from the shelf over the stove, shook some into a cup, and added hot water from the sink's instant hot water dispenser, the steam rising in the cool kitchen air. He had forgotten to turn the heat on last night. He didn't have to figure out why. The caffeine almost immediately brought new life to him. He opened the refrigerator to find only vomit-inducing food: yogurt, cottage cheese, fruit. Not a donut or pastry to be found.

"Shit."

"What?" It was Diane, at the kitchen entrance, bending at the waist, adjusting her breasts as she buckled her bra behind her back. She had on her jeans and shoes; her sweater was bunched around her neck.

"I have a 7:30 aerobics class," she said, "and need to go home and change." She straightened up, pulled on her sweater, and yelled, "Call me again next time Angus needs a walk," as she ran out the door.

McManus, dumbfounded, watched her go. He had no more than half a minute to pull himself together before headlights flashed into the driveway. It was Marcia pulling up in her '95 Grand Am. He quickly entered the living room to make sure Diane hadn't left anything behind. He straightened up the mess, except for whatever might be beneath Angus, who continued to sleep at the end of the couch.

Marcia parked in the garage and entered the house through the kitchen. McManus checked his watch: 7:03. "You're home early."

"You sound disappointed. Did I interrupt something?"

"Like what?"

"Were you and Angus having a moment?"

"Angus and I have stopped dating. We're just friends now."

"Speaking of which, was Diane still around when you got home last night?"

"Diane? Diane? Oh, yeah. Diane. The neighbor's kid, the dog walker. She was watching some old movie."

"Right. She said she'd brought over a DVD of *Lolita,* the old version, with James Mason."

"*Lolita,* right."

"Odd choice for a teenager, wouldn't you say?"

McManus couldn't tell whether his wife knew everything or had no suspicions whatsoever. What he did know was that, in general, she took great pleasure in jerking his chain. "Guess she has a thing for Kubrick."

"As long as you're here, I've been meaning to tell you: I've found a counselor."

"Counselor?" Did this mean their marriage had a chance of making it?

"She helps couples divide up their assets. We'll save a bundle on lawyers' fees if we keep it amicable."

McManus felt he was being railroaded into a divorce he did not want. He loved Marcia and was sure she still loved him.

"She's getting back to me today about our appointment. I'll leave the info in the usual spot." She meant on the refrigerator. Maybe he wasn't so sure she still loved him.

She walked into the bedroom and closed the door.

Thank God I cleaned up the living room, thought McManus. He walked to the door and picked up the leash, causing Angus to spring from the couch. On the space the dog vacated was a pair of bikini panties—pink, with blue flowers. McManus stuffed them into his jacket pocket.

ONCE HE GOT BACK WITH Angus, McManus saw that the bedroom door was still closed, so he left the house, got into his car, and headed to the Cross Island Parkway. He right away noticed he was being followed by a maroon four-door sedan. He pulled off the parkway into a the parking area of the Bayside Marina. The sedan pulled off behind him and parked about 20 feet away from him.

McManus put his hand on his Glock as he released his seatbelt. The windows of the sedan were blacked out, obscuring the occupant. McManus scanned the parking area. No one else was to be seen here this early on a Saturday morning. As he was about to exit, he realized there was something familiar about the vehicle. In fact it looked just like . . .

The driver's side window rolled down.

It was McCarthy.

The inspector pointed at McManus, then waved him over. McManus relaxed his grip on his weapon, but his heart began to pump even more furiously, his hungover temples pounding with each beat. McManus nodded, got out of his RMP, and walked over to her window.

"Get in, McManus." It was an order.

Here it comes: demotion and transfer. He was sure of it.

He got in on the passenger side and closed the door. He heard the locks click shut—the inspector must have hit the button on the driver's side armrest. McManus sat there, looking out onto the bay, the fog thick and still, waiting for his superior officer to drop the hammer.

"I didn't see Detective GQ at Clancy's last night. I had to drink alone," she said.

McManus sat silent, looking out the front windshield at the mist-shrouded bay, measuring the response he would give.

He never had a chance.

McCarthy turned her whole body to McManus, causing the skirt of her electric-blue suit to ride up her thighs, revealing the lace at the top of her glittering gold stockings.

She reached over to bend her right arm behind McManus's head, and drew him near, as if she were a python. She then grabbed his crotch with her left hand. McManus, in his weakened condition, was powerless to resist as he locked lips with his superior officer. One part of him, however, was anything but weak: his hard-on was immense and pulsated in tandem with his heart and temples.

McCarthy scooted over the center console, the police-band radio squawking as her 3-inch heels pushed a variety of buttons. She ripped open her jacket and pulled her skirt up to around her waist. McManus could see a thin lace panty peeking out between her thighs, soaked in anticipation.

McManus quickly and clumsily undid his belt and trousers, pushing them down around his ankles. He then yanked at the thin wet panties, popping the sides, and dropped them to the floorboard.

"Always the impetuous hero, Pat."

By now, she was straddling him. McManus took a buttock in each hand and slid her down his thighs. He entered her on contact as both inspector and detective moaned in depraved ecstasy.

Minutes later, a Highway Patrol officer pulled off the parkway to check out the two lone parked cars facing the water in the parking area. Running their plates in the database, he found they were unmarked department vehicles. He smiled as he saw one car, the one with the blacked-out windows, bucking as if its engine were idling rough, even though its engine was off, its exhaust quiet. He shook his head, turned, and reentered the parkway.

Twenty minutes later, in his own car, the dazed detective was back on the parkway. He reached into his pocket, pulled out the pink-and-blue panties, and dumped them out the window. He then reached into his other pocket and pulled out the damp lace panties. He smiled and tucked them into the glove compartment.

"For safe keeping," he said to himself. He checked his watch. "On time." He smiled.

He switched on the radio to hear the traffic report, but instead heard the news about the call girl whose throat had been cut open after she'd attended the hospital benefit. After flipping the switches for the lights and siren, he drove at injudicious speed through the thick fog toward Manhattan.

69

PEAR

IT HAD BEEN AFTER 1:00 when he drifted off; now he looked at the clock: 4:36. As he lay face up in bed, with his wife sleeping soundly next to him, he imagined the headlines in the papers on the stands right now: "Devilish Dissector on Death Spree" in the *Post* and "Surgical Slayer Stalks Sin Sity" in the *News*. The *Times* would be more sober but no less damning: "Murderer Loose at Eastside Medical Center."

He sat up, swung his legs over the side of the bed, slid into his scuff slippers, and rose. He shivered for a moment, then picked up his robe from the foot of the bed, and put it on.

He walked silently to the door, exited the master bedroom, and went down the stairs to the living room. The blinds were open, and the glare from the street lamps below illuminated the ceiling with an eerie yellow glow that cast shadows over the crown moldings.

He headed toward the bar and poured himself a Glenlivet. This was not his routine, but this was not a routine week. He walked over to the large window overlooking Fifth Avenue and the park. The fog-shrouded street was deserted. A sip of the Scotch burned the back of his throat and warmed his chest almost immediately. He thought back to his earlier years at the medical center. Life was so much simpler back then, and so was death. He tended to his patients, taught students and residents, and made what he thought was a good amount of money. Doctors were still doctors, not "providers." The insurance companies didn't tell them which pill to prescribe, which test to order, and how much they could charge.

But it wasn't the changing practice of medicine that had turned Pear into the curmudgeon he became. That started the week the first body went missing in 1986. The news media and the NYPD didn't connect the dots, but he did. And, with the help of Murtaugh, he had stopped the murders, though they both had thought the maniac was dead, washed down the East River and out to sea.

Pear saw a hint of light in the sky. Dawn was coming—he dreaded the new day and the new misery it would bring. He'd kept the whole thing quiet back then. This time it was all public, but he'd do what he could to minimize the damage to the medical center.

He figured it was time to shower and head to the hospital. He finished his drink, went back upstairs, and entered his bathroom. When he and his wife had renovated their apartment, they'd installed his-and-hers master bath and dressing suites. This way he could shower and dress without disturbing her. She usually slept well past 8 while he was in the office by 6:30 or 7, even on weekends.

He slid the pocket door closed and turned on the shower. Within seconds, the glass was fogged, and Pear stepped in. He looked at his aging body and the inevitable effects of gravity. As the water ran over his paunched belly and the sagging skin on his arms and legs, Pear decided that they didn't bother him in the least. Power had come to him through meetings, lunches, and golf games, not feats of strength. Every wrinkle on his face, every inch added to his waist reflected another step up the ladder of influence, another badge of courage. He hoped to go up many more before he was done in this world. He'd already been promised the job of state commissioner of health if the governor won reelection next year.

After finishing in the bathroom, he dressed in his usual gray pinstripes from his Hong Kong tailor and left. Breakfast would be black coffee and a scone, delivered by the Eastside Center Diner after he got to work.

Dan was waiting downstairs with the Benz warmed up. As they drove, Pear's cellphone rang. It was Murtaugh telling him the news about Andrew Feld's hooker.

Another murder. And it wasn't even 7:00.

AFTER DAN LEFT HIM AT the rear entrance to the hospital so he could avoid the press, he got on his private elevator. Designated for the president and chairman of the board only, the lift had been built in the early 1900s out of solid walnut and elm, with hand-carved ebony detailing. The door was an old brass gate that folded to the side, and the control was a manual slide lever, right for up, left for down. The smell of motor oil and humidity on the lower floors gave way to an aroma of wood oil as the elevator moved upward.

The lights in the top-floor corridor were dimmed, as was normal at this hour and on this day. He walked to his office, his footsteps silenced by the thick carpeting, his breathing echoing slightly off the paneled walls. He didn't bother to turn on the lights to his office—he knew every inch. Opening the closet, he switched his gray jacket for his white lab coat. He then sat at his desk and checked the time. Murtaugh would arrive in minutes.

He reached into his right pants pocket and pulled out a small key, which he used to unlock the small cabinet built into the right side of his desk. He placed his hand on the rubberized finger pad of the safe he'd had bolted into the desk. He pressed the buttons in sequence then heard the slamming sound of the spring-loaded door opening. He reached in and pulled out a Smith & Wesson .38 snubnose revolver.

Some of the snubbie's bluing had worn off, and there was a hint of rust near the trigger, but all in all, it wasn't in bad shape for a gun not touched in twenty-five years.

He tucked the weapon into his pants pocket as Murtaugh entered the room.

70

DEMETRI

THE HEAT WAS NOT YET on, so the wooden floor was cold on his bare feet. The tiled floor in the bathroom was even colder. He wanted to shower, get dressed, and leave with as little fanfare as possible. Before entering the shower, he caught a glimpse of his face before the bathroom mirror steamed over. His left eye and forehead were so black and blue it was a veritable hematomata, to use the vernacular.

He carefully shampooed his hair to get out the residual dried blood. The wound was tender but covered in a waterproof clear spray, so showering was not a problem.

He dressed, picked up his backpack from his bedroom, and went down to the kitchen for breakfast: leftover French toast dunked in his mother's honey concoction. He wrote a note to leave on the refrigerator, telling his parents he had research to do and needed to go back to school. No doubt he'd hear from his mother as soon as she saw it.

The train station was only a short walk away, but the chilly wind starting up made it feel longer than usual. He got there just a minute prior to the train's arrival from Oyster Bay and Locust Valley. In Jamaica Station, he changed trains, and from Penn Station in Manhattan, he took the subway uptown a couple of stops and crossed town on foot. The sun was low in the sky, sweeping its light from east to west along the midtown streets. The city was slowly coming to life. The stores and street vendors were preparing to open.

He bought a copy of the *News* at the stand outside the medical center and entered the building. He expected to flash his ID and breeze through security as usual, but things had changed. The guard stopped him, scrutinized his ID, and combed through his backpack.

"Since when do the guards have guns?" Demetri asked.

The guard looked at Demetri and stared for several seconds before saying, "Since yesterday." He held his stare, saying no more, until Demetri walked on.

He figured he'd sit in the library to scan the paper before commencing the day's explorations. He was astonished to read about the murder of the HR clerk in a clinic waiting room. And then another killing, at a tony restaurant on the East Side. The MO was the same for both: throat sliced wide open. One was on premises; the other, off but with a hospital surgeon involved. Both had to be related to the Pervis affair. On page 5, there was a short item on the death of a subway worker decapitated in the tunnels by a train. The location was right near the medical center. Hmm.

Just then a classmate, Hillary Winston, the school's source of all information, misinformation, and just plain gossip, sat down next to him.

"Demetri, my darling, you're back. For a while there, everyone thought you were a victim of the Doctor."

"The Doctor?"

"Yeah that's the nickname we've chosen for the murderer. All the blogs have picked up on it." She looked at Demetri's newspaper. "So you know about Feld's hooker."

"Hooker? It says 'escort.'"

"Such a child you are, Demetri. It's sweet."

Demetri rolled his eyes.

"Listen, little boy, I bet there's nothing in the paper about a certain Dr. Toll."

"Toll?"

"He overdosed on Fentanyl and crapped out."

"Dead?"

"As a nail, door that is, my love." She got up and shook out her long black hair. "No time to dawdle, Demetri. I'm scrubbing in on a craniotomy. I'll put you on my e-mail list serve to keep you up to date."

"Sure, do that, thanks," said Demetri. In fact, he was already on her list and had instructed his Gmail account to route all her messages directly to his spam folder. "Bye."

"Bye, Hillary!" Demetri was sure she was the one in need of the craniotomy, or maybe just a lobotomy, like Jack Nicholson in *One Flew Over the Cuckoo's Nest.*

Demetri's thoughts shifted to the news at hand.

Toll dead? The hooker at the restaurant? The security guy? The HR clerk? Maybe even the subway worker? Demetri began to think about these disparate events. When he took his physical-examination course over a year ago, his professor had given him some good advice. It was on Demetri's first day examining a patient—a surrogate patient, actually, an actress. The professor was speaking while he was between the young woman's legs giving her a pelvic exam. "If you have a patient with multiple symptoms," he said, "don't assign a different diagnosis to explain each of them. Try to find the one diagnosis that encompasses most or all of the symptoms, and you will invariably be correct."

All of the deaths in the last week, as well as the injuries to Demetri and his father, weren't hard to connect. But the medical center's earlier murders and missing bodies, and the contemporaneous citywide murder sprees— several episodes, occurring at intervals of twenty or twenty-five years—were much harder to put together. A thorough review of the facts the night before with his dad pointed them to a succession of several killers: a cult of some type performing these evil deeds over decades. But doctors slaying people for no apparent reason? And a medically precise brain dissection?

It made no sense.

Demetri knew he would not solve the problem sitting in the library. If he wanted any answers he had to get downstairs, way downstairs, to the subterranean labyrinth of the medical center. He took his backpack and white coat and headed for the stairs in the main corridor. Although he thought of returning to the library stacks to continue his search there, his forehead dissuaded him.

As he approached the door to the stairwell, a hand grabbed his backpack and pulled him backwards, throwing him off balance.

"Sorry, old boy."

It was Carter.

"You scared the shit out of me."

"Yeah, we're all jittery. These murders are . . ."

"Unbelievable?"

"No."

"Terrifying?"

"Not that."

"Sick?"

"My thoughts exactly, Demetri boy. You and I—great minds locked onto the same wavelength. Which is why it was fated that we run into each other now."

"What is it this time? Another seven-minute flyby with the X Factor?"

"No, much better than the Factor. Barroca has a hip fracture he needs help on."

"Barroca, oh." Not again, Demetri thought.

Altan Barroca routinely was in over his head and then depended on the house staff to save his bacon. He rarely took advice, so even when a fellow or senior resident was present, he usually compromised the result. Demetri remembered Barroca doing a leg-lengthening procedure he'd never done before and had only watched once. Most surgeons would observe several, take training courses, and even ask an expert to scrub with them before doing their first on their own. But Barroca knew no fear and had even less common sense. The leg lengthening was uneventful until the surgical drapes came off and the foot was malrotated outward by 45 degrees.

"There's no one else to cover the case, Tom? Really? Besides, it's Saturday. I just came in to pick up my belongings. I'm quitting school and moving to Bangkok as a purveyor of fine young boys."

"The child pimping will have to wait. Summers is the chief resident on call, but he hates operating with Barroca. Ergo fourth-year medical student who wants to become an orthopedic surgeon."

"What about the great man of medicine who stands before me?"

"Me? My Saturday-morning squash game, of course. Never miss it."

"Of course."

"I knew I could count on you, Demetri boy. Just remember, keep your hands out of the wound when Barroca has a knife or drill in his hand. You'll need all your fingers if you're gonna be a filthy-rich Park Avenue orthopedist."

Demetri watched Carter run off toward the elevators and waited for him to get in before walking to the elevator himself to go up to the OR. As he entered the car, he noted an impeccably dressed man, in the typically decadent style of European chic: loosely knotted tie, off-color sports jacket, pinky ring, and those funny-looking loafers.

"Hello, Dr. Barocca, I'm medical student Makropolis."

"Yes, yes. I remember you helped me on that lengthening two months ago." Barocca spoke in a definitely European but still not quite placeable accent. Maybe Croatian trying to be Italian and French.

"Yes, sir, and I am helping you today."

"Ah, wonderful, boy. Wonderful." He said the word as though he were auditioning for a part in *Grand Hotel*.

"How is that patient from two months ago doing?" Demetri immediately wanted to retract that question, but it was too late.

"Very well. Yes, very well, boy. I have her doing therapy. Working to get her foot straight when she walks."

Demetri smiled and nodded, but he knew all the therapy in the world would not compensate for a 45-degree rotational deformity. Four or 5 degrees, yes. Forty-five, not a chance.

"What is the case today?"

"Eighty-year-old woman, boy. Subtrochanteric comminuted hip fracture. We'll be doing a Gamma Nail."

"Sounds good," said Demetri, who knew that those fractures could be a bitch to fix. They were hard to reduce, to line up in anatomic position—even experienced trauma surgeons had a hard time with them. Had Barocca ever done one before?

They entered the locker room and changed into their scrubs. Barroca went to see the patient while Demetri wrestled with his backpack as he squeezed it into the narrow locker. He took his wallet and pen from the top shelf of the locker, where he'd put them when he'd emptied his pants pockets before changing, and exited the room. He left his cellphone.

Half a minute later, a notification tone emanated from his locker, indicating the receipt of a text message.

But by then, the phone's owner had begun to scrub.

71

THE DOCTOR

DESPITE THE NEAR-PITCH BLACKNESS, his magnificent eyesight allowed him to see every aspect of this delicious morsel in perfect black and white as she sat against the wall by the elevator. With complete lack of light, he knew she had nowhere to go.

He'd heard her periodic sighs over the past two hours as he worked in his laboratory. His color vision needed a minuscule amount of light to function, so he'd seen the color of her magnificent eyes only briefly, when he'd approached her earlier—her face was illuminated by the screen of her cellphone before she flipped the device closed. Of course it was pointless for her to call for help from down here in the lowest of subbasements. Besides, the battery was certainly dead by now, making the device useless.

When he'd come close that first time, as he was turning the lights off in succession, he'd allowed her to detect him, then left, allowing extra time for her fear to marinate and grow. The terror enhanced the chemical processes in the hypothalamus, thus strengthening the dosage for use after harvesting.

Now, again, he stood not 5 feet in front of her. He smelled her perspiration and smiled. He also smelled that she was mid-cycle: most receptive. He smelled her life force. The silence of his footsteps and stealth of his body made him nonexistent to her. But then he let out the slightest of chuckles—just enough to sharpen her feeling of dread.

The girl popped up her head and got to her feet. "Who's there?"

Silence.

"Is any one there?"

He admired the curve of her body and the taut sinew of her legs.

"Help me, please! I'm stuck down here!" She turned and pounded on the elevator door. "Let me out of here!" She was indeed special. So special, the Doctor had not yet decided on her special end.

The Doctor silently backed away and headed down the long corridor, passing multiple doors, all identical, on the way to his lab. He had more work to do in preparation for the next procedure. Review of his extensive records had revealed that the method of harvest was critical to the success of the infusion. The surgical technique, as well as the specimen's degree of dehydration, were the two elements most crucial to achieving maximum effect. In his early years of research and trial and error, he'd needed as many as a donor every week to sustain the youthful effect, but that frequency proved unsustainable as the local populace became more sensitive to murders and disappearances. Fortunately, in 1913, construction on an extension of the Lexington Avenue Subway delayed his harvesting tissue from a particular donor; by the time of the sacrifice, the donor's system was characterized by extreme dehydration. The effect of the resulting infusion lasted two years, probably due to its higher concentration in the dehydrated patient. Further refinements led to an unprecedented twenty-plus years of unremitting youth, but he still lamented the quick dissipation, only a few weeks post-infusion, of his hyper-senses. The Doctor likened it to the use of methadone in addicts. Even though methadone lasts a long time, it doesn't supply the same high as heroin.

The Doctor hoped that the recent weakening of the infusion's strength was due to a technical error on his part. If the problem was his changing biochemistry, he'd need to acquire donors more often—a major problem in a city now grown accustomed to a much a lower crime rate than that it endured during the era of his last harvest. He thought of moving to Iraq or Somalia, someplace where life is cheap, but the horrific lifestyle did not appeal to him.

No, he would figure out the issues and solve them. He always had.

He entered his lab but did not bother to turn on the light. He checked on the cell chromatography. The test was proceeding nicely and would help in the next go-around.

The Doctor's next task was to get something to eat—he was famished after his busy evening. He exited into a short corridor that ended in a large steel door. As he grasped the handle, he felt it vibrate and heard a low rumble; the intensity of the vibration and the pitch of the noise told him it was a Number 5 subway train, traveling uptown. He opened the door and a rush of cool, damp air passed over him. He stepped out into the tunnel as rats scurried away. Above him, he could see the steel-beam suspended tracks of the Lexington Avenue Line and the last of the train as it headed north. If he walked farther west, he would be under Grand Central Terminal and its myriad of tracks. Instead, he turned east and headed for the river.

He walked along the tracks of the old coal shuttle used, way back in time, to ferry materials from East River barges to the medical center. Now the tunnels were traversed only by the Doctor, who needed to move about without notice, using connectors to various buildings for exits. He even made use of the small coal cars to convey bodies to the water's edge for disposal. The entrance to the tunnel from the river was hidden beneath the FDR Drive and all but submerged at high tide. As he walked along, the pitter-patter of little feet and the dripping of water preceded him. He did not need a light to find his way; his superior vision showed him the tracks, the rats, and everything else. He was careful to walk on the rail ties to avoid mud and water on his shoes. He approached a well-hidden side corridor overgrown by roots with a door that led to a staircase. He pulled out his multilock key and unlocked the door, which he was careful to lock behind him. He avoided touching the rusted and slimy handrail as he walked up several flights of stairs. The locked door at the end opened to a private garden near Tudor City. On the garden side, the door was covered with ivy and so grown over that, once closed, it was never noticed. The ivy he had chosen for this part of the garden was a variety that retained its leaves year round, turning rust red in the fall and winter.

The doctor walked across the garden to a patio door, which he never locked. He slid it open and walked toward his elevator, which he opened with the turn of a key. He went up to the townhouse's fifth floor. All the blinds in the home were drawn, allowing only small slits of light to illuminate the interior.

The floor was as he left it. Every layer of dust was allowed to remain in order to help him detect intruders. In truth, though, he did not worry about the possibility of trespassers. His alarm system, plus the garden's 10-foot walls, topped with razor wire that was camouflaged by more ivy, provided airtight security. He did not really need the services of the security agency he employed, but found no reason not to take the extra precaution. The company, which specialized in the protection of dignitaries associated with the nearby UN, had armed guards stationed less than two minutes away. Purchasing the home, many years ago, from an African ambassador and maintaining its foreign-soil designation helped a great deal. Maintenance on the building was conducted by a housekeeping firm that cared for little-used homes of diplomats. The agency had access to the garden and exterior of the building and to all but the fifth floor inside.

The Doctor looked at the wall clock he'd bought at Cartier in the 1890s, when he first turned thirty. It was still early morning, and although he could do without sleep for several more hours or even days if needed, he had a long weekend planned and wanted to be in top form. He stripped to his shorts, admiring in the mirror his lean, muscular body. He loved his hands especially. A professor once told him that the part of the body people look at the most is their own hands, which is why people seek attention from doctors for any condition that alters their hands' appearance in the slightest. The Doctor's hands were large yet delicate. They could perform the most intricate feats of surgery or they could snap a spine in an instant.

Pleased with himself, he lay down to rest.

As he stared at the hand-painted fresco on the ceiling, he replayed the dissection of Pervis in his mind down to most minute detail. He recalled it as flawless. Pervis was at the most extreme level of pain at the moment the Doctor harvested the hypothalamic tissue, which turned out to be perfect in every way and which he processed in an expedient and efficient manner. He could find no fault in the preparation, harvest, and processing, so why had the effect been so short-lived? Perhaps the victim lacked sufficient Substance R, as he called the neurotransmitter, to give the Doctor a full and effective dose. Perhaps the cocktail he'd used to feign Pervis's death had had an adverse effect.

What he suspected and feared most was the development of antibodies making him more "immune" to the effects of the infusion. In other words, he worried, his body was becoming resistant.

But he had used the same cocktail several times before.

He had discarded Pervis in the anatomy lab rather than abandoning him to the rats or the river because he was bored and wanted to have some fun. He enjoyed seeing that portly Pear and his oily minion Murtaugh squirm under the scrutiny of the press. The Doctor couldn't have asked for a more entertaining diversion.

Entertainment was one thing, work was another, and he needed a new donor to provide a booster. He was not yet sure if the girl would be the one. Perhaps he would keep her alive as a plaything to fulfill his desires. Whether the girl or someone else ended up as the donor, this time the bloodletting needed to be especially slow and painful to maximize the neurotransmitter's presence in the tissue—so excruciating, in fact, that whoever the specimen was, he or she would rather be drawn and quartered.

Hmm. It had been years since he'd had the pleasure of trying that on anyone. The Doctor smiled as he dozed off.

72

McManus

"MCMANUS. I WONDERED WHEN YOU'D show up." It was the chief of detectives. The Crime Scene Unit had arrived at the café two hours after the discovery of the call girl's body. They were still working.

"And what brings you out on a Saturday morning?"

"After the disaster at One PP yesterday, McCarthy's been reassigned. I'm supervising the investigation now."

"Welcome to the nuthouse, Jack."

"The commissioner is breathing down my neck because the mayor is breathing down his. I want the case solved by Monday, or you and McCarthy both will spend the rest of your career investigating child pornographers from behind a computer screen on Staten Island."

McManus took a moment to hope he hadn't just committed a similar act of child pornography with the eager dog sitter.

"Another thing, Pat. Mick Makropolis called me. He says these murders may be connected to . . ."

". . . the Ripper murders of 1986? Yeah, the thought occurred to me, too."

"Gotta get up pretty early in the morning to keep up with the great Patrick McManus."

Or be Inspector McCarthy, thought McManus. "About time you noticed."

"And watch out for Pear and Murtaugh. They were both involved in some way back then."

"Yeah, Pear's easy to make: a classic big-time politico bullshit artist. And Murtaugh—well, you know Murtaugh."

"Yep."

"So, anything from this Feld about his girlfriend?"

"Park Avenue call girl. Otherwise unremarkable. But the doc thinks he saw someone suspicious—says he looked like James Bond."

"Anyone else?"

"The bartender. He saw the same guy get up to follow the girl to the bathroom. He thought the guy was going for a five-minute, slam-bam-thank-you-ma'am hook-up. Apparently she conducted business regularly at the restaurant."

MCMANUS FINISHED TALKING TO FELD and left him sitting in the back of the unmarked RMP where the chief had stashed him for safe keeping.

He went back into the restaurant and found the bartender seated on a stool behind the bar, wiping glasses that had come out of the dishwasher.

"Barkeep, don't you know you know it's a felony to tamper with evidence?"

"Tamper with . . ."

"The glasses. You've heard of the concept of fingerprints, I imagine."

"These glasses were washed last night. I put them in the washer after the police got here; I wasn't going to leave the mess. That's not how I run my bar."

A moron, McManus thought.

"Did you see a man here last night: a tall white male, blond hair slicked back, muscular, good looking? Had on a tux."

"Sure. Intense eyes, not very talkative. Looked like James Bond, the new one. Had eight martinis and was still walking straight when he left. Dropped a great tip." The bartender pulled out and waved a $100 bill.

"I'll take that for evidence. You'll be reimbursed by the department." McManus placed the C note in his pocket on the slim chance there was a usable print on it.

"Hey, I need a receipt for that."

"Sure. Call 311 and ask for the Receipt Bureau. By the way, I assume you wiped down the bar in addition to doing the dishes."

"Not a smudge to be found."

McManus shook his head and called over a patrolman. "Officer, take this man to the precinct. We should be able to get a decent sketch of the murderer."

"The murderer?" said the bartender, his legs beginning to quiver. "He was the murderer?"

"You got it, pal. You're the only one to see him face-to-face and survive."

73

MAKROPOLIS

HE STEERED HIS JEEP OFF the Long Island Expressway and onto the Cross Island Parkway, driving north to the Bronx and Rodman's Neck, the NYPD shooting range.

Getting off the parkway, he took the first right off the traffic circle and passed a line of Harleys parked in a lot. Loud Latin music was playing, despite the early hour. No one paid attention to the Jeep; every car that passes on the way to a short unmarked lane is police. He drove down the lane to the gate and came up against a large steel plate set up to prevent unauthorized entry. A heavily armed officer stepped out of the security booth as Makropolis showed his credentials. "Wait for the green light," the officer told him.

Makropolis nodded as the steel plate lowered and the red light turned to green. He drove through then turned left toward the armory. Even with his windows rolled up, he heard the *crack-crack-crack* of gunfire from the shooting range as police officers either practiced or were taking the yearly test required to keep their firearms. Back in his heyday, Makropolis would shoot a perfect score year after year with gun after gun as the department switched from revolvers to semiautos. He was invited to join the marksmanship team but declined, preferring to shoot at bad guys rather than paper targets.

He exited his car and walked past several officers, on their coffee break, lounging at picnic tables. The armory was a boxy, imposing structure made of cinderblock; it resembled nothing so much as a reinforced bunker. Makropolis was familiar with the armory's contents, including a collection of historic weapons, handguns as well as rifles, dating back to before World War I. He'd fired a few of them: the Thompson Submachine gun, the "Tommy Gun," of the Prohibition era; the "Grease Gun" used by American troops during World War II.

He approached the entrance and knocked. An officer appeared at the half-opened Dutch door.

"Ah, the legend himself," the cop said.

"Bishop, you old son of a bitch" said Makropolis, shaking the man's hand.

Bishop opened the bottom half of the door and ushered Makropolis in. They passed an armorer working at the lathe. Bishop pointed to the man and said, "He's making a firing pin for an old Pocket Nine semiauto. We can't find the parts anywhere so we manufacture them ourselves. I have an old British Webley. The cylinder was cracked so I made another one from scratch."

Makropolis nodded. He appreciated good workmanship when it came to a gun—a misfiring weapon could be costly when your life was on the line. He noticed a Sig P226 on Bishop's hip as they both continued to move down the aisle to Bishop's workstation. Sitting on the workbench was an HK MP5, the modern equivalent of the Tommy and Grease Guns and the main assault weapon of special-ops police around the world. It was fully disassembled and undergoing a thorough evaluation. "We didn't have these back in the day."

"It purrs like a pussycat, Mickey. Easily controllable even with one hand in full auto mode."

"Impressive."

"Tell me something. You notched a perfect score every year."

"I did."

"How? Most of the time you were firing those shitty 2-inch snub-nose revolvers."

"Pure talent, my friend."

"What stance did you use? Chapman?"

"Modified Weaver, although in the early years, it was single straight arm."

"Single straight arm? You shittin' me?"

"I'm as honest as the day is long."

"I don't believe you . . . but maybe I do." He opened a drawer and pulled out a plastic bag containing a gun and a spent shell casing.

"Here's your gun. After I got the call from your pal the chief of detectives, I thought, 'I'd better clean it up nice and polish it, if the great Mic Mak is on his way.' You're one lucky fuck to get this thing back after what happened."

"Not lucky, my friend, just good-looking."

"And here's a box of Speer Hollow Points. My gift to you. Don't spend it all in one place."

74

DEMETRI

THE CASE WAS UNEVENTFUL UNTIL it was time to place the rod into the femur. Barocca had started the surgery after the anesthesiologist, Richard Queen, an expat from Down Under, had administered a spinal anesthetic.

"You'll do this right quick, won't ya, mate?" he said to Barocca.

"Yes, yes, boy," said the surgeon in his vaguely Middle European accent. "Only an hour and a half."

Queen put on headphones and cranked up his iPod. He preferred to listen to loud music on speakers during surgeries, but no surgeon in the hospital, including Demetri, could stand the maudlin country-and-western ballads he played. As Queen monitored the patient's vital signs, he performed a not-so-silent karaoke number behind the anesthesia screen. Demetri looked at Barocca, who rolled his eyes.

Positioning the patient on the fracture table and doing the prepping and draping of the surgical site took fifteen minutes. Demetri had his sterile gown placed on by John, the scrub tech. John then took a glove and stretched it open for Demetri to place his right hand.

"Stick it in, papi!"

Demetri smiled under his mask as his hand was driven into the glove.

"Aye, papi!" John exclaimed as Demetri laughed.

Demetri then asked Barocca, "Don't we need the C-Arm fluoroscope for the procedure?" Barocca realized he had not yet set up the C-Arm.

"Boy, I have been doing this for forty years. Where you learn this at such young age?"

Demetri shrugged.

"Okay, you re-set up since you know how and I come back in fifteen minutes." Barocca threw off his gown and gloves and left the operating room.

Queen looked at Demetri and cranked up his headphones loud enough for the entire staff to hear followed by his bombastic sing-along.

Later Demetri held the soft-tissue retractors while Barocca surgically approached the greater trochanter. He placed his starting hole in the correct position for reaming the femur and quickly placed his intramedullary guide wire down the shaft of the femur, checking its position via frequent fluoroscopic X-ray images. He then quickly reamed with the reamers, placed an overly large rod down the femur, and placed a screw through the rod into the femoral head, locking the rod and, presumably, the fracture in place.

"That was quick, no, boy?"

But something did not look quite right to Demetri on the fluoroscopic image. Careful not to contaminate his sterile gown, he stepped up to the video screen and saw on the AP film that the rod appeared to be too big for the canal of the femur and overlapped the bone edges excessively.

"What's the matter boy? You can close. I have a massage appointment."

"Uhhh, Dr. Barocca," said Demetri, "can we get a lateral image?"

"Lateral?" said Barocca. "What for, boy?"

"We've never gotten one. We need one for documentation of rod placement."

Barocca rolled his eyes. "Okay, boy, get the film. I will be in the lounge if you need me." Barocca then broke scrub and exited the OR.

Demetri called the radiology technician over to retrieve the C-Arm, which had been pulled back after the initial imaging. The technician pushed it into place, locked the wheels, and slowly rotated the flouroscope beam into the desired lateral view.

"Everyone covered? Get lead or be dead!" the technician yelled. He looked around the room and found everyone nodding affirmative that they were wearing lead gowns. The technician pressed the flouro button, which was followed by a beep. A second later, the image appeared on the screen. Everyone in the room, including the dancing Queen, stopped and stared. The lateral radiograph showed the rod was outside the femur, in the soft tissues, with the fracture displaced 100 percent. Barocca had never reduced or set the fracture.

"Ohhh, piss off!" Queen exclaimed, jumping up and down at the head of the table as he ripped his headphones off. "Where is that suhgeon? Nuhse, go fetch his hoyness from the lounge."

Demetri stood motionless, realizing that this morning's surgical case would probably take all afternoon and he'd be lucky to resume his investigation by dinnertime. He hoped that the sciatic nerve and deep femoral artery hadn't been damaged by the misplaced rod. Demetri's shoulders slumped under the weight of the lead gown. He was exhausted, and the real case had yet to begin.

After what seemed like hours, Barocca stormed into the room. "Impossible, boy. What have you done?" Demetri demurred, then heard Queen behind him mumbling something like, "Have you ever done one of these before?"

Barocca looked around, obviously miffed at the overheard remark. "Gown, please!"

"But you haven't scrubbed yet, Dr. Barocca," said the scrub nurse. "And you don't have a mask on."

Barocca tilted his head up as a sign of exasperated superiority and glided out of the room to scrub. Queen set his sights on Demetri. "Hey, get going and do this case before he gets back. We have only twenty minutes of spinal anesthesia left before I have to put her to sleep."

Demetri turned towards the circulating nurse. "Can we page the chief resident on call?"

"Dog Lab strikes again," said Queen. He put his headphones back on and resumed his performance.

A minute later, the phone rang. The circulating nurse picked it up: "OR 12. Yes. Yes. Uh-huh. Thank you." She hung up and spoke to Demetri. "Summers is busy in the ER. He said to call Carter."

"He was, um, in a meeting earlier. Page him and see if he is finished."

"Oh nuhse, while you're at it, I need a unit of packed RBC's," said Queen. "And a koala sandwich."

Demetri smiled and placed a self-retaining retractor in the wound, feeling for the tip of the rod. After four or five tries, he was able to lock the remover on the rod. With a mild tap of a mallet on the inserter, he had the rod out. Barocca entered and approached the patient when the scrub nurse noticed he had no lead on. "Doctor, you are unprotected."

"What? What, girl? Oh, no lead." He threw his arms up in frustration, put on a lead gown to shield his nether regions from X-rays, and headed back to rescrub.

A moment later, Carter walked in, wearing a mask. "Closing already?"

Queen ripped off his headphones. "Fuck you, Carter. Can't you see the rod is sitting on the table?"

Carter, a quizzical look on his face, looked at Demetri.

"Barocca placed the rod without getting laterals and missed reduction of the femur. It went out posteriorly. He's in there scrubbing again," he said, tilting his head toward the scrub room.

Carter walked over to the C-arm screen, scrolled through the images, and shook his head.

The scrub-room door flung open as Barocca stepped into the room. "Carter, you WASP boy, you. Why you send me student and no real assistant? He ruined the case."

Demetri wanted to object, but Carter waved him down.

"Well, I'm here now," said Carter. "Let's get this over and done with." He rushed past Barocca to put on a lead gown and scrub. He returned, donned a sterile surgical gown and gloves, pushed Barocca to the side, and turned to speak to Demetri. "We can place the rod in the femur and use it as a joystick to reduce the fracture. And we can place the guidewire down the shaft, then ream and put in a smaller rod."

Barocca nodded. "Good idea. Who said all WASPs are stupid?" Barocca roared with laughter at his comment. No one else cracked a smile.

Soon the fracture had been reduced and the new rod placed. Before it could be locked in place, Barocca was out of the room to tell the patient's family what a great job he'd done. Once Carter and Demetri finished the internal fixation and closed, the patient was wheeled out to the recovery room.

"About bloody time," said Queen. The patient's spinal anesthetic had worn off. Her toes were wiggling and pink.

Carter and Demetri headed to the locker room and saw Barocca at the open door of the lounge, in his street clothes, with an unlit cigarette in hand.

"Everything else okay, boys? Ehhhh, you Greeks and WASPs." He reentered the lounge as the door to the lounge automatically closed behind him.

"What did he mean by that?" asked Demetri.

"How the hell should I know?"

"Exactly who is this guy? And where the fuck is he from?"

"Some say he's a long-lost prince from some small Central European country that hasn't existed for a hundred years. I say he may be from Brooklyn." They both laughed as they entered the locker room.

Carter grabbed his white coat and headed for the door as Demetri unlocked his locker.

"I'm off to the ER," said Carter. "I need to do of all the shit work Summers deems below his status. By the way, thanks for helping in there. You saved the patient from disability and Barocca and the hospital from one ginormous lawsuit. Enjoy the rest of the weekend. I'll see you Monday at 6 A.M. for rounds."

Once Carter was gone, Demetri threw off his bloody scrubs and changed back into his jeans, sweater, and lab coat. He threw his backpack on, pinned his ID onto his coat, and was about to kick the locker door closed when he noticed that he'd left his phone on the shelf. He grabbed it, slammed shut the locker, and headed for the exit, dirty scrubs in hand. He stuck them into the deposit bin and walked toward the elevators.

He could finally get to what he'd intended to do hours before, prior to his detour through the Dog Lab's chamber of horrors: a thorough search of the basement and subbasement halls for the old connectors shown on the plans he had in his pack. He knew the sub-subbasement would be locked by now—he'd have to wait till tomorrow to search down there.

The elevator door opened. The car was packed with friends and family of patients so he decided to take the stairs. About halfway down, he reached for his phone—it had been hours since he'd checked his voicemails and text messages. The stairwell was empty so he sat down to go through them. The first voicemail was from his dad telling him not to do anything stupid. The second was from his mother telling him he was dead meat for heading back to the medical center. "*Vlaka!*" The third was his mother calling back to continue berating him for breaking his promise to spend the weekend at home. He then checked his texts: he had only one. It was from an unknown phone number—it must have been sent to him in error:

Help me tr ped sub ment.hurry pls Mar a

Mara, he didn't know any Mara. Was it a spam ad for offshore Viagra? He looked at it some more, then noted the space in the name. Marla? No. Marta? No. Maria?

Could it be her? He went into the front pocket of his backpack and pulled out the small slip of paper she'd given him two days earlier with her phone number on it. It matched the number on the text. Maria Bassias was trapped somewhere in the bowels of the medical center, he was sure of it. According to the time stamp on the message, she'd been down there for over twelve hours.

He hoped it wasn't too late to save her.

75

MURTAUGH

"I'VE HOPED AGAINST HOPE THAT we got the bastard back then," said Pear.

"I've told you for the last twenty-five years, I got him. He staggered. We tried to wade out to catch him, but he collapsed into the water. The current had to have taken him out to the river—there was no way he could have survived. Of course, I would have gotten another shot at him while he was still standing if not for your spasm of conscience."

"I deflected your hand because I wanted to take him alive. I've regretted that action all this time, wondering if the monster would return. And now he has."

"It can't be the same guy. It has to be a copycat."

"How could it be? Only you and I know the truth about him and about what happened in '86. The missing body, the murders—all connected to each other and to a physician at the medical center."

Pear reached into his pocket, pulled out his revolver, and placed it on his desk.

"I didn't know you had one of those," said Murtaugh.

"I've kept it locked away all these years hoping to never see it. But you and I, my friend, are bound to this maniac by blood and time. We have no choice but to go after him. And this time, we will not fail."

"Your plan?"

"Only you and I know of the tunnel to the river. We tracked him there last time—I'm sure he'll reappear there. We'll head to the basement and open the bricked-over, rusted steel door."

"We'll need a sledge hammer."

"There's one waiting there for us."

"And all the racket? Do you want everyone in on this?"

"I've informed the engineers to expect some noise related to the police investigation and to ignore it."

"You expect me to lift the sledgehammer? I'm too old for that shit."

"Not to worry. Dan, my driver, is a bodybuilder. He'll do the grunt work and then leave. Are you sufficiently armed?"

Murtaugh stood and patted his right hip. "Glock 9mm with two spare clips and 2-inch .38 special detective's snubbie on my ankle."

"Then let us begin our trip to hell." Pear stood, picked up his revolver, and placed it into his pocket. The two men both walked down the long corridor to the main elevators.

"I assume you know how to use that thing," said Murtaugh.

"Korea and the Reserves teach you a lot of things. For your information, I've loaded it with +P hollow point .38 Specials."

"I guess you don't want to take him alive this time. Assuming I never get to talk to him, why don't you clue me in on who he is. You always said you'd tell me."

"I can tell you only his assumed name, as his file was found to be entirely fictitious. Before the killings in '86, he'd apparently been around the medical center for over twenty years as voluntary faculty and had worked in an obscure lab on the third floor of the medical school. But no one could recall anything about him, and by the time we went to look at it, his lab was empty. It was as if he never existed, although many people had faint memories of seeing someone like him around. A few retired professors even remembered lunching with him but never got past his veneer. An oncologist told me he saw him a few days before he disappeared. Said he hadn't aged a bit since he'd first noticed him a dozen years before. His name at the time was Matthew Zella. Methuselah, get it? How that name got past everyone is beyond me."

The elevator door opened and Mortimer emerged. He mumbled a hello and tried to maneuver around Pear and Murtaugh without making direct eye contact.

"Hello, Joe," said Pear. "Working today?"

"The Residency Review Committee is breathing down my neck. I need to get ready for them."

"You okay, Joe?"

"The murders, Toll's death—I guess I need some rest."

"You should get some, Joe," said Pear, patting Mortimer on the shoulder before joining Murtaugh in the elevator.

Pear waited for the door to close before he spoke. "What a dowdy old fart he is. If I'm lucky, he'll commit suicide and save me the trouble of firing him."

Murtaugh stared at the elevator door without comment as the two men descended.

76

McManus

HE LEFT THE WEST SIDE and was on his way east when his phone rang. It was the ME.

"McManus."

"Winter. You owe me—big time."

"You have something?"

"Get over here. We'll have show and tell."

"Ten minutes."

He hung up the phone and turned downtown with light blazing and siren blaring. What the hell, he thought.

When he got out of his car, the wind blew his tie over his shoulder. He looked up and saw the sky darkening then remembered his raincoat was at the cleaners. Damn dog, he thought.

Winter was in his office, hunched over a small glass-walled box, prodding something in it with a tongue depressor. He motioned McManus to a chair opposite his desk. McManus sat and remained silent as Winters continued what he was doing.

After what seemed like minutes, McManus realized there was a dead mouse in the glass case.

"I didn't know you do animal autopsies."

"Only in my spare time." His deadpan delivery had McManus believing him for a moment. Then the detective rolled his eyes.

"Behold, McManus. A dead mouse. Right?"

"Right."

"Wrong. It looks dead, it feels dead—except it isn't dead."

McManus leaned forward to look at the mouse.

"You're losing me, Doc."

"The propofol vial that was tampered with had a cc of fluid left in it. I used half for analysis and injected the other half into this mouse last night."

"Yeah, and?"

"First, let me tell you about what we found in the fluid."

"Sure, Doc. But in English, please."

"We were able to confirm what I'd suspected: a modified form of curare, the paralysis drug, as well as a combination of neurotransmitter-type drugs. Not that they were in any form ever described in the literature, but it stands to reason that an injection of this concoction would induce a unique form of coma, something akin to suspended animation."

"Suspended animation? I'm Captain Kirk and you're Bones. Beam us up, Scotty."

"Have you ever heard of the dive reflex?"

"The drive reflex?"

"No, dive, as in diving into water. In medical school, one of the first tests you do in physiology lab is to induce a dive reflex in the student next to you by having him dunk his face in ice-cold water."

"Still waiting for the point, Doc."

"Patience, my friend. I'm sure you've heard of people falling through broken ice on a pond, being submerged for half an hour or more, and then being miraculously resuscitated with brain function intact."

"Ponds and mice. Got it, Doc."

"They survive because of a primitive nerve system common to vertebrates called the lateral line system. It dates back to when we were fish."

"Ponds, mice, and fish. Ah, now it all makes sense."

"Sharks use the lateral line nerve system to find prey in the water even when they can't see or smell it, almost like it's sonar. Humans have the remnant of a lateral line nervous system, but it serves a different purpose. There are receptors located in the skin of the face. Once activated by cold water, the system slows the heart down to one or two abnormal beats per minute. The body goes into ultimate survival mode: blood is pumped to the brain and away from the rest of the body. The whole idea is to keep the control center alive as long as possible at the expense of everything else."

"So you're saying that . . . this is what happened to Pervis? But there was no cold water—ah, but there was the drug. Our Mr. Pervis was one undead mouse."

"Go to the head of the class. To the unsuspecting, the condition looks like a cardiac arrest with only an occasional meaningless beat. But in fact, Pervis, like the mouse, was alive when he left the operating room. The drug combination excited his lateral line system while inducing coma and paralysis in other ways. It's sick, McManus. I mean, really sick. But I have to admit, it's brilliant."

"So who is our perp?"

"A remarkably good neurochemist or neurologist, with extensive work in stupor and coma."

"A doctor—and one of the hospital stars, to boot. I knew Pear was trying to protect someone." McManus stood and held out his hand. "You're right, Doc. I owe you."

"We're not done, McManus. The killer left a thumbprint on the vial. It doesn't match that of Pervis's anesthesiologist, who yesterday conveniently died of an overdose, but it does match prints taken at the scene of the murder at the doctors' offices and—wait for it—at the restaurant on the West Side."

"How the fuck did you get that information before me?"

"No one else bothered to connect the crimes and look at the prints. They just sent them off to the databank. Fine sleuth that I am, I placed them all on screen at the same time, and I say they match. Don't quote me, but one killer committed all these crimes."

"Do me a favor. Don't advertise the fact that you found the fingerprint match prior to yours truly."

"My lips are sealed, Detective. It'll cost you dinner, though."

"I should arrest you for blackmail."

After the two men shook hands, Winter escorted McManus to the front door.

"One thing, Doc. If this guy is so smart, why is he leaving his prints all over the place?"

"For starters, I don't expect the prints to match any name in the databank. And maybe . . ."

"Maybe?"

"Maybe he just doesn't intend to get caught."

77

BASSIAS

THE BLOW WAS SO HARD it knocked her unconscious instantaneously. She hadn't seen or heard it coming—she hadn't heard a sound as she sat in the dark by the elevator bank. She came to in a well-lit room, lying on something cold and hard.

Her vision was blurred, her eyes bone dry. She wanted to rub them but as she tried to reach up, she found that her wrists were tightly strapped down. Her mouth was dry, too—it felt as though it were lined with cotton. The last time she'd had anything to eat or drink had been before she'd gotten trapped in the darkness—at least twelve hours ago, she figured, recalling the time on her cellphone before it died, although in fact she'd been on this table for another eight. She also felt very, very cold.

"Good afternoon, Ms. Bassias." The ethereal voice floated over her. "I trust you had a nice nap. I certainly did. I'm now refreshed and ready for the festivities."

"Whe—omm I?" The words struggled to form on her dry tongue and swollen, cracked, bleeding lips.

"A little tongue-tied? I wouldn't worry. No one else will ever hear, let alone see, you again."

Nausea welled up within her, but try as she might, she expelled nothing, producing only a series of dry heaves. She tried to look down at her body, but her head was strapped down, too, as were her torso and legs.

"Why?" was all she could muster.

"Why, indeed."

The voice continued to float around the room, which slowly came into focus. It looked to Maria like a laboratory but an old one, like those seen in old pictures from the medical center's infancy.

"Convenience, desire, need, lust. All happened to intersect at you."

Lust. The specter of violation caused Maria to spasm and flex in an attempt to break her bonds. She began to lapse into unconsciousness.

"It is useless to struggle. Men more than twice your size have been unable to break those bonds. You're uncomfortable, I know, but your discomfort is exactly my intention. It came to me in a flash of brilliance as I slept. Dehydration concentrates the factor, but it is pain that purifies it. The neural pathways for pain, you see, once excited, produce neurotransmitters. The more pain, therefore, the better the result. Yes, pain is the answer to the ultimate question. It has taken me 100 years of research and study, 100 years of trial and error, to reach this point. Longevity is based on the degree of pain inflicted prior to harvest, and you, my dear, will be my experiment to determine what a human can ultimately endure. Funny, isn't it? I wanted you originally for my enjoyment as a plaything. Now I get to have my cake and eat it, too."

The Doctor checked his watch, "It is almost time for the harvest." He paused, lifted his head, and listened. "We may be having company. How delightful. I haven't had a class to teach in a dog's age."

He turned and exited the room, leaving the unconscious girl to dehydrate further.

78

PEAR

THE BRICKWORK CAME DOWN IN two blows—Pear noted Dan was clearly enjoying the chance to do something other than open and close car doors. The mortar had been weakened by years of steam emanating from the room's valves. But, considering that the job had been done in haste, Pear was pleased to see, as he examined the area under the room's sole light, a bare 75-watt bulb, that the brick wall had until today remained intact. The thought that there were other entrances and exits to the ancient labyrinth beneath the medical center did not interest Pear at all because he already knew where to find his ghosts.

"Dan, clear the bricks away."

Dan's gloved hands began to work furiously at the pile, moving them to the side of the rusted metal door.

"What about the noise?" Murtaugh asked. "He might have heard us."

"I doubt it," said Pear. "It's quite a distance to that tunnel."

When the path was clear, Murtaugh grabbed the door handle and pulled. "It's locked. I don't remember it being . . ."

"I locked it before we bricked it over," said Pear. "Here is the only key." He pushed Murtaugh aside, inserted the skeleton key into the lock, and turned. There was a loud screech and clunk as the key did its job. Pear grabbed the door handle and pulled. Nothing happened. He tried again, then finally motioned Murtaugh and Dan to help. Still, there was no give to the door. It was obviously rusted into its frame.

"Fucking shit!" said Murtaugh. "We're screwed!"

"Patience, Murtaugh. Where you see problems, I see solutions." He picked up two large crowbars that had been leaning behind a steam valve just above the floor and handed one to each of his compatriots. "Use the sledge-hammer to jam them between the door and the frame, here and here," he said, pointing to spots high and low. "Then while I pull, you two pry."

Soon all three were sweating profusely. There was a large groan of distressed metal as the door begrudgingly opened.

Pear pulled out what to the others seemed an odd-looking flashlight and illuminated the dark entrance before them. The three looked in to see a small landing and a dark metal staircase heading down.

"Dan," he said, "go to my office. If Murtaugh and I are not back within the hour, call for help."

"But, sir . . ."

"No buts, this is something Murtaugh and I must do ourselves. If we don't return, there is a letter in the middle drawer of my desk that will explain everything to the authorities."

"I have him covered," said Murtaugh. "Go." Dan, though doubtful, exited toward the main hallway.

Pear motioned Murtaugh forward and handed him the flashlight.

"I hope this thing doesn't die on us," said the security chief.

"It's my otoscope, with lithium ion batteries. It'll last."

"We won't be checking eyes and ears tonight, Doc."

Murtaugh stepped onto the landing, which squealed under his weight. As he turned the light downward, the halo it created lent him a saintly glow. "I hope this doesn't collapse," he said as he took the first step down the rusted staircase. "It's deteriorated since the last time we used it."

Pear waited by the door at the top of the landing, expecting to hear Murtaugh's okay for him to proceed. As moments passed, he tensed. He placed his hand around the grip of the revolver sitting in his lab coat pocket. He slowly stepped onto the metal landing and heard it squeal once more.

"Murtaugh? Are you there?" He peered into the darkness below. *"Murtaugh?!"*

With no answer, he placed his finger on the trigger and started down the steps.

79

McManus

HE FLASHED HIS ID TO the guard as he bypassed the line of twelve people waiting to get in. "Hey, he jumped the line!" yelled a scrawny lab tech waiting to pass. "What is this?" The security guard simply rolled his eyes at the tech as McManus kept moving.

His first stop would be the top floor. He needed answers from Pear and Murtaugh and wasn't leaving without them. He neared the main elevator banks and realized he was limping. It's going to storm today, he thought. It always did when his knee hurt that much.

His movement hampered, he missed one elevator and had to wait two minutes for the next. When he got on, he was followed in by a group that included the lab tech. As McManus pressed the button for the executive floor, the geeky tech stared at him from across the cab. McManus noted he was about 5 foot 3, probably 130 pounds, with a small pot belly, a caved-in chest, and a bad set of severely coffee-stained teeth. McManus turned to face the front of the elevator.

"Hey, you!"

McManus continued to look forward as everyone turned to look at the angry technician yelling at him.

"I said, 'Hey, you!' You think you're hot shit?"

McManus couldn't believe what was happening. Was this guy overworked? Had he not taken his meds this morning? The detective tried to ignore the tirade, but everyone else on the elevator wanted no part of it and exited at the next floor. The door closed as the two squared off inside.

When the elevator door opened on the executive floor, McManus exited calmly, smiling at his stealthily executed plan. As the door closed, he heard the technician yell from inside, "I'll have your badge for this!" then plead, "You aren't going to leave me here, are you?" McManus figured it would take fifteen to twenty minutes until the guards found the guy inside the cab, then another thirty to find a key to unlock the handcuffs attaching him to the handrail.

As McManus walked the carpeted hallway to the CEO's lair, he passed the office of the orthopedic department. The door was open; the secretary, Peabody, was seated at her desk. She nodded in acknowledgment as she continued about her duties. McManus proceeded further down the hall and knocked on the door to Pear's suite. After receiving no answer, he opened the door to find the secretarial office dark and empty but the light to Pear's personal office beaming under the closed door.

McManus didn't bother to knock this time. When he entered, he found Pear's desk chair empty. Scanning the room, he saw neither Pear nor Murtaugh.

Suddenly he realized someone big was standing directly behind him.

80

DEMETRI

HE RAN DOWN THE STAIRCASE, two, sometimes three, steps at a time, his heart racing after reading that text message. He tried to call his dad. The building's steel structure prevented his getting much of a signal, but he did manage a voicemail telling him to get help.

Once on the main floor, he ran to the lobby. The overworked guard, faced with at least twenty people awaiting entrance to the building, told him to call security extension 2500 to report a missing person.

Demetri ran to the information desk, grabbed a house phone, and dialed security. He was put on hold.

"Shit!" He looked about the lobby and noted the entrance to the staircase going down. He took his laptop from his backpack, switched it on, then tapped the shortcut he'd labeled "ESMC." The schematics of the sublevels came onscreen instantly. He scrolled to the one for the main building.

He ran to the stairway door and started running down as fast as he could while balancing the laptop in his hand. He walked past the morgue, then past the kitchens, which were bustling with activity as the patients' meals were being prepared. He trotted by the central supply rooms, where dozens of hospital support personnel were moving carts full of equipment scheduled for delivery to the various floors.

The corridor then made a sharp right turn and narrowed slightly. Demetri stopped and consulted his laptop. Satisfied with his direction, he continued on, past the inpatient pharmacy windows. He expected to find a staircase on the left, about three-quarters of the way down the pharmacy hallway. The carts and crates filling the area made seeing the side doors difficult, but as he approached the area, he noted a door marked "Stairwell E to Subbasement."

The stairs were narrower than those of the main staircases but still well lit and maintained. He took them down to where they ended, at the subbasement level.

As he opened the door, the warmth and dampness hit him like an invisible wall—very different from the air-conditioned air in the rest of the hospital. He stepped into the hallway, realizing he had never been down here. He knew from the blueprints that this level connected many of the medical center's buildings and also housed the meat and potatoes of the complex: the heating, electrical, plumbing, and main engineering infrastructure. The corridor he entered was claustrophobic, despite its high ceiling, due to the myriad of large conduits and pipes dropped from the ceiling and hugging the walls. He had to duck occasionally to avoiding hitting a pipe or conduit with his already aching head. Industrial gas-vapor lights mounted on the walls lit the corridor brightly but cast many shadows and were blinding to look at directly. He noted two signs with arrows: one read "Main Engineering," with an arrow pointing to the right corridor; another pointed to the left toward the medical school. Checking the diagram on his laptop, he was able to pinpoint his location. About 50 yards to his left was where the stairwell to the even older sub-subbasement should have been, if it still existed. He walked in that direction, past a pair of engineers working on a steam fitting.

"Hey, you shouldn't be down here," said the gray-haired one. "It's only for staff."

Demetri turned, looked the engineer straight in the eye, and tried to drop his voice an octave. "I'm from the Department of Buildings." He pulled out one of his father's old NYPD IDs that he kept as a souvenir and flashed it briefly in the direction of the engineers. "We have an application for modification of the corridor."

"We're always the last to know," said the same engineer, who waved Demetri on. The entrance to the stairwell was supposed to be 10 yards ahead, but the pipes and conduits continued uninterrupted along the wall. Upon closer inspection, Demetri noted that behind the pipes was a patch of newer brick and mortar surrounded by older.

He sat on the floor to reevaluate his situation, knowing time was of the essence. Placing his computer in front of him, he began to scan the schematics looking for another stairwell nearby, but he couldn't find one. He then remembered the old paper plans that he'd hidden in his backpack and pulled them out. He spread them on the floor and started to examine them.

After a few minutes, he noticed a large shadow blocking the light of the lamp. As he looked up, he was momentarily blinded by the lights on the wall. When his vision returned, he saw a man standing over him with a long blunt object in his hand.

81

PEAR

"MURTAUGH," HE MURMURED TO HIMSELF, "where the hell are you?"

Near the bottom of the steps, Pear saw a bulb hanging from the ceiling and pulled the thin chain hanging with it. The darkness was immediately illuminated to a state of what could at best be described as near darkness. The ancient, feeble bulb sizzled and snapped.

"Murtaugh, where'd you go?" he yelled out.

In the silence broken only by the hiss of steam valves and the dripping of water, Pear heard Murtaugh's voice, coming from way off, down the corridor to the right. He scanned with his flashlight down the corridor and saw the ceiling and walls lined with ancient terra-cotta pipes, with decaying asbestos and thousands of cables wrapped in tar paper; the ceiling and walls closed in on Pear the moment he brought his light down to the floor in front of him, allowing the darkness to envelop everything else. He noted footsteps in the layers of old dust and knew that Murtaugh must be up ahead in the old coal room by now and that he needed to catch up fast. He did not relish being in this subterranean hellhole alone. Once he met up with Murtaugh, they would take the rail line corridor that led to the East River. Pear had found the Ripper there once and would catch him there again.

As he headed toward Murtaugh, his footsteps became progressively drowned out by the sound of running water inside the walls. It was probably raining above, he thought, and the city's sewers were doing their job. That must have been the reason Murtaugh was unable to hear him.

When he approached the coal room door, he found it ajar. The room was well lit by Murtaugh's flashlight. Pear entered, revolver in hand.

"Murtaugh. Why did you . . ."

Murtaugh responded in gurgles from the floor as blood poured from his throat and air slurped and spit from his trachea.

82

McManus

PIVOTING ON HIS BUM KNEE toward the big man behind him, he intended to elbow the guy in the face. Instead, McManus's knee buckled and he went down, assisted by a shove in the chest from the big man. The detective scrambled backward on his hands to give himself some distance but to no avail, as the man walked over and stood above him, hands on hips.

"That was a stupid move."

"Huh?" was all McManus could muster as he rubbed his knee and focused his eyes on the man. He was a large Asian bodybuilder, as far as McManus could tell, wearing a chauffeur's outfit covered in soot and dust, with a pair of contractor's work gloves in hand.

The dirty chauffeur reached down and helped McManus to his feet. "I said it was a stupid move. You should have stepped forward and away from me before turning. Especially if you have an unstable knee. Old ACL, huh?"

"Who are you?"

"Dan Lee, Dr. Pear's driver. I'd shake your hand, Detective McManus, but my hands are filthy from doing some demolition."

"I see that." McManus looked down at his own fine white shirt and silk tie with a big hand print across them. He tried to brush it off. "Where's Pear?"

"In the medical center."

"The medical center's a big place, Dan Lee. I need to speak to him now, before more murders are committed. A female worker is missing, and your boss has some answers."

"He is . . . unavailable at this time."

"Look, we can do this the easy way or—"

"—the hard way. Yeah, I'm a former PD. Look, whether I like it or not, I have my instructions from my boss. I'm to wait an hour since I last saw him before I summon help."

McManus looked at Lee, cocked his head, and smiled. "But former officer Lee, your watch is running a bit fast, is it not?"

"Now that you mention it, it appears an hour has passed."

"I thought so. Now tell me."

Lee spent a minute explaining what Pear and Murtaugh were doing. He also told McManus about the letter.

"Let's see it."

Lee walked over to the desk, followed by McManus limping. Lee opened the drawer and took out the sealed envelope.

McManus ripped it open and read. As panic showed up on his face, he turned to Lee. "Take me there now. If I'm right, we may already be too late."

As they turned for the door, Lee said, "I hope you can keep up, with that knee of yours."

"I'll keep up. Just move."

The two men ran down the hallway as the founders of the medical center looked down upon them from their perches on the walls.

83

DEMETRI

"CAN I HELP YOU?"

It was the gray-haired engineer standing over him with a large pipe wrench in hand. His compatriot was behind him. "You look lost."

"There's supposed to be a stairwell right here, going down," said Demetri, sounding despondent, "but I can't find it. I *must* find it!"

The younger engineer snickered. "Take it easy, kid. This is the lowest floor. Where did you say you're from?"

The older guy slapped the younger guy in the back of the head. The younger engineer winced in pain as he looked at his compatriot. "Hey . . ."

"There's another subbasement below this one," said the older one, "but it was closed off years ago. I've never seen it in the twenty years I'm here."

Demetri brightened. "I need to see that floor and its supports. Is there another way down?"

The engineer rolled his eyes and let out a big sigh. "No one has wanted to go down there in over thirty years, or so they tell me. It's rat-infested, with old diseases in the air. The chief engineer says there may be smallpox. And I was told it's mostly submerged because of the rising tides and global warming."

Demetri smiled. Global warming was true enough, but Manhattan was made of solid rock, so it was unlikely that the groundwater level was that high. And he doubted that smallpox persisted in the tunnels below, since the virus had been declared eradicated in 1980 and now existed only in the refrigerators of two labs, Plum Island in the U.S. and another equally desolate location in Siberia.

But Demetri kept his skepticism to himself. "Right. That's why it's so important that I get down there. Think. Any other way you can remember?"

The older engineer's eyebrow arched as he placed his wrench on the floor with a loud clunk. "Follow me," he said as he turned and walked down the hallway. He made a left then stopped in front of a door. He checked his innumerable keys, picked out a large brass one, and turned it in the lock. "This is a steam room that used to house a coal-burning boiler. There's a metal hatch on the floor that leads to a coal room. It's been closed for decades." The rusted door hinges protested loudly as the door slowly swung open. As the three men entered the room, the senior engineer flicked on the light switch. Demetri's forehead immediately began to bead with sweat.

"Hot enough for ya?" asked the none-too-bright junior worker.

His colleague flicked on a flashlight and scanned the floor, holding the light still after it found a 2-foot-wide metallic green protuberance. "There it is. Let's hope it still opens." They walked over to the item, which turned out to be a metal hatch similar to those on ships, with a central wheel to open it. The gray-haired man gave it a try, but the wheel wouldn't turn. He looked up at his coworker. "Well, what are you waiting for? Give me a hand." Trying together, they still couldn't make it budge. "Rusted shut," said the older man. He looked at Demetri. "Sorry, kid."

"How about using that big wrench you left out in the hall?"

"Good idea. I guess you Department of Buildings guys aren't all dumb, after all." The gray engineer nudged the younger one, who took off out the door and returned seconds later with the wrench on his shoulder. Demetri saw both engineers' uniforms soaking through with sweat. They wedged one end of the wrench between two spokes of the handle and pulled on the other end, hoping the longer lever arm would pry the wheel loose. Nothing.

"All right, let's put our backs into it," said the older man. There was a slight screech of metal, but then it was full stop again.

"Hey, kid, this handle is long enough for three."

Demetri walked over and stood opposite the two engineers.

"We'll pull from this side, and you push from that side," said the senior man. "Ready? One, two, three, now!"

Just at the point of their giving up, a squeal of metal rang up from the floor as the wheel began to move in earnest.

"That's it, kid. Keep going." Soon the wheel was moving, and the locking bars were retracting. After the two engineers removed the wrench, Demetri pulled up on the hatch. It resisted at first then gave suddenly, causing Demetri to fall back onto his rear as the engineers burst out in laughter. Demetri crawled over to the edge and looked down. It was a deep, dark hole. Demetri hated deep, dark holes.

"What's the matter, kid? Scared of the dark?"

"N-no. I have my flashlight, I can take it from here."

"You sure you're okay?"

"I'm fine. I have the blueprints to guide me." He pulled them out of his pack.

"These buildings have been built and rebuilt so many times I hope you have the right ones," said the older engineer. "Good luck, kid." The two men exited, leaving Demetri alone above the hole.

Demetri pointed his flashlight down. The narrow beam reflected off the cast-iron ladder leading to the room below. The room's floor looked rough. It took a moment for Demetri to figure out that it was covered with old coal. He leaned into the hole with his light and scanned the room. It was cavernous, with coal everywhere. And it was black, completely black.

Demetri stepped into the hatch, placing his right foot on the ladder. There was a slight groan as the age-old metal adjusted to the weight. He placed his flashlight in his mouth and started down. At the bottom, his foot landed on some coal, which gave way with a fine crunch, followed by the same as his other foot planted. Switching the flashlight to his hand, he looked around. He saw dozens of piles of coal, most from one to 10 feet high, although in one corner, the pile reached the ceiling, about 20 feet up. The beam of his light reflected the fine dust floating in the room, the cause of black lung in decades past, before modern filtering equipment, now but a memory for all except the few men who work the coal mines of middle America and for their fathers, forced by the disease into early retirement.

He scanned the far reaches of the room but, with everything black, had trouble finding the doors. To his left, he saw the light reflect off some metal on the floor; he realized it was a set of rails that must have been used for carts transporting the coal from its delivery site at the river. He walked up to the rails and followed them as they curved around a pile of coal. He bumped into a pair of wooden swing doors that squeaked as he pushed through them. It was then that Demetri noted the complete silence in the hallways leading from the coal room—those creaking doors had announced his arrival to anyone within earshot. He threw his beam of light along the rails, noting their continuation as far as his eye could see, apparently making a slow descent, probably toward the river. Since he saw no other hall or tunnel, he figured he would follow the railway as far as possible. He noted an occasional rat at the periphery of his beam, but few of the rodents lingered, preferring the darkness. Thank God for that, he thought.

As he walked, he realized there were multiple alcoves but none had a door or passageway to any other area. After a few minutes of slow progress, Demetri was startled by a rumble overhead. It must be the Lexington Avenue subway, he thought as his flashlight beam was dimmed momentarily in the dust stirred by the passing train. He now knew he was headed east toward the river. He wiped his forehead of what he thought was sweat but was in fact, he realized when he shined his light above, muddy water dripping from drainpipes. Looking back at the rails, he noticed a flowing stream of water heading between them in an easterly direction. He started to grow concerned about the water's effect on his footing in the darkness.

Demetri soldiered on as the tunnel continued a slow downward descent, and the silence he'd noted earlier was replaced by the whoosh of an increasingly large flow of water and the scurry of rats seeking higher ground. Soon, as the water torrent increased, Demetri knew it was raining and realized the white noise of the running water eliminated any possibility of his hearing anything coming his way.

His light began to dart left and right and front to back as fear filled his mind and cold water filled his shoes. He was no longer sure of what he was down here for, other than some fool kid's quest for the truth and maybe an infatuation with a pretty girl. He began to walk faster as he heard splashing behind him. Was it just the flow of the water, or did it signify footsteps? Was someone following him? Was it the murderer?

Demetri wasn't sure and wasn't about to hang around to find out. He began an all-out run toward the river, hoping Maria would be down that tunnel.

84

NATHAN

HE PICKED UP THE PHONE. "Bigelow? I just got a call from a little bird in building services by the name of Lombardi, who is now on my payroll. It appears the game is afoot in the subbasement. Apparently Pear and that ass Murtaugh are using a sledge hammer and crowbars for a little project down there. Care to have a look with me?"

"Meet you at the main entrance in ten minutes."

HE GRABBED BIGELOW BY THE arm, pulling the reporter under the awning out of the rain.

"All right, Warren. What gives in the basement?"

Nathan grinned as they entered the main hallway. "It's not the basement, it's the subbasement, and even lower. Apparently Pear and Murtaugh have been doing some excavating downstairs in search of the . . ."

"The Holy Grail?"

"No. A Pulitzer for you and a tenured full professorship for me." Nathan's eyes were wild as he was gesticulating furiously. "If we uncover what they are up to and how it ties in to the murders, you'll have the story of the year, and the medical center, to keep me happy, will beg me to accept an appointment—maybe even as department chairman.

"Are you okay, Warren? You sure you haven't been snorting something?"

"There's a gold mine down there, Jack. Trust me."

Nathan practically pulled Bigelow down the staircase. "It's two flights down. And apparently they've taken a staircase that goes even lower." As they neared their destination, Nathan turned and handed Bigelow a small flashlight.

"You'll need one of these."

"Thanks. Uhh, so what's . . ."

"There it is!" Nathan was bouncing like a ping-pong ball. He entered a room to find a pile of rubble in front of a door that was ajar.

"Well, whaddya know? Warren, you may be onto something."

"Let's go!" The giddy doctor walked through the doorway and found a staircase. He started clambering down. Bigelow shrugged, turned on his flashlight, and followed.

At the bottom of the staircase, Bigelow looked up at the hanging light-bulb. "Looks turn of the century to me." They both scanned the maze of pipes and hallways, "Which way from here?" said the reporter.

Nathan put his index finger over his mouth. "Shhhh!" He stood still and listened. Bigelow froze and listened as well. Hissing and electrical buzzing were all they heard. Occasionally a valve would snap open then close. In the distance, there was an occasional rumble.

"I think Grand Central is that way," said Nathan, pointing to his left. "And Lexington Avenue is that way," he said, pointing to his right.

"So which way do we go, Sherlock?"

"Elementary, my dear Watson, to the right."

"Because?"

"Lombardi overheard Pear and Murtaugh mention a coal room. Look." He shined his flashlight on an old fading sign to his right: "Coal Room."

Nathan began to walk quickly with Bigelow close behind. As they approached a door, Nathan exclaimed, "This is it! And now for the unveiling."

He pushed the door open, stepped aside, and looked at Bigelow, who shivered then passed out. Nathan turned to look in the room and found Murtaugh—bloody, undoubtedly dead—face up on the floor. Nathan began to feel nauseated but steadied himself. He looked around the room and found no one else. But he did see something on the floor next to Murtaugh's body: two lit flashlights. One of them was odd-looking. He picked up: it was a Welch Allyn light source.

"Holy fucking shit!"

85

McManus

MCMANUS AND LEE ENTERED THE subbasement from the elevator at a full run. They nearly knocked down Lombardi, who was walking in the opposite direction. Lombardi directed them to the door leading to the coal room then continued on his way.

McManus entered the room to find rubble strewn all over. "You let your boss go down there?" he asked Dan Lee.

"He had Murtaugh with him."

"Murtaugh? Then Pear is fucked for sure." McManus pulled out his Sure-fire light and his Glock as he entered the staircase. Lee followed, taking his licensed Heckler & Koch P7 from his waistband. Upon reaching the landing, they both assumed standard operating procedure in covering the area. Once the area was secured, they both stopped to look and listen.

"Which way?" Lee whispered.

McManus pointed his light down to the right, illuminating multiple footprints in the dust on the floor. "Let's go," he said, as quietly as possible. They proceeded in methodical fashion toward the coal room. Just ahead, McManus noted a body on the floor, the legs of which were keeping the doors slightly ajar. McManus doused his light as they approached, weapons at the ready position. There was a faint light cast from inside the doors.

McManus approached the body. It was Bigelow! The detective checked for a pulse and found one. Peering inside the door, he saw a man stooping over another body—and holding a bright shiny object. As McManus readied himself for the attack he motioned for Lee to grab and swing the door open.

Lee grabbed the door with his unarmed hand and swung it open abruptly. Crouched in an isosceles stance, McManus raised his weapon as his finger curled over the trigger. The figure over the body quickly stood and turned to face him, shining a bright light in McManus's eyes.

Temporarily blinded, McManus reflexively fired off two quick rounds.

86

MAKROPOLIS

THE PELLETS OF RAIN WERE drumming on the top of the Jeep as he pulled in front of the emergency room. He had not felt the prickles earlier in the day, but now, along with the bad weather, they hit him hard.

Before exiting the car, he racked the slide of his Kahr to chamber a round, then removed the clip and replaced it with a full one. He attached the halo sight atop his gun then zeroed the sight before placing the gun in his pocket. The sight was a bit over the top for such a small gun, but the halo made dark and close-quarters gunfighting much easier. He looked out the car window to see the wind-driven rain pounding the glass at the emergency entrance. As he dashed from the car, the rain soaked him and the wind howled. The glass doors hesitated a second before opening; once he was inside, the doors closed to lock the storm out.

A guard approached him. "You can't park your vehicle there."

Makropolis held up his police ID, holding his finger over the word retired. "Oh, sorry."

"That's okay, son. Just tell me how I can get to the main hospital."

The guard told him to follow the green line on the floor. With his soaked trousers dripping onto his workboots, Makropolis left a trail of wet shoe-prints on the floor as he walked. Just as he passed through the double doors into the main hospital, he heard "Hey, Mr. Makropolis!" from behind. He turned and saw a young doctor. He looked familiar.

"I'm Thomas Carter," said the doctor, shaking Michael's hand, "a friend of your son's. We met briefly the other night."

"That night was kind of foggy for me."

"Yeah, I guess it was. I'm here looking for my girlfriend, Beth, an ER nurse. She hasn't answered her calls since last night. Are you looking for Demetri?"

"Have you seen him?"

"He was heading down to the basement on some kind of research. He's been obsessed with the Pervis murder."

"Show me."

Carter led Makropolis to the main lobby and then down the stairs. "He was heading down here earlier today before I stuck him in the OR for a few hours to fix a leg. I'll bet he got downstairs less than a half hour ago." Once they were in the basement, Carter looked around. "I'm not sure where he would have gone from here. The morgue? You know, return to the scene of the crime?"

Makropolis shook his head. "No, we discussed it last night. Pervis's body was stolen from the morgue and later placed in the anatomy lab—a perverted joke, apparently. But the deed was probably done elsewhere, although not far from the anatomy lab, I suspect—most psychopaths get lazy when they dispose of their bodies."

Carter grimaced. "Sorry I asked. The anatomy lab is this way." They headed past the kitchens and entered the corridor to the school. They stopped at an intersection.

"We're under the medical school," said Carter. "Beyond that, all I know is that from here, it gets complicated."

Makropolis was oblivious to Carter's uncertainty. His face and chin set as his brain started to review the blueprints he'd gone over the other night with his son. Carter, unsure whether to leave or stay, stood there waiting. After a few moments, Makropolis said only, "This way."

They took the corridor facing them. After a few turns, it became clear to Carter that his friend's father was running on pure instinct. They passed two engineers, who directed them down the hallway.

Makropolis stopped. "It's one of these doors."

"Which one?" said Carter, as they both tried turning various doorknobs.

Makropolis then halted at one of the doors. "This one," he said, facing a closed door.

"The sign says it's a steam room."

"How many steam rooms have a huge pipe wrench outside their door and dirt trailing out of them?"

Makropolis tried the door. It was locked.

"I can call security for the key," said Carter.

"I have the key," said Makropolis, as he hefted the wrench and started to swing it as a sledgehammer.

87

Bassias

SHE AWOKE. HAD SHE SLEPT minutes or hours? One thing she was sure of was her extreme thirst. Her lips were crusted, and when she moved them, the taste of blood immediately became apparent. The room itself now felt quite warm, even though, as she realized, she was nearly naked. She felt completely vulnerable and very, very scared.

Suddenly she heard a door open.

"We have a guest." It was *him.* "No, not just a guest but a student of the fine art of medicine."

She tried to look around, but her head was immobilized. Then she cringed as the battered face of an unconscious man was shoved in front of her eyes. Blood dripped from the man's nostril onto Maria's cheek and mouth. The salty taste of his blood mingled with that of her own. The Doctor quickly pulled his prize back from the table.

"Don't you recognize your boss, my sweet, the venerable Dr. Fredrick Pear, Physician in Chief and CEO of this grand medical complex around us? But of course you do."

Maria realized it was Pear and started to retch from the taste of bile in the back of her throat.

"Leaves you speechless, Maria, my darling? I am sure you are honored to be the first of my specimens to be harvested in front of a live medical audience. Such a shame he will not live to tell the rest of the medical profession about my success at prolonging life. Well, I can always send a monograph to *Lancet* or the *New England Journal* when I think they are ready."

Arching her eyes and head as much as possible, Maria could see some of what was happening. The Doctor was binding the unconscious Pear's arms to his body with duct tape. He then placed Pear on a counter across from the table to which she was strapped, then propped him up to a sitting position, resting his back against a set of shelves packed with specimen jars holding all sorts of organs. The Doctor bound Pear's feet then placed a loop of rope around Pear's neck. The rope hung from what looked like a meat hook on the ceiling. Clearly, if Pear struggled or slipped off the counter he would hang himself.

"There. That will keep you out of trouble, Herr Professor, yet still in full view of the operation."

Moments later what seemed like two firecrackers resounded from the doorway through which the Doctor had just entered with Pear. The Doctor's cheerful face gave way to a menacing frown as he turned toward the door.

"It would appear we are to have more guests, my dear. Let us see if they are in the mood to watch as well. But then, perhaps it would be better to eliminate them. Too many guests spoil the broth, as it were. Wouldn't you agree?"

As he spoke, the Doctor ran his slender but strong hand along Maria's naked torso. She tried to pull away but was tied fast. His hand ran down from her breast to her abdomen and down to her pubic area. As his fingers slipped under her still present panties, Maria arched her back and tried to scream for help, but her dry vocal cords and swollen tongue made it impossible to produce a sound. As his hand began to probe, the girl tried to cry, but the contortions of her face simply cracked her parched lips further, the taste of blood again in her mouth. She knew it was futile to fight.

"A bit dry down there, my love? Nothing I can't fix." He continued to grope her genitals. "And a virgin! A rarity these days. Soon you will be begging me to end your life, but, alas, you must bear the burden of your femininity to the very last second." He ripped the panties off in one powerful yank. But then he stopped and listened.

Abruptly, the Doctor pulled his hand away. "I have some unfinished business to attend to. It will take only a few minutes, and then I shall return to finish you."

And he was gone.

88

MAKROPOLIS

THE WRENCH-AS-SLEDGEHAMMER DID ITS work, blowing the door inward to lean top end first. Makropolis then took a step back and slammed his body into the door, sending it to the floor of the dark room with a loud thud. As he was about to enter, a man shouted from down the corridor.

"Hey, what are you guys doing down there?" It was the silver-haired engineer.

Makropolis eyed the engineer, flashed his badge for a split second, then entered the room. Carter, just behind him, hesitated a second longer, then smiled at the engineer. The engineer yelled back to his coworker, "More from the Department of Buildings."

A large arm reached out of the open doorway, grabbed Carter by the arm, and yanked him in as the engineer turned away.

After adjusting to the dark interior, Carter and Makropolis began to search. Carter soon eyed the open hatch. "This way!" he said as he pointed it out to Makropolis, who seconds later was down through the opening, sliding down the ladder like a fireman on a pole. Carter eyed the hatch and the soot all over and then looked at his white doctor's coat and his semiprecious khakis and loafers.

He remained frozen until Makropolis popped back up. "Coming?"

"I, ah, am a bit . . ."

"Look, Carter, if you're not going to come with me, at least make yourself useful and call 911. I need backup."

"Got it. I'll call right now." Before Carter could turn, Makropolis had already slid back down and was searching the floor for evidence of Demetri's movements.

He passed a door and found the rail line. He noted the disturbed soot on the rail ties—it led east. He started to run in that direction, kicking rats out of the way as he went. Soon his footsteps were joined by splashing as his feet began to hit running water. He noted the trickling of water down the walls of the tunnel and the increasing flurry of rats. Makropolis paused a moment as the overhead rumblings of a subway train passed, then he continued east. He came to a track switch and a bifurcation of the rails, with one set breaking off and cutting back west, toward the medical center's Park Avenue buildings into a separate tunnel. He knelt to look at the ties. He saw no footsteps to the west but plenty of activity east. Just as he rose to renew his pursuit of Demetri, he heard the echo of shots ring out. They were coming from the west, in the tunnel he hadn't come from. He felt prickles on the back of his neck.

East or west? Someone—maybe Demetri—was in obvious trouble back toward the medical center. Shots were fired; enough said. Makropolis turned and headed west. As his flashlight illuminated the tunnel, he pulled out his Kahr. He kept it in the low ready position, this time with his finger off the trigger.

89

McManus

IT TOOK A FEW SECONDS for the temporary blindness from the muzzle flash to go away, and a few seconds longer to be rid of the temporary deafness from the gunshot echoing in the small space. By then, McManus realized he'd made a terrible mistake. The man he shot was holding a flashlight in his hand. He was still standing and yelling in McManus's direction.

". . . motherfucking idiot! I'm gonna sue you and the city! You'll be my doorman for the rest of your fucking life if you ever fucking get out of fucking jail!"

It was Nathan. McManus soon realized he'd missed or, at least, hadn't hit any vital parts of the man's body.

"Look at my fucking jacket! Look at that hole and the burn marks! Do you know what this jacket cost me?" He lifted the jacket edge toward his flashlight to examine it.

"Ten bucks, tops," said McManus as he holstered his weapon. "It's a Chinese-made lab coat."

Bigelow, lying behind McManus and Lee, came to and slowly propped up his head and shoulders. "What happened?"

"You wimp," said Nathan. "You passed out at the sight of this body here. And don't tell me you didn't witness this imbecile of a detective shoot at me."

"Sorry," said the reporter, rising unsteadily to his feet. "Who's that on the floor?"

Nathan turned and knelt at the side of the body. "It's Murtaugh." Not wanting to go near the man's bloodied neck, he felt for a pulse at the wrist. After a few seconds, he looked up at the threesome surrounding him. "There's a pulse, but it's shallow. He's fading fast. He needs blood and fluids and needs to be gotten to an OR. Otherwise he'll be dead in minutes."

They heard an agonal gurgle from Murtaugh's neck. Nathan stood and grabbed the silk handkerchief from McManus's breast pocket. "I need this." He knelt again and applied pressure to parts of the neck. "I repeat: we need help fast."

McManus checked his phone. "There's no cell service down here. Someone needs to go upstairs."

"You're Pear's driver, aren't you?" said Nathan. "Go to the ER. Bring some EMTs and nurses down here with a crash cart and a stretcher. And tell them to make sure the trauma room is ready."

"But Dr. Pear was down here with Murtaugh. I need to find him."

"No, what you need to do is get help immediately, or this guy is dead. Bigelow, you stay with me. Detective, you can go look for Pear. But this time, look before you shoot."

McManus opened his mouth to object but knew Nathan had a point. He nodded to Lee to get moving. Lee hesitated a moment then took off back the way they came.

Nathan called to Bigelow. "Raise his feet. That will send blood down to the body and head." Bigelow did as instructed. Nathan felt Murtaugh's pulse; it was minimally stronger. "Good. Hold them there. Detective, why don't you stop standing there looking like an alcoholic window-shopping at a liquor store and go find that fat cat Pear?"

McManus was about to object again but again stopped himself. He'd never seen Nathan act this professional. "Shout if you need me back here" was all he said.

Nathan looked up at the detective, nodded, and smiled ever so slightly, then turned a serious face back to his patient. He placed his fingers in the gash and cleared a large clot from the trachea.

McManus scanned the room with his flashlight and saw disrupted layers of soot on the floor leading away down the corridor. He took out his Glock again and held it in the low ready position as he followed the trail.

90

DEMETRI

AFTER A FEW MINUTES OF running, Demetri stopped to listen. He heard the flowing and dripping of water, the squeaking of rats, and his own panting, but the sound of someone possibly following him had stopped.

His heart pounded and his legs ached ferociously. He was scared as he had never been before in his sheltered life. Demetri swore he heard what sounded like gunfire back where he'd come from; he had no desire to go back and investigate. He felt he would find the girl further east.

He began his easterly trek again. He passed several alcoves to either side, but none led anywhere. They appeared to be places for men to step aside as trains of coal carts went by. He passed several more alcoves, careful to ensure there was no one in them who could do him harm. He finally passed an alcove that looked deeper than usual, at least 20 feet deep and 10 feet wide and high, and covered by roots from trees above. His light revealed large roots popping through the bricks of the ceiling and walls, making the alcove narrow toward its back, completely grown over. Satisfied that no one appeared to be hiding there, he began to continue east but a metallic flash from the alcove's vegetation caught his eye. He turned back to check it out.

Entering the alcove, he noted that the floor was dry, and worn from years of use. He ducked under a big clump of roots then crawled over another. The alcove was even deeper than it had seemed at first glance, and very well camouflaged. He shone his light on the far wall and saw a door. He stood up in front of the door, ducking so as not to hit his head on the low-hanging roots. The door was old, probably cast-iron, with huge hinges. It might have been at least 6 inches thick. Then the glint of brass caught Demetri's attention again. It was a lock—and it was new, incongruous with the aged door. Demetri pulled out his keys from his pocket and, although he doubted it would open the lock, figured he had nothing to lose. He took the key to his medical school locker and tried to place it in the lock with no luck. He then tried the key to his room. It slid in two-thirds of the way. He tried to turn it.

Snap! The key had broken in the lock. "Shit!" He tried to pull it out but there wasn't enough sticking out for him to get a good grip on. "Probably a utility room," he said to himself. He walked back out to the rail corridor and resumed his journey east. His head was now getting soaked by the water dripping overhead.

Chinese water torture, he thought. The water was cold and muddy gray. It smelled of the city's refuse, and Demetri was soaked to the bone with it. He began to shiver.

Time was running out, he feared. Maria was somewhere down here, and if he didn't find her soon, she would probably wind up another victim. He vowed that, once he got to the end of the corridor, he would turn back and do another search. If he saved her, he vowed to give up on this detective stuff. Becoming a doctor was hard enough.

91

THE DOCTOR

IT'S GETTING CROWDED DOWN HERE, the Doctor thought to himself as he approached the coal room. He knew from the voices and smells that at least four others were in the room. He weighed his options. Killing them all risked bringing the entire NYPD down here, which would mean discovery of his labs and possibly his home. He could not take that chance. Such exposure would require his moving to another city or even another country. He had more than enough funds to move a hundred times if need be, but he'd been comfortable in New York since he'd moved here to enter medical school in 1891.

When he'd received his letter of acceptance to the school, he was overjoyed that he was leaving the dull confines of his home in Chicago and the small commuter college he'd spent four years attending. He had nothing to lure him back to Illinois. He'd had no siblings. His father died of the flu in 1897, and his mother withered away in a nursing home from Alzheimer's, eventually dying in 1903 of sepsis due to a bed sore. Once he completed his internship, he turned his attentions to research and the study of aging and neuroanatomy, which got him appointed to the medical school's faculty. His obsession with aging soon led to his isolation from the mainstream faculty, but his research, which included experimentation on himself, led to success, albeit at the cost of his sanity's being forever altered. The Doctor considered it a reasonable trade, especially since the added physical and mental abilities of his new persona more than offset the negatives, which his mind perceived but did not object to. He knew that psychotics are often aware that they have some type of mental illness and that some try futile attempts at self-treatment with alcohol or narcotics. The Doctor, on the other hand, was content to enter cycles of maniacal depravity to prolong his life. No, not just content—he relished those cycles.

In light of the intruders present, the Doctor came to a decision: it was best that they find no trace of him and his human lab rats; a harvest would have to wait for another day. He would dispose of the girl in the river and would leave Pear in the tunnel, to be found with a "self-inflicted" gunshot wound to the head. In the meantime, he'd lock down and camouflage the entrance to his labs as he had done in the past. A well-placed suicide note on Pear's computer outlining the CEO's sad involvement in a cult of medical satanists, Pear being the last, should end the story. In the maze of the tunnels and storage rooms, his labs would never be found, even if the police were right in front of them.

Despite the darkness of the tunnel, he saw as well as heard an officer begin his walk toward the coal-tunnel entrance. Lithe as a cat, the Doctor turned and was gone in an instant, back toward his labs to initiate his plan. He would have plenty of time to complete his tasks.

As he strode towards the laboratory, he became increasingly aware of the rain at street level. The white noise created by the water rushing into drains and sewers and into the subterranean tunnels was interfering more and more with his auditory sense. His visual acuity in the dark, however, was still spectacular. As was his sense of smell. The subtle change in the tunnel breezes told him the East River entrance was now closed and under water, probably due to the storm surge up the river. No matter, he thought. I'll place the girl's body into the water after I paralyze her, and it will go out with the tide. An unfortunate drowning death due to the storm, tomorrow's papers would read.

Then he would cuddle up next to the fireplace with a nice book and ride out the storm in his humble abode.

92

PEAR

HE VOMITED ON HIMSELF AS he awoke, seated on what felt like a counter. His vision out of his left eye was fuzzy and his cheek ached, both no doubt due to the blow he'd taken earlier to that side of his head. As his right eye began to focus, he saw a body lying before him. It was a naked woman, beautiful, strapped to a stainless steel table. Upon closer inspection, it was an autopsy table specially configured with straps and locking blocks; the poor woman's head was held in a viselike device. He lifted his head and looked around the room. It was clearly a laboratory of some type, with multiple anatomic specimens in jars and an entire counter covered with surgical instruments. There was an electron microscope at the far end of the lab. Pear tried to move but found himself bound and immobile.

"Miss?" he whispered. With no response he repeated, more loudly, "Miss? Are you all right?"

Bassias opened her dry eyes. "Dr. Pear?" She spoke in a bare whisper, the most she could manage through her dry mouth and throat. "Please . . . get me . . . out of here. He's . . . a maniac." She began to cry, although she produced barely any tears.

"Who are you?"

Her crying stopped for the moment. "Maria Bassias . . . Medical Records Department."

"I'm sorry I let this happen to you," Pear responded. "But help is on the way."

"Too late to save either of you, however." It was the Doctor, storming through the door. Maria started to cry again, convulsing against her bonds.

The Doctor walked over to the counter opposite Pear and picked up a syringe. He cleared the air from it, letting the fluid spritz his two captives. "We wouldn't want either of you to die from an air embolus, would we?"

He walked over to Maria's side and placed the needle of the syringe into the IV hep lock in her arm. After the Doctor had injected half the syringe, Pear noted that her crying in the room had stopped.

"You monster. I should have let Murtaugh kill you back then."

"But Dr. Pear, I did die. And then I was reborn. You see, neither a little lead bullet nor the East River can kill me. I have been dying and reviving since this venerable medical institution was in its infancy."

Pear grimaced. Only now did he begin to understand who and what this man really was.

"Don't fret, Dr. Pear. She is only immobilized. She can see, hear, and feel everything. Not quite the condition that I imposed on that lump of lard Pervis. With him, I had to fool your best anesthetists and slow the heart rate to next-to-nothing. No need to deceive you now, is there, Dr. Pear? No, I want you to be aware of the medical miracles that I perform. Your mind will be fully awake, and your senses will be fully aware, but you will be trapped in a body fully paralyzed. A human prison, in other words. I know how impressed you are by groundbreaking research. Mine is well documented in these labs. Over 100 years of meticulous work to perfect the elixir of life!" The Doctor bowed several times to an imagined audience. He then turned and approached Pear. "You are next, my good friend. My apologies for not using sterile technique, but I am sure you understand, under the circumstances." The Doctor seized Pear's left arm as Pear struggled in vain to free himself from the maniac's powerful grip. "Now, now, Dr. Pear, you are not afraid of a little needle, are you?"

Pear felt a pinprick in his arm followed by some burning. The Doctor smiled at Pear, who started to spasm mildly, his arm and facial muscles literally rippling under the skin. Then his body relaxed completely.

"That's better. Now, let us begin." The Doctor turned and unbuckled the straps holding down Maria. "Such a shame I don't have time to ravish you before I drown you, my love. But such is the schedule of a busy doctor these days. Managed care has made our lives miserable." He began to whistle a ditty from the Gay Nineties—"Charge of the Roosevelt Riders," a popular war tune of the time.

The Doctor then turned to Pear. He removed the revolver from Pear's pocket and placed it against the helpless CEO's swollen cheek. "This will make quite a mess, so we'll do it in the tunnel." He pocketed the weapon, then with one hand grabbed Pear under his arm and lifted him off the hook. Tossing the limp body over his right shoulder, he said, "My friend, you've gained some weight since we last met face to face." He then turned back to Bassias, grabbed her by the hair, yanked her upright, and threw her over his left shoulder. "We won't be using the coal cart today, boys and girls. We don't want to create much of a racket, let alone get Dr. Pear's white lab coat any dirtier than it already is."

After turning out the lights, the Doctor exited the self-locking door of the lab. With his two bundles on his shoulders, he began to trot eastward, toward the river.

Pear's head faced downward as he bounced along, feeling his guts pound against the maniac's clavicle and acromion. He was powerless to say or do anything, although he could still move his eyes, which slowly became accustomed to the dark. The blackness was almost absolute, lessened only by an occasional diffuse gray glimmer from overhead, in all likelihood from shafts to the street level.

The bouncing had continued for several minutes when Pear noticed a silver and gold Mont Blanc pen begin to slip from his lab coat's breast pocket. He was unable to help it fall, but after a few moments, it dropped onto a rail tie. If Pear could have smiled, he would have, hoping the pen would lead Lee and any other rescuers in this direction.

Suddenly the bouncing stopped, and Pear felt himself being swung around as the Doctor halted then turned and took a few steps back. Without putting down either of his loads, he bent forward and picked up the pen.

"Mont Blanc," the Doctor said. "Can't leave such a fine writing instrument lying around. You never know who might pick it up."

The Doctor stood and spun and headed east again. Pear's face was still, but inside he wept.

93

McManus

USING HIS SUREFIRE FLASHLIGHT, HE followed the disrupted dust on the floor of the coal room. Judging from the streaks adjacent to the footprints, it appeared someone was being dragged.

Once out of the coal room, the maze of dark corridors and tunnels increased his disorientation, as did the sounds of the subway and running water. As he passed under a rumbling overhead train, he noted the foot trail had disappeared due to the dripping water muddying the floor.

"Shit." *Where to now?* He flashed his light down a corridor to his left. It was dark and devoid of any signs of recent passing. He looked down the corridor to his right. He noticed some footsteps and followed them for a short distance until he found himself standing on a metal grate overlooking a torrent of sewer water. It was flowing at great speed, no doubt toward the river, carrying with it the flotsam and jetsam of New York City's inhabitants.

He reversed his steps and was back on the tracks of the coal rail. He felt he had no alternative but to follow the rails east. Perhaps the murderer, with Pear in tow, was headed for the river. McManus had found that even poorly conditioned psychopaths can perform amazing physical feats.

McManus knew he was at most minutes behind the perpetrator and was going to get him one way or the other. He quickened his pace, but as side alcoves and corridors appeared, he systematically cleared those areas with flashlight and gun in hand. His knee was aching at a 10 out of 10 with every step, but it was adrenaline that kept him moving.

94

MORTIMER

HE PASSED BY DR. PEAR'S office and found it open but empty. So much the better: he was in no mood to chitchat with that angry man. This last week saw Mortimer's usually effusive demeanor deteriorate in a downward spiral, and the murders just added to the depression. He had never felt so down in all his life as he did at that moment. He was a failure, as an orthopedic surgeon, as chief of his department, and as a husband and father. He felt that now to his very soul. After downing a few drinks in his office, he felt even more somber, so much so that he became lethargic, moving slowly and with great effort.

The thick carpeting in the main hall slowed his footsteps even more as he headed for the exit; the hospital and departmental chiefs mounted on the wall looked down upon him as he padded by, the weight of responsibility on his shoulders palpably crushing him to the floor. As he passed Louis Woodrow Stinton II, the enigmatic but powerful chief of surgery at the medical center in the 1950s, Mortimer could stand it no longer. He made an about face and headed back toward Pear's office then straight for the executive private elevator. The cab was not on the floor, just as he had hoped.

He looked down the shaft through the brass gate. He took a deep breath and placed his hand on the gate door and pulled to find it locked. He examined the mechanism and saw the trip switch required to unlock it—it was behind the gate, out of reach of his fingers. He took his bandage shears from his lab coat and used it to reach in and depress the switch.

Mortimer swung the gate open and peered into the depths of the elevator shaft. Pear will be really annoyed, he thought, when he finds his hand-carved elevator cab damaged. Mortimer smiled as he stepped closer to the edge.

Suddenly a hand appeared over his shoulder.

95

Makropolis

AS HE HEADED WEST, HE encountered several side tunnels. He followed a number of them—all dead ends. After his fourth detour, he turned back to the main coal tunnel and decided he would not stray off course but rather move directly west. Makropolis was now racing west, gun in hand.

After a few moments, he stopped and listened. The din of machine and nature conspired against him; he could not tell which way to go. With every step west, the prickles grew more insistent. He knelt and looked at the floor. There was water between the rails, but the ties themselves were still dry in spots. He looked at several until he found what he was looking for: a fresh shoeprint, adult male, probably an Italian leather sole, heading east.

He immediately turned and began to run in the shoeprint's direction.

96

THE DOCTOR

AS HE APPROACHED THE ENTRANCE to his abode, he decided to deposit Pear in one of the shallow alcoves opposite.

"I will return to finalize your suicide in a few minutes, my dear old friend. No one will bother you here." He tossed Pear like a ragdoll into the dark alcove. Pear landed on his hip with a sickening snap and crunch. Unable to scream or yell, Pear passed out.

The Doctor smiled. His revised plan was simple: dispose of the girl in the pool created by the storm's high tide. There she would drown before being swept away with the receding tide of the estuary called the East River; return and kill the fat man; disappear into his nearby home before the intruders arrive. He'd be listening to Sibelius on his Krell/Wilson X-2 audio system while the police searched for him in vain.

The Doctor readjusted Maria on his shoulder and started east again. As he approached the entrance to his home, he had a change of heart. "Perhaps my dear, we can have a tête-à-tête in my little domicile." He pulled her under the massive roots. When he approached his well-concealed door, he noted a disturbance in the area and smelled that Makropolis boy. When his key wouldn't enter the lock, he realized what had happened. "Well, Ms. Bassias, back to Plan A."

He began his lope toward the river with Bassias still on his shoulder. "Such a shame I can't show you my home, my dear. It is quite beautiful, particularly a room on the top floor that I use for entertaining male and female guests every few years. But alas, it is not to be. Perhaps in another life."

As he approached the tunnel's eastern exit, the smell of the sea overwhelmed most other scents, but he caught the whiff of a something familiar.

"It appears your medical student–cum-detective has gotten here before us, my pretty one."

97

MORTIMER

HE WAS YANKED BACK, OFF his feet, landing on his rear end. "Careful, Dr. Mortimer! You could have fallen in!" It was Carter, breathless with excitement. "Are you okay?" he asked the quiet department chief.

Mortimer looked up at him. "Yes, Tom. I . . . I was absorbed in thought. But . . . thank you. Why are you here?"

"The student Demetri is in the subbasements. I was down there with his dad, who sent me to get help. When I reached the main floor, I called security. Then I ran into Pear's driver, who already had called the police because Murtaugh was attacked down there. I came looking for you to give you the heads-up."

Mortimer roused and took a deep breath. A moment earlier, he'd been about to commit an unspeakable act. But now he looked up at the excited junior resident and said, "If one of our students is down there, we need to be there, too. Let's go!"

Carter pulled Mortimer back onto his feet and looked down the shaft. "How about that. Pear has his own private elevator."

Now Mortimer grabbed Carter. "Careful!"

Soon they were on one of the main elevators. When the door opened to the main floor, they were greeted by Pear's driver, Lee, and a contingent of heavily armed police, plus EMTs, nurses, and equipment. Mortimer asked Lee et al, "Need some company?"

Lee looked at the Emergency Services Unit sergeant in charge of the unit, who shrugged his shoulders in response. Carter and Mortimer stayed in the cab as Lee and the rest got in. Once in the subbasement, the sergeant directed the nurses and EMTs, along with a cadre of officers, to follow Lee to the injured security chief. The sergeant ordered the rest of the ESU unit to follow Mortimer and Carter in the other direction, where Carter had told them he last saw Makropolis. The two engineers, still hard at work on their valve, stood in awe as they saw Mortimer and Carter run past, followed by the ESU officers with shotguns and machine guns in hand.

98

PEAR

AS HE LAY PARALYZED WITH half his face buried in coal, his leg twisted, and his hip fractured, he counted the merits of his life. *I have been a good man,* he thought, *I have done many good deeds.* But as the clammy cold seeped into his clothing, he began to believe hell would be his final resting place.

A large rat eyed him, wondering no doubt what a tasty morsel his eyeball would make, but the eye's occasional reflexive blink held the rat back. After what seemed like hours, Pear heard footsteps then saw a beam of light pass. This was followed by another beam of light and the nearer footsteps of a much larger man. Obviously Dr. Ripper was being followed, though not by Murtaugh, who by now was certainly dead.

If he could have cried out, he would have, but the injected drug made it impossible. His soul however, wailed for Murtaugh, Bassias, the people killed twenty-five years ago, and the myriad other victims over the generations.

As he began to slip back into the blissful black of unconsciousness, he heard many footsteps and much splashing. And then: "Hey, I think I saw a reflection. This way!"

It sounded like Mortimer.

Suddenly there was light. And then there were people and commotion. A couple of men lifted him. There was blinding pain from his right femur, shattered when the Doctor tossed him into the coal like a sack of potatoes.

"Is he alive?" It was Carter.

"He has a pulse, but I think he's paralyzed or comatose or something." It was Mortimer again. "He's also fractured his femur. Let's get him to the ER."

Suddenly the commotion was silenced by the sound of gunshots echoing from further down the tunnel.

The sergeant yelled to his team. "Let's move! I'll take the point!"

99

DEMETRI

THE COAL RAIL TUNNEL ENDED in a pool of water. Demetri realized the exit was submerged due to the rainstorm and high tide. Brightening the tunnel was an eerie light—originated by the headlamps of the cars speeding past on the FDR Drive above, then filtered through a manhole cover and reflected by the pool of water. He shut off his flashlight and readjusted his backpack, hoping to keep his laptop dry. He stood on one of the rails to avoid the stream of water running between the rails toward the exit. He was cold, wet, and miserable and still had failed to find Maria.

Demetri watched the water level at the entrance for a few moments. It continued to rise, although the rate seemed to be decreasing. The noise of the rushing water and of the cars passing overhead made his head ache. Finding nothing of further interest, he decided to head back toward the medical center. As he turned, he slipped off the rail and fell against the wall, getting soot and mud over his entire outfit and submerging his shoes. "Damn," he muttered under his breath. He got back on the rail, hoping to avoid the water until he reached drier ground. He carefully walked the rail for another 10 feet then slipped again and fell full speed to the side. Rather than hitting the wall, he stumbled into a small alcove filled with a pile of old lump coal. He lost his footing even as he tried to regain it, and fell over the pile face first. Moments later, he scrambled to his knees to find himself covered in soot from head to toe. As he turned to climb over the coal pile back toward the main tunnel, he spied a figure bounding past him in the main tunnel, going toward the river.

Demetri reflexively cowered behind the coal pile. He realized it was a creature of malice.

The eerie light from the water outlined the tall figure in a halo of cool blue. Demetri saw that it was a man in a lab coat was not alone but was carrying a person on his shoulder. As the muscular figure pulled the apparently lifeless, naked body off his back, the body's head flopped around for Demetri to see. It was Maria! Demetri wasn't sure if she was alive or, perhaps, in a catatonic state. Her eyes were wide open, their static expression full of dread and helplessness. He must get her away, but how? The river entrance was flooded, and it was a long way back to the medical center.

"Here you go for a swim, my dear." The Doctor tossed her into the water. The splash echoed in Demetri's ears. "Goodbye, my love. The tide is turning. Enjoy the river view of the city while you can."

Demetri dumped his pack and exploded from the alcove with the ferocity of a caged lion. Expecting to hit the Doctor amidships, Demetri only flailed through the air and into the water as the Doctor sidestepped him.

"There you are. I thought I smelled something familiar." The Doctor roared in laughter as Demetri found himself flailing in cold water next to Maria, who was face down. After gulping and then coughing up a mixture of water and air, Demetri found he could stand neck deep in the water. He grabbed Maria and flipped her onto her back, propping her face above the water.

"How touching. Perhaps the police will find the two lovers permanently embracing as their bloated bodies wash up on some rocks downriver. A tragic accident by all accounts. Such a shame that her virginity—and your rectum—are still intact to the end. If only I had more time, I would do you both. But it is time to end this pathetic charade."

Demetri struggled to stand upright as he felt the deeper water pulling at his legs. The tide was beginning to move out, and he and Maria with it. Demetri needed to buy some time. "What shithole did you crawl out of? You dress like a doctor, but you're a psychotic maniac." He realized his insult sounded totally lame, but he'd said the first thing that came to mind to distract the Doctor while he searched the pockets of his jeans while trying to balance himself in the water.

"Maniac? Me? I know perfectly well what I am doing. I have been a great physician and a world-class surgeon since your great-grandparents were in diapers. But enough of this!"

With the speed of a gorilla, he scaled the side wall of the tunnel, planted himself on a small ledge above the water pool, and pulled out a hyperdermic needle. "This is in case you can swim." The Doctor leaned toward Demetri, extending his arm with his thumb on the plunger in preparation for the paralyzing injection that would lead to Demetri's drowning death in the water. The Doctor grabbed Demetri's arm in a vice-like grip and began lifting him out of the water with ease. "This works faster intravenously but works intramuscularly nearly as well." Demetri frantically searched his pocket with his free hand and, to his relief, quickly pulled out what he was looking for: his Spyderco folding knife. Suddenly there was a flash of metal and a streak of crimson in the water as the Doctor's arm retracted in pain and Demetri fell back into the water. Blood was pumping furiously from his forearm. Demetri was sure he'd cut an artery and some tendons, but the Doctor made no sound. Instead his face transformed: it became a feral thing, pure animal, pure death. The Doctor stood on the ledge, hunched like an eagle eyeing its prey below. "Well, the kitten has teeth. I normally like my hands on my prey when I kill but now . . ."—the Doctor pulled out Pear's revolver with his uninjured hand and pointed it at Demetri's head—". . . this will have to suffice!"

The gun blasts filled the end of the tunnel, followed by only the silence of running water.

100

MᴄMᴀɴᴜꜱ

IT WAS HARD TO DISCERN noises as he was running east in the tunnel because of the scurrying rats and the dripping and running water. His depth perception was off due to the darkness, which was exacerbated by the black soot that covered the walls and ceiling. He could see with his flashlight that at multiple points, the black brick gave way to chiseled stone—evidence of the tunnel's having been blasted from New York's bedrock generations ago.

As he increased his speed, his footing became more tenuous, and his bad knee caused him to limp, preventing an all-out run. He did notice more light in the tunnel leaking in from the streets above. He knew he was nearing the surface. But how much further he had to go he did not know. He kept his firearm in the low ready position despite the weapon's feeling heavier and heavier as his arm tired. Just when he was about to stop from exhaustion, he saw, about 45 feet ahead, his most dreaded scene. The perpetrator was pointing a gun at Demetri Makropolis's head while the boy was up to his neck in water.

McManus had no intention of yelling out to the perp to drop his weapon. The detective let go of his flashlight, raised his gun held in a perfect isosceles, and placed his finger on the trigger. Zeroing in on his front sight and leveling the rear, he centered on the perpetrator's torso. As he began the Glock's long trigger pull, the Doctor, perched on a ledge, suddenly turned his head and his weapon toward McManus. His body was outlined by blue light giving McManus a great target. The murderer's eyes were afire, and he laughed heartily. The laughter and the view were then obscured by the noise and flash of

McManus's gun—noise and flash that, oddly, seemed double what the detective was used to. As his vision returned, McManus looked toward the end of the tunnel. The Doctor was gone. "Damn! I couldn't have missed him!"

"*I* didn't," McManus heard from behind.

McManus turned quickly, his knee nearly collapsing. It was Makropolis, standing 10 feet behind him on one of the rails. The retired cop, holding his weapon up in the old-fashioned Weaver position, ran up to McManus, then passed him. "Cover me!" He ran up to the end of the tunnel at the water pool's edge, with McManus scanning the area for signs of the murderer or other movement and followed as quickly as his knee would allow.

Seeing the Doctor floating face down in the increasingly blood-filled water, McManus holstered his weapon. He watched as Makropolis stepped into the pool, pulled his son out, and hugged the boy tight. McManus carefully stepped into the water's edge and grabbed the naked girl, somewhat embarrassed at seeing her like that, and brought her to the water's edge.

Demetri turned from his dad's embrace toward McManus. "I don't know if she's dead. The Doctor kept talking to her as if she heard everything." Demetri knelt down, pulled her further up out of the water on to the rails, and felt her neck. "Hard to feel a pulse." Demetri grabbed his father's flashlight and checked her pupils. "They're reactive, she's alive!" He took off his wet bomber jacket and placed it over her naked body.

McManus, recalling the medical examiner's mouse, smiled. "Yeah. The nut has a special injection that feigns death. Keep her warm. Here." McManus handed Demetri his sooty jacket—at least it was marginally drier. McManus then turned to Makropolis, "Thanks. You never should have retired."

Makropolis placed his hand on his son's wet scalp. "I guess I wanted to spend more time with my kids, although I think I can spend more time with this one on the job than off." He smacked the back of his son's head, lightly but firmly.

What seemed like an eternity later but was really only a minute, a group of hospital security and NYPD ESU officers came running down the tunnel with Carter and Mortimer in tow and, not far behind, a host of ambulance personnel.

Carter grabbed Demetri and gave him an uncharacteristic hug. Mortimer then did the same. Demetri pulled Carter aside. "How did Mortimer get involved in all this?"

"It's a long story," whispered Carter. "Later."

The ESU officers spoke with McManus, who pointed out the body of the Doctor, still floating in the water. But as they turned to look, they saw the body and the water surrounding it being sucked out with the tide.

"What the fuck?!" McManus exclaimed. With the tunnel now open to the outside air, the roar of the Nor'easter outside kaboomed. The officers ran up to the opening but found no sign of the body in the rushing river. The ESU Sergeant got on his radio calling for immediate air-and-water search-and-rescue. Then he yelled back to McManus, "You sure you got him?" McManus glanced at Makropolis for reassurance, then nodded in the affirmative. "Make that a search and recovery," the sergeant shouted into his radio.

Bassias was wrapped in blankets by the hospital EMTs and placed on a stretcher. As the group headed back towards the Medical Center through the tunnel, Mortimer brought the detective and the others up to speed on what else had happened.

"We found Dr. Pear and carried him back. It appears his hip may be broken. It looks like I'll be in surgery tonight."

A call came in on the sergeant's radio: Murtaugh was still alive and in surgery. "Nathan surprised me with his professionalism back there," said McManus. "If Murtaugh survives it'll be thanks to him."

Mortimer shook his head. "So the jerk is a real doctor after all."

Just then another call, heard by all in the tunnel, came in over the radio to the ESU Sergeant. "A nurse's disemboweled body was found in a dumpster outside the medical center. Her name tag read 'Beth . . .'"

Hearing Beth's name, Carter collapsed against a wall. Demetri grabbed him and propped him up.

"Tom, I, I know . . ."

Carter shrugged him off and stood up straight, looking into the tunnel darkness ahead. "She was an occasional trim, that's all," he said before staggering away.

Mortimer looked at Demetri and the receding form of Carter. "Demetri, go keep him company, he needs it." Demetri's dad, who still had his arm around his son, gave Demetri a polite shove, and Demetri walked to catch up with his friend.

Soon Demetri, Mortimer, and Carter were back in the Medical Center and McManus was on his way to One PP to see the chief.

THE NYPD HAD TWO HELICOPTERS—a Bell 412 and an Augusta 119—search the East River for bodies once the storm had subsided, but without success. The scuba team dove in off a launch after an RMP spotted some debris floating just south of the Battery Park Terminal. It turned out to be a bloody, tattered doctor's lab coat, which was submitted for evidence.

McManus was called in for a full debriefing by Adamo, the chief of detectives,—with a demotion or promotion to follow, the odds being 50-50. Makropolis, on the other hand, had been escorted to Police Plaza for a talk with the commissioner. What was that all about?

McManus spent half an hour sitting outside the chief's office, listening to a loud commotion behind the closed doors. The commissioner was inside—he was known for loud outbursts at his underlings and for micromanaging every aspect of his department of 35,000 officers. McManus did not know what the noise signified other than its having something to do with him. He shut his eyes and recounted his current state of affairs: his marriage was a shambles, he may have slept with the neighbor's daughter and *had* slept with his inspector, his imported clothes were a mess, and his knee was aching for attention. And every one of those problems was most likely not fixable.

McManus checked his voicemail and text messages. He found a text from his soon-to-be-legal dog sitter telling him how much she enjoyed the evening; a voicemail from his soon-to-be ex-wife saying she had an appointment scheduled with the counselor on Monday; one from his ex-inspector turned present lover wanting to meet for dinner; and a text from his soon-to-be ex-partner reading, "Whassup? Doin betr." He shook his head and closed his eyes. He opened them as the door to the chief's office swung open.

"McManus, get your ass in here."

McManus realized he was in deep shit. The police commissioner was present, seated next to Makropolis. The PC grinned and commanded McManus to take a seat.

Silence ensued for a second as McManus squirmed, expecting the worse.

"Mick here filled me in on what happened underground. McManus, I expect a full report by 8 tomorrow morning, since I have scheduled a full press conference for 10:00. Both you and Makropolis here will take full responsibility in front of the press. Understand?"

"Yes, sir." McManus figured he might as well bid farewell to his career as a detective in front of half a dozen TV cameras. In his head, he began calculating commute times to Staten Island.

The PC continued. "Good. Now, I can't believe you managed this case on your own with no back-up. As usual, you're a loner and can't be trusted to follow department policies and procedures. As your punishment, Thompson is no longer your partner. Detective Special Operations McManus, meet your new and newly rehired partner, Micky Makropolis. If anyone can keep you in line, he can."

The PC shook the hand of the mute and pale-white McManus then turned to Makropolis. "Welcome back. If you're going to do any shooting, I want you to do it as a full member of our team, not as some half-cocked retiree."

Makropolis turned to shitfaced McManus. "Partner, this could be the beginning of a beautiful screwed-up friendship."

101

THE MAKROPOLI

THE NEXT MORNING, SUNDAY, DEMETRI was seated at the kitchen table with his dad and his siblings. His mom was putting the finishing touches on the French toast while Yia Yia sat in the living room mumbling to herself as she half-slept in her comfort chair.

"Here you go!" said Sophia as she placed a huge platter of French toast and another holding a perfectly browned pound of bacon on the table. Like a flock of pigeons pecking a slice of stale bread, the forks attacked the food; within seconds, the platters were empty. The family was quiet except for the occasional "mmm" and gulp of milk.

Sophia Makropolis smiled as she stood behind Demetri and watched. At times like these, she thought all was right with the world. Glancing at the Sunday paper lying on the counter, she saw the headline, "Dr. Doom Done In." She picked it up and turned to page three to find the lead article, written by Jack Bigelow. Her eyes opened wider with every paragraph she read.

Smack! Wielding the paper as a weapon after finishing the article, she whacked Demetri in the back of the head.

"Ouch!" yelled Demetri, rubbing the site of the assault. "What was that for?"

"That's for being stupid and almost getting yourself killed!" She waved the paper in front of him as she talked.

Then she turned on her husband. "And you! You let your own son, *your own son,* act as dumb as you. He's a medical student, he's not some *vlaka* police detective, and you encourage this type of behavior! Why didn't you tell me?"

Makropolis shrugged. "I didn't want you to worry. Look, it's over now, and we are all safe and sound."

"What else have you been hiding from me?"

"Well . . . come to think of it . . . the Police Commissioner has . . . rehired me."

Sophia lifted the paper in preparation for a backhand smack then dropped it on the floor and hugged her husband. "That's the best news I've heard all week!"

"Huh?"

"I love you and want you safe, but this past year you've made me miserable trying to help with the dry cleaners. You're terrible at running the store; you're late when you make deliveries. Do you want me to lose all my customers?"

They all laughed as they returned to their breakfast.

EPILOGUE

MATCH DAY

LATE BECAUSE HE'D OVERSLEPT FROM working on a presentation, Demetri ran past the guard, entered the library, and stopped behind the mass of students.

He drew a deep breath and tried to relax. It was March 18, Match Day, the day all U.S. medical students learn where they will be going for their internships and residencies.

The Dean was smiling as he handed out the envelopes. Demetri took his but was too nervous to open it immediately.

"Demetri," said the dean, "Dr. Pear asked me to thank you."

"How is he?"

"Recovering well since his hip replacement by Dr. Mortimer two weeks ago. It's a shame the initial pinning after the accident failed, but Dr. Pear says he'll be back to work soon."

Demetri wondered if Murtaugh would ever return to work. The security chief had survived his throat wound but was now undergoing speech therapy to learn how to talk again. Demetri had seen him in the hospital the other day looking gaunt and frail; they saluted each other.

"That's great, Dean," said Demetri as he eyed the envelope in his hands.

"I'm sure you will do well no matter where you go," said the dean before turning to the next student.

Demetri stepped back to check out his classmates. Most were exuberant, but a few had long faces.

Konrad Tofski walked past Demetri on his way to the dean. "Hey, Detective, what's happening?"

Meanwhile, his roommate Cheryl was yapping and beaming while Allan, his other roommate, stood in a corner pretending to read his letter but actually peering at his classmates with disdain over the top edge of the paper. Allan's and Demetri's eyes met for a second. The animosity between them was intense. They'd never liked each other, but in the four months since the killings, Allan had become Demetri's antagonist, jealous of Demetri's coming career in surgery, an avenue no longer possible for himself due to his eye injury. The jealousy consumed Allan. The two no longer spoke, and Demetri did everything possible to avoid being in the apartment at the same time as Allan.

Demetri averted his gaze and headed for the exit. What did the Dean mean by his remark that Demetri would do well wherever he went? Was he headed for some poverty-stricken orthopedic program in a Third World country? Was he on his way to a general-surgery internship with no future in orthopedics? The possibilities were many, and his hands began to shake.

After he left the library, he entered the main hospital. Security remained tight but was less stifling than it had been last fall. He flashed his ID then took the main stairs down. A moment later, he bumped into Warren Nathan.

"Watch out!"

"Sorry."

Nathan eyed him up and down. "Hard to believe you're actually going to finish med school. Do you even know how to tie surgical knots?" He rolled his eyes and shook his head before he brushed Demetri aside and walked away.

Nathan appeared to have reverted to his usual rotten-tempered self, Demetri thought as he headed toward the Health Information Management Department. He couldn't believe the luck of that jerk. The guy had tried everything to undermine the hospital and still landed on his feet. He became the hero who not only saved the near-dead chief of security but did it in front of one Jack Bigelow, who wrote the two-page article headlined "Eastside Surgeon Solves Murders and Saves Ripper Victim." The spread, which included a huge picture of Nathan, had not only landed a Pulitzer nomination for its author but had also caused Nathan's surgical practice to explode. What a strange world, thought Demetri, considering that it had been the Greek medical student who risked everything to solve the case.

He pulled on the door to the HIM Department and opened it to see the clerk behind the counter beaming.

"Well?"

"I didn't open it yet," Demetri said, feeling his worries fade as he drowned himself in the pools of Maria's eyes.

He'd cherished every moment with Maria these last few months. Even his mom was getting used to her, although Sophia was still not comfortable with her son dating a non-Greek. Greeks were one of the most clannish ethnic groups in New York, and his mom was leader of the pack. But now Demetri was afraid he would be leaving the city and might not see Maria for months at a time. Or maybe ever again.

"Oh, silly, come here." She flipped up the counter top, opened the low door underneath, and walked out to Demetri. "Let's go over there." She guided him into a dictation booth, where he sat and fumbled with the envelope. Maria grabbed it. "I'll do it, you dolt." She tore it open, read, then shrieked and started jumping up and down.

"What? Tell me!"

Maria stopped jumping, hugged Demetri tight, and whispered in his ear, "You're staying here at Eastside another five years!" She then kissed him, long, hard, and deep. Demetri took it in, elated on all counts.

"Did you ever think anything different?" she said when the kiss finally ended. "The number-one orthopedic program for my number-one man." She kissed him again. This one was even longer, harder, and deeper. It left Demetri an oxygen-starved, dimwitted boy. It would take minutes—no, make that years—for him to recover.

TWO HOURS LATER, A TALL redhead was walking uptown along First Avenue in front of the United Nations building. She had just finished her lunch break and was heading back to work. Her boss, the CEO of a small telecommunications firm, had just hired her as his vice president and chief financial officer. Normally she would have kept him enthralled as they lunched at a cozy little restaurant downtown, but he was in Singapore on business, so she had decided to take a stroll.

It was a gorgeous day, warmer than usual for March, so she took off her jacket as she walked north. The tête-à-tête daffodils were just opening along the UN fence, and the city's residents were emerging from their long hibernation. Feeling that spring was in the air, the redhead radiated sex. She'd removed her jacket, allowing her white chiffon blouse to ripple with the breeze and her nipples to harden under her bra. Her long, slender legs made the edge of her skirt bounce with a playful intensity as her hips swayed east and west. She spied two men across the avenue who gave her the once over and she smiled.

Life was good. She had a great job, a steady boyfriend, and, at age twenty-eight, was a man magnet. Even keeping her married boss at arm's length was appealing.

Suddenly she caught a chill. She became self-conscious, and stopped to look around. Shivering even though the sun was still out and the temperature was holding steady, she put her jacket back on. She saw no one strange, just a very old man walking with a cane on the UN property behind the fence. He appeared to have once been tall and muscular, but he limped as if he were recovering from an injury.

At first he didn't seem threatening at all. But he was hunched over, almost as if he were a bird of prey—specifically a vulture, she thought.

And then she realized he was staring directly at her.

Those eyes . . .

Printed in the USA
CPSIA information can be obtained
at www.ICGtesting.com
JSHW022207140824
68134JS00018B/901